Ghosts of Summers Past

By Katie Jane Newman

Friend
Noun
A person with whom one has a bond of mutual affection, typically one exclusive of sexual or family relations

Frenemy
Noun, informal
A person with whom one is friendly despite a fundamental dislike or rivalry

For Austin, with love always xxx

PROLOGUE

My dearest Jessamy

I always thought I'd live forever but while we drift through life taking it for granted, we don't notice the ticking of the clock. Time has run out for me and I wish I could see the sun set over the bay one last time, that you and I could be sat under the tree like we did so many times, if only just once more. There isn't enough time to tell you everything I wish I could.

I miss you already.

I'm hoping I went on the wave of passion with a dashing younger man but I fear that my fantasy was unfulfilled and it was this vile disease that took me. I hope it was peaceful and quiet and I hope I could hear the waves crashing on the shore as I left this life. In these final days, it has become more and more clear that you have always been the best thing that ever happened to me. If I were to have been lucky enough to raise a child, I hope that she would have been just like you. I don't think you realise how much you saved me.

The passing of time fades memories but I remember so clearly all those summers that we spent at The White House. Two lost souls, the proverbial black sheep strangely fated to be part of the painfully perfect and painfully dull family that we ended up with. Our summers gave me a reason to smile and laugh and dance and be joyful. They gave me a peace I didn't ever find in all the doomed marriages and the endless love affairs.

I think my heart broke for the final time the day you decided not to return. I understand fully your reasons and in the same situation I would have done as you did. But I couldn't leave the house, not entirely, there was too much of my soul in those bricks. I wish I had the chance to tell you my story but sadly time has run out. It's there, Jessamy, at the house, it's there for you to find.

Everything I have is for you. You and your beautiful daughter.

Find the painting, Jessamy, the one that we hung for the sheer hideousness of it (do you remember?) and when you find it, look closely at it for that's where you'll find my legacy. You may wish to send the painting onto Count Vlad once you've taken what you need, it would suit Vlad Manor very well and irony of it hanging in that godforsaken hell hole would keep me amused for eternity.

The house, of course, is yours. It's time for you to go back because there is no other worthy custodian of its future. What you seek you will find there. Your story has yet to be written and the house will show you the way. There is a new chapter waiting for you but I fear that all you know will change before you feel ready.

The house will be there for you and I will be there for you. Always.

Listen to the whispers in the eaves and the calling of the trees, you will hear me amongst the spirits. They will tell you all you need to know, you just have to let them in. Turn up the music, dance and laugh, take the house into a new future and give it its light back.

Scatter me under the tallest oak tree where the sea breeze can be felt. That's where I wish to be. I don't want anyone else there, just you. My sisters can shed their false tears at whatever ghastly memorial London society will expect them to host, but they cannot shed them at my grave.

I wish I had the time to tell you how much I love you, how much you saved me, how much our summers meant to me and how immensely proud of you I am. You have such fire in your soul Jessamy, let it burn for all to see.

No more hiding.

A new path beckons you, you just have to look for it.

Go to The White House, sit under the trees, breathe the scent of the sea and listen carefully to the whispers and know I will always be there alongside you.

Be brave, darling girl, be brave.

I love you

Forever, your Great Aunt

Lily x

CHAPTER ONE

I'm sitting at the entrance to Hades.

The rain is hammering down, great fat drops fighting for space on the windscreen, weather with such a destructive temperament that I'm expecting Noah to come sailing past. The leaves, ripped violently from the trees, whip past looking lost as they are picked up by my headlights.

"It's July for fuck's sake," I grumble through gritted teeth as the rain finds its way in through a new leak in the window seal. Drip, drip, drip onto my elbow until it stiffens painfully from the cold. I stretch it out in front of me, rubbing the damp skin to regain some warmth.

Be brave, she said.

I don't feel brave. I feel sad. Lost. Alone. I've not been here for years, shutting out The White House until it became a memory from which I could hide, buried for two decades until it crept back at my lowest moment, back into my dreams and holding on to my unconscious with a vice like grip. The dreams of him, his face, young and beautiful, smiling at me from a time long gone.

Memories that were buried until the day Lily died.

"You're being silly Jessamy." I reproach myself firmly. "The past is over, gone, there's nothing here. It's just a house."

The past is here.

It's not, it's gone.

You know the truth Jessamy, why lie to yourself.

I can almost hear the dark voices calling me from beyond the wrought iron gates, their menacing whispers mixing with the endless tap-tapping of the downpour on the roof until I long to turn the car around and flee.

I want a child Jessamy, before it's too late.

Go to Lily's, give me some space.

I don't know if I want 'us' anymore.

The tall gates look imposing as the headlights pick out the twisted shapes of the gargoyles and demons that decorate the metal. It was Lily's idea of a joke, to wind up the Vicar who lived opposite, the Vicar who both adored her and equally despaired of the debauched lifestyle that she made no attempt to hide. In the strange gloom brought on by the lashing rain they look like the doorway to hell and I wrap my arms around myself squinting through the bleak night to try and make out the house.

"Just open the gates Jess, it's just a house. Only a house." My words may be quiet but they sound more untrue now than ever. It's not *only a house.* I know it, Lily knew it which is why she bequeathed it to me and Phil knows it. The outcome of Lily's will has given my husband of twenty-one years the chance to give into the resentment that's been quietly simmering for the entire duration of our marriage. *I can no longer deal with the ghost you keep in your head.* It was mid-argument that the call came to say that Lily had died and he stood there watching me, as my heart shattered in my chest. No comfort, no kind words, just the perfunctory hug that he felt obliged to give while my Grandma failed to contain her relief that her vivacious, rule-breaking younger sister had died.

"The house is yours of course." Grandma had snapped, sounding furious that she didn't inherit it, "…seems rather fitting all things considered."

I didn't hear her words properly, instead I crumpled as Grandma prattled on unconcerned, talking about Lily's final wishes, angry that no provision had been left for the memorial service that London's Society expected to attend. I stopped listening and shut out the venom that Grandma hissed at me down the line. It's only now that I replay her words, *all things considered* but I'd never give Grandma the satisfaction of questioning what she meant.

I feel scared of what is beyond the gates. The emptiness and the silence. I'm scared of what is trapped inside my head, the memories that I have buried for so long. Since Lily died they have been coming to me in my dreams, showing me the past and blocking the way to the future.

*What you seek, you will find...*I hope so Lily, I hope so.

Resignedly I open the car door, pushing it with my feet to open it against the wind. The angry rain beats its way in drenching me in seconds. It's a cold rain and the droplets are like little shards of glass that scratch my skin. I pull my hood up and run quickly to the gates. Up close the gargoyles look even more disturbing, their crazed grins mocking me. I struggle with the entry panel, the numbers too small for my cold, wet hands.

"Goddamn it!" I shriek, hitting the number pad and rattling the gates. "God bloody damn it!"

"Jessamy Summers wash out your mouth!" The Vicar comes through the gloom, his miserable looking dog hanging its head against the rain and suddenly I feel thirteen again, being told off for saying something similar at the church fete, the first summer I came to Otterleigh Bay.

"Hi John." I say sheepishly, hanging my head almost as low as the dog.

The Reverend reaches behind me and punches in the number code. The gates creak open. "No need for damnation today. The weather is doing just fine on that score." He smiles gently. "Gosh, Jessamy, it's been years…I didn't think we'd ever see you back here. I'm so sorry about Lily, so desperately sorry. The world is a quieter place without her…"

"You know?"

"Of course I know, dear child, she was here."

"Here? At the White House? Lily was here? Grandma said…Grandma said she died in London." I say stunned.

"London? Oh, goodness no! She'd never go there."

"No, she wouldn't, would she? I don't know why I didn't even question it when Grandma said." I twist my face into a grimace. "It would seem that everything I've been told over the past few months has been a lie." John looks confused so I continue with an explanation. "Lily told me she was spending the summer in Venice with friends, which was why we weren't meeting in Florida. I had no reason to think otherwise…It didn't ever cross my mind that she would lie to me. I mean, why would it? She never did before." I rub my forehead. "I had no idea she was dying, she didn't tell me. I don't think I've caught my breath yet. I can't believe she was here all alone…"

"Oh, she wasn't alone…" The Vicar says cheerfully, then stops himself. "Oh."

"She wasn't? Who was here? Not one of the husbands?"

The Vicar looks almost sheepish. "I'm sorry Jessamy, I was sworn to secrecy, and as a man of the cloth, retired or not, I'm afraid my promises reach all the way up."

"I suppose it's not the done thing to fall out with your boss when your boss is God!" I manage a slight grin all the while my mind is whirling. Who would look after her? Why not me? Fat tears roll slowly down my cheeks mingling with the rain. "I should have been the one to look after her, I was her family and she was everything to me but I didn't know."

The Vicar reaches out for my hand. "My dear Jessamy. She didn't tell you because she wanted you to remember her as she was, a bright, bright light that shone for all to see. She didn't want you to see her old and ill, a shadow of herself, her light dimming day by day. She made her choice to protect you but mostly, I think, to protect herself. You were her whole world and you meant more to her than all the husbands and lovers and friends that she had. She had your love, that's only ever what she needed and it kept her warm when the end was nearing." He smiles, his kind face soft. "It will be nice to see some light back in the house, it's been under darkness for too long. Go inside child, it's too cold to be crying in the rain."

I look beyond him to the house squinting through the rain to make out the outline. I've never seen it so bleak, so full of despair. "I'm not sure I can."

"Of course you can! There is nothing to be scared of. Bring the house back to life, Jessamy, that's what Lily wanted. Get out of this hideous weather and go inside." He looks at his watch. "I must go, the Archbishop is calling shortly, something to do with a golf tournament against the Church of Scotland. They seem to forget that I'm retired, old and grumpy!" He grins and squeezes my shoulder. "You'll be fine, Jessamy, just fine."

He turns away from me to cross the road where the cottage lights blaze. "You know where I am if you need me."

"I do. Thank you."

"You know, Jess, even in the darkest moments there is…" He pauses and chuckles. "…still light, somewhere."

"Did you just make that up?" I ask wiping my face on my sleeve and giggling.

"Yes, I decided mid-way through that my most profound religious statement may not have the desired affect!" He chuckles. "Lily…you…two peas in a pod, surprisingly so." A look of sadness fleetingly masks his gentle face. "Yes, a light really has dimmed. Goodnight Jessamy."

"Good night John. Give my best to Winnie."

"I shall. And Jess, I'm just across the road, remember that."

"I will. Thank you. Thank you for everything you did for her, she adored you, you know."

"She took great delight in winding me up. It's little wonder my hair fell out!"

I watch him cross the road, his wellingtons squeaking on the wet tarmac, until I can't see through the rain water dripping into my eyes. I blink furiously and move to push open the gates, they creak as I do, the sound is loud in the empty space. "Here goes nothing," I shake my head slightly. "Well Lily, I hope you're right."

I hurry back to the car, cursing my stupidity at leaving the door wide open. The seat is soaked and a puddle has formed in the foot well but I climb in and move the car slowly through the gates and onto the gravel drive. Quickly I get out of the sodden vehicle to close the gates, which shut with a bang before easing the car forward onto the shingle. The headlights shine through the downpour, no more than a metre ahead, and I keep my speed as low as I can without the engine cutting out entirely. At the end of the drive I park against the wall and close my eyes.

"Come on Jess, you can do this."

With a weary sigh, I switch off the engine and force myself back out in the rain. I feel cold, painfully cold, my teeth chattering from the unending chill of the rain. My car boot creaks as I lift it to retrieve my suitcase and with difficulty I feel my way in the darkness to the front door. I wrap my hand around Lily's key in my pocket but as I near the door I reach above the doorframe padding my hand along the wood to the little nook. My key is still there. I take it down surprised at how heavy it feels in my hand. The key has probably been up there since I finally closed the door on the summers here. I leave Lily's key in my pocket and use my own. "Here goes nothing."

***

The house smells strongly of floral scented air freshener.

9

It's a sickly-sweet synthetic smell that has been sprayed so liberally it stings my nose but it doesn't quite mask the mustiness of a tired, grieving house. The scent will forever remind me of death and the loss of Lily. Despite the downpour outside, I leave the door open, the rain taking advantage and splattering noisily on the tiles. I feel along the wall to the light switch and pull it down, the lights dotted around the room chinking as they heat up.

I wrinkle my nose against the stinging scent and throw open the two windows uncaring about the rain. The wind blows in, chilling the room further and I wrap my wet coat tighter around myself.

I move into the centre of the room on trembling legs.

The silence is overwhelming. The house doesn't even creak. It's in mourning, the sadness is touchable somehow and as I look around me the shadows of memories filling my mind with faded colours of happier times, of the jazz that forever spilled from the speakers dotted around the house. I feel a crushing weight in the centre of my chest. It's too quiet. Wrong. It's wrong. I can't feel her here at all. The hallway is too tidy, the tiles too polished and the staircase too varnished. Lily didn't live neatly. I should be tripping over discarded shoes and smelling the Chanel perfume she favoured or the delicate smoke of the French cigarettes she enjoyed. Empty champagne glasses from her many parties should be making rings on the antique furniture and sticky patches from spilled drinks should be marring the floor. No, this feels very wrong and I want to leave.

Now.

I close the windows, shutting out the rain, and back away from the room to the door, walking stiltedly through it and closing it softly behind me. I can't do what Lily wants me to do. I can't be here with the ghosts in the room, the ones that are stroking me with their cold fingers, because they scare me. I don't want to do it alone.

I feel so alone.

My husband is having a mid-life crisis, my daughter is living her life in London training to be a doctor and my best friend is busy juggling her successful events business with her family. I lock the door and pull my hood up against the rain, hurrying back to the car to sit in the wet, cold seat. I'll go to a hotel. I passed one on the way here. I'll come back tomorrow. When it's light.

Maybe.

What you seek you will find.

I'll scatter Lily as she wanted and I'll go home.

Back to Phil. Make him face the mess our marriage has become and I'll finally stop apologising for my life before him.

I turn the ignition on and slam my hands down on the steering wheel.

If I go, I'll be letting Lily down. Lily who gave me sanctuary over and over, who sheltered me from parents who were always so disappointed. Lily wants me to know her story. *It's there for you to find.* I sit here until my limbs ache from the cold. The rain has worsened and the sky is now a strange colour sitting between lilac and grey, so dark that it looks hell-like and fearsome. I fumble in my pocket for my phone and ring Phil.

"Jessamy." He says curtly when he finally deigns to answer.

"I'm here."

"Good. You left ages ago..."

"The weather made the motorway slow going. It's dreadful here..." There is a long, uncomfortable pause. I imagine Phil raking his hands through his salt and pepper hair as he searches for something to say and I wonder how our relationship turned us into strangers. It was so good once, or it appeared to be - strong, dependable Phil stepping up to a role as husband and father, never showing how much he resented it all, until now. *I'll never be the one you long for.*

"Is everything alright with the house?"

"It seems so sad and feels all wrong. Will you come down? I don't want to be here alone and you know, we could talk, sort things out..." I don't like the pleading tone I'm using, I sound needy and it bothers me.

"No Jessamy, no. Sorry, but no. I don't want to, I told you, I need space. I need time and I want to be on my own for now. I'm going to go away." He pauses. "I've decided to go to France..."

"France? Why...?"

"I can't think here, there's too much of you in the house..."

"Of course there is, it's my home..."

I can hear him thinking, the deep breaths that echo down the phone line. Eventually he says, "I've done this, I know it's bad timing with Lily and I'm sorry, really sorry. You've done nothing wrong Jess, it's me. All I wanted in life was a family, a child of my own..."

"You have one." I interrupt quickly. "You have Rachel."

"It's not the same. She's your daughter, not mine." I hear a door close in the background. "I have to go."

"Is someone there with you."

"Don't be silly." The phone clicks and I sit listening to the high-pitched wail of the discarded line until a branch smacks the car window and I yelp in shock. I fiddle with the radio trying to find something to take away the sound of the storm but my hands shake too much and I can't see beyond the tears that are falling.

"Come on. Come on!" I yell at the radio which finally springs to life, picking up a local station where the overly cheerful presenter says, "...lock the doors people of Devon, the storm is getting worse. The local met office advises no travel unless absolutely necessary but don't worry, we're here to keep you company. And..." He says his DJ voice bursting with enthusiasm, "what better song to play you than *Let It Rain* by East Seventeen."

"For God's sake." I seethe. "Don't be so happy you piece of shit DJ." I shut the ignition off cutting off the boy band and battle the weather back into the house, pulling my sodden case behind me.

"Well house," I mutter crossly, slamming the door. "Looks like we're stuck together for tonight."

I drop my case at the bottom of the stairs and cross the room to the door that leads to the kitchen. The door is stripped oak with ornate carvings of roses covering every inch of it and I gently run my hand over the flowers, feeling the knots and imperfections in the wood under my fingertips. Lily loved roses. The house was always filled with them, great arrangements of delicate cream flowers that perfumed the air with such a sweet scent. I asked her once why she always chose roses but her face closed and I never pressed to know more. Now I wish I had. I wish I'd asked every question and got every answer, had one more gin and tonic sitting on a deck chair under the trees, had one more conversation and laughed one more time. I push the door and walk into the dark corridor behind. It is eerie and the shadows seem to reach out for me making my heart race. "Oh, for God's sake woman!" I tell myself crossly. "It's nothing. Man up!" I switch the lights on and hurry down the long corridor to the kitchen at the end.

The kitchen is in darkness. I find the switch beside the door and the lights push the darkness away. The room is spotlessly clean, the faint smell of bleach hangs in the air. I drop my phone and keys on the scrubbed kitchen table and sit down. This was always my favourite room, situated at the back of the house with wide doors and a wall of windows that let in the light. It looks out over the garden and down to the three giant oaks that separate the garden from the cliff edge and from the neighbouring farm. The walls are bright red contrasting with the creamy flagstones that cover the floor.

I stare into the darkness outside.

I swear I see someone moving and press my face up against the glass peering into the night, my tired eyes searching the shadows. "It's your mind playing tricks." I say to myself. "That's all."

I'm tired, physically and emotionally, suddenly longing for my own bed and the warm, large body of my husband. I move stiffly across the kitchen to the cupboard where the glasses always used to be kept. I turn on the tap but the water is discoloured as it comes out of the faucet so I leave it to run. I'm so hungry, my service station coffee and pastry is a distant memory. Stuck to the front of the fridge is a scrawled note.

Food in freezer
Wine in fridge
J

I pull open the fridge and take out the wine sending a silent thanks to whoever 'J' is. I pour a generous amount into a glass and drink half of it quickly before opening the freezer and rummaging through the packs of frozen food. I choose a pie and turn the oven on to cook it, my stomach rumbling loudly.

I take my glass and the bottle back to the table and pick up my phone. Maybe I can persuade Phil to change his mind about France. Perhaps he'll come down and it will all be ok. I press his number on the screen grimacing at my reflection in the windows. I look worn out and ancient. When did I start looking this way? Yesterday? Last week? Last month? I don't recognise the person looking back at me and Phil's words taunt me. *You've let yourself go...used to have pride...used to be so sexy...*

I got complacent.

I spent my days writing books, romance for women of a certain age, stories with dashing heroes and beautiful heroines, eating packets and packets of biscuits dipped in hot, sweet tea whilst battling with plot lines that would keep my readers happy. I didn't notice the weight going on, didn't notice the passing of time nor did I notice that I was no longer being noticed.

How much of this mess is my fault? All of it? Some of it? None of it?

Go to Lily's, he said, *give me some space.* I feel ashamed. I am ashamed of the reflection. I am ashamed of who I've become. I'm ashamed that I proved my parents right. I'm ashamed that I didn't fight harder. I'm ashamed that my body stopped working. Mostly, I'm ashamed that I wish, more than anything else, that the ghost was still here.

***

Phil answers eventually. I sink down into my seat and rest my forehead on the table. He doesn't say anything but I can hear him breathing.

"It's so empty." I say quietly. "There is nothing here." I begin to cry again, my tears dampening my cheeks and pooling on the table. "I feel so sad, that everything is changing and I want to press pause, to stop it for a while, catch my breath...you know?"

"Yeah I know. I'm sorry I made you sad, I'm sorry that I've been a selfish prick and I'm sorry that I've never been him..."

"Oh Phil." I sigh deeply and sniff, wiping my cheeks as I sit up straight. "Phil, he's only ever been inside your head, because of Rachel, because she's a reminder of what was before. I've always been happy with my life...I wish I knew what was going on inside your head, why now..."

"He's not just inside my head Jess, please don't insult my intelligence. I don't want to talk about him or us or anything now. I'm sorry for upsetting you and I'm sorry that Lily has gone." He sighs. "I can't deal with any more confrontation because I don't know if..."

"If you want me?"

"It's not that simple anymore, things have changed... I've changed Jess, we've gone in different directions, the closeness we had isn't there anymore and I don't know if we can get it back. I'm sorry Jess." He whispers and I close my eyes against the pain in his voice.

"You're making me feel that this is all on me. That this is all my fault."

"Sorry."

"Sorry? Is that all you can say?"

"There isn't anything else to say." Phil says coldly. "I've told you I need space but you keep ringing…"

"When did you become such a bastard?" I snap. "Fine, have your space, whatever…leave me to cope with all this by myself, I don't care. I DON'T CARE."

I press the call end key and with a sudden wave of fiery rage I hurl the device across the room where the glass screen shatters against the floor. "Fuck, fuck, fuuuuuuuuuuuuuuuck." I scream at no one and promptly burst into hot, angry tears. How dare he just assume I'm going to sit and wait for him to make up his mind. There is no marriage if it's so dependent on conditions.

***

My phone rings loudly in the silence of the room and I jump spilling my wine onto my lap, "Shit." I grumble reaching for the mobile on the table. "Phil?"

"It's me." My daughter laughs down the phone. "Have you gone mad?"

"Sorry Rachel, I broke my phone and I thought it was Dad ringing. Are you ok?" I ask mopping my trousers with my hand.

"Yeah, I'm ok. I just wanted to make sure you arrived in one piece." She says, "I've seen the news, the motorway looked awful. Are you there yet?"

"Yes, I arrived about an hour ago. The drive down was hellish and the weather is only going to get worse. I can't imagine how, it's hideous enough now."

"Are you ok Mum? Down there on your own? Can Dad not come down?"

"I'm fine Rachel, really I am. There's no need to worry…"

"Will you and Dad be ok?"

15

"I'd like to think so…"

"Mum?"

"Yes?"

"Do what is right for you." My daughter says softly. "Don't do anything because of me or because you think you should. Life is too short to not be completely happy."

"When did you get so wise?" I ask.

"I learnt from the best. I must go Mum, the med students left behind this summer are going to a pub quiz in Walthamstow and it's a war with the nurses! They won last time, we have to win this time or we'll never be able to hold our heads up again!"

I laugh. "The NHS needs to be fearful for the future if it all depends on a pub quiz!"

She giggles her tinkly laugh. "Do you remember the hot consultant from my last placement, Juan? He was my mentor? Well he's invited me to attend a limb amputation he's doing tomorrow and I'm so excited. He looks amazing in blue scrubs…"

"Aren't you supposed to be learning something, not letching at your teacher?"

"I will learn and letch! You should see him Mum, smouldering, Spanish good looks. You could use him as inspiration for your next book!"

"Oh, could I?"

"Yeah! And if he were to get naked we'd all buy it!"

"Argh stop, you're my daughter, I can't listen to this! Tell me about the amputation!"

"You're gross Mum!" Rachel gives a big belly laugh. "Really gross. Do you want me to send you photos?"

"God no!" I shudder.

"Can you imagine losing a limb? Gross! I must go, the quiz won't win itself! I'll ring you soon. I love you Mum, and if you're not ok down there, just say and I'll get the first train out of London."

"I love you too baby and please don't worry, I'm old enough to cope with down here..."

"Yeah, I know but with Dad being an arse…"

"I'm fine Rach, honestly. Go and have fun, beat the nurses to an intellectual pulp and remember your mascara for tomorrow!"

"I wish. Scraped back hair and a clean face is the limit! Bloody hygiene." She giggles. "Bye Mum."

"Bye darling."

The phone clicks and I put the handset back down on the table. When did it all go so wrong?

***

I feel so tired.

Emotionally and physically worn out. The wine, delicious and cold, is beginning to make me feel sleepier than I'd like right now. I don't want to sleep. I want to get to know the house again, make it feel like the home it was rather than the unfamiliar bricks and mortar it has become. Without Lily here the house seems too big, too empty and quiet, it smells wrong and there is no laughter.

There hasn't been any laughter in my life for too long.

I've never been melancholy, always been a 'glass half full' girl but recently I've felt my identity slipping further and further away and I've no idea who I have become. I wish I could blame Phil, hold him responsible for all of it and forgo any part I may have played, but that would be unfair and untrue. The real fact is impossible to ignore.

I don't love my husband.

I wrap my cardigan around me tightly and walk through the cold, still house. A faint layer of dust has begun to settle on the furniture but the scent of polish remains potent in the air. I keep to the ground floor, opening each room and walking in and out with just a cursory glance.

It's so quiet. There is no music. There was always music but now there is just the sound of the ever-worsening storm. The rain taps on the windows, making me increasingly more nervous that someone is trying to get in but the house remains in mourning.

I stop in front of a painting of Lily hanging on the wall outside of the lounge. I've never seen it before but it is the most stunning portrait. She is young, in her teens I think, her mass of raven hair tumbling around her shoulders, a beaming smile on her full lips. She has a look on her face of unadulterated happiness, her face is so full of love that the feeling seems to emanate from the frame. It's in her eyes, the curve of her mouth, the way she dips her head…I squint at the signature drawn in gold pen, but it's merely a squiggle and I've no idea of the name. I run my finger lightly down the thick, bold strokes, the oils bumpy under the tips. Fleetingly I wonder if the artist is the secret she has kept all these years but likely I'm just grasping at straws.

I walk into the lounge and balk at the chill. It's the largest room in the house and north facing so feels colder than the rest of the house but tonight, with the imposing silence, it feels arctic. I can see the ghosts in here, the memories of the parties that Lily was so fond of throwing, dancing in front of my face. The jazz that played on the gramophone, the one that still sits on the sideboard in the middle of the far wall, the plumes of smoke that rose from the endless cigarettes that were smoked, the laughter and the chinking of glasses as they were filled over and over again. I can see my friends, looking cool, laughing together, drinking more alcohol than their parents would approve of. It's all here. The stories of my past and somewhere buried away for me to find, are the stories of Lily's past. I just have to figure out where to look.

It's for another day.

I switch all the lamps on and close the curtains, shutting out the night. Opening the gramophone lid, dark oak painted with gold leaf, I blow the dust from the deck and cough as it bellows up in my face. I wonder when it was last used, what the last record was that Lily played on it. It's a beautiful piece of craftsmanship and it appears to have been painted by hand, long strokes of gold leaf and peacock blue in delicate swirls that twist up to the horn. The swirls trail underneath and I lift it up to follow their lines. Underneath is the smallest heart, painted in gold, and inside the heart are the initials J & L. J? Who was J? I lower the gramophone and look at it for some clue. J? She never spoke of anyone named J and I'm pretty sure it cannot be the same J who left the food for me. My heart begins to thump. *I'm not a detective, why didn't you tell me what you wanted me to know?*

I open the sideboard and peruse Lily's records, each of them protected from the air by plastic cases, before selecting one and pulling it from the cupboard. The case is heavy but I rest it on the top of the sideboard and take the record from it, putting it onto the turntable. I wind the gramophone up and lower the needle, waiting for the ancient machine to start. It's crackly but sounds earthy somehow, and I sit down on the sofa and close my eyes. I remember this record.

18

I remember dancing to it.

One drunken night when I'd been cast aside in favour of my friend and I thought my heart was breaking.

Swaying in the corner with the skinny, carrot haired boy who always made me feel better.

Always.

I've not thought about him for years.

The house is doing strange things to my mind.

I turn off the music and close up the room for the night. The memories can wait.

***

I tentatively climb the staircase, my suitcase dragging awkwardly behind me. The bannister has been freshly varnished and feels sticky to touch so I use the wall to negotiate the steps. I've climbed these stairs so many times but not as nervously as I do now. The ghosts of the past walk beside me, Lily's raucous laugh lingering in the bricks.

...too much of my soul is in those bricks. "I think some of my soul may be here too." I whisper as I puff up the stairs. I walk down the landing, my suitcase making a rattling sound on the stripped oak floor. They need attention, the varnish patchy in places and in other areas, stains mar the wood. Another job for my mental to-do list. I sigh.

The radiators clunk and clank as the water in the pipes heats up, attempting to thaw the chill of the house that has been sitting empty for a while. The once-white walls have a faint yellow tinge and it smells mustier up here, a couple of miserable looking flies dart around and I wave them away with my free hand. I hesitate outside of Lily's room, my hand on the knob wondering if to go in, but tonight it's a step too far. I'm already feeling her loss all too keenly but to enter her room and not find her sitting at her dressing table liberally painting on glossy red lipstick is more than my fragile spirit can handle right now. I carry on down the corridor to my room and open the door.

It looks the same as it always has. Posters of Morten Harket and the Goss brothers, Corey Haim and George Michael stare down from the walls, faded and curling around the tacks that pin them to the plasterboard, unchanged from the days when they were the idols of teeny boppers. I can almost smell the white musk in the air, a favourite of mine in a time gone by and I sit down heavily on the bed suddenly winded from the rush of memories, the colours, images and feelings that have been buried for so long. Lily was right, the whispers of the house hold all the secrets, gripping them tightly in the old wood and ancient stone.

On the side table is a photo. I pick it up and feel a sprinkling of tears behind my eyes. The frame is typical of a seaside gift shop, decorated with shells covered in iridescent paint. Smiling up from the photo are my summer friends, the only real friends I had during my teenage years. I can hear their voices, the laughter and the tears, if I listen hard enough, all tiptoeing in to remind me of warm summers days. Life was simple, the five teenage girls giggling over dirty paragraphs in Jackie Collins' books, swooning over white toothed pop stars and dancing to Madonna while singing into hairbrushes – yes it was perfect back then. Those summers at Lily's took me away from my demanding and overbearing parents for whom their only child would never be good enough, not smart enough, not pretty enough, not the son they so desperately wanted. It was safe here, for a long time it was safe but as with all great things, the sanctuary can never last long. At least, not for me.

My bed has been made and coming from the sheets is the perfume of fabric softener. On top of the bedspread is a small basket of toiletries, toothbrush and paste, small sachets of cleanser and moisturiser and, I smile widely, a small bottle of white musk bubble bath. I open it and inhale the scent. Suddenly it's nineteen-eighty-nine again and I'm going to a party at Debbie's. I take another deep inhalation and it's nineteen-ninety and I'm sitting on the beach. I click the top back down and lie back on the bed.

The ceiling needs painting.

Flecks of discolour run across the ceiling and I've never noticed before how wonky it is. It's nice, being wonky, the high ceilings were never going to be perfectly straight. It's quirky. I like it.

I should unpack.

Groaning I wriggle up to sitting and give my suitcase the evil eye. There isn't much in there, I only packed what still fits and it's a limited selection. With a big sigh, I cross to where I left my case and unzip it grimacing at the meagre items inside. Part of me wonders if I avoid unpacking, can I still go home?

Can I still call it home?

Do I want to go home?

I put the clothes on hangers and look at what I dress myself in. *When did you let yourself go?* Phil's words, so harsh and painful to hear, are truer than I wanted to believe. I have let myself go, there is nothing hanging in the wardrobe that would suggest that I used to be so alive, so spontaneous and fun, yes even sexy. It's all frumpy, oversized and middle aged. Where is my personality? When did I lose it? When did I lose me? When I settled for 'like' not 'love', or when I realised that there would never be the baby that Phil wanted so desperately. Did I lose myself when I began to lose my marriage?

I want a baby before it's too late.

We can have tests…

I'm not a lab rat Jessamy.

"Fuck off Phil." I say angrily, slamming the wardrobe door. It doesn't catch and swings back open quickly, forcing me to stand aside. I take a couple of steps back and fall over a box I'd not noticed beside the wardrobe, landing painfully on my bottom and feeling the rising pain ricochet up my back.

"Ow." I kick out at the box, childishly, but as my foot makes contact the box turns ninety degrees and on the side, written in big, black letters, JESSAMY SUMMERS 1984-1992.

I pull my foot back quickly, as though a monster was reaching to pull me into a strange, alternative dimension.

I told her to burn the box.

Goddamn it Lily, the one thing I asked…

I grab the basket of toiletries and rush out of the room, into the bathroom that is across the hall. My hands shake as I lock the door and lean against it.

No monster you can't come in.

The taps splutter and spit as they pull the water from the depths of the house. I yelp as the hot scalds my hand squashing it protectively under my armpit as I liberally flood the bath with the musky bubbles. The little pops of white foam dance across the water, twisting and spinning as the water pours from the faucet.

I sit on the edge of the bath until it is full, the steam fogging the mirror.

"What do you think the box is going to do Jess?" I ask myself and like an addict to a drug I leave the bathroom, the door wide open, and cross the landing to my room.

The box sits staring at me.

Come on, it taunts. *Take a look.*

"Alright monster, do your worst, I'm not afraid of you."

***

A musty smell seeps from the box as I rip the brown tape from the lid.

"Oh!" It comes out as a gasp followed by a rush of breath. I hadn't realised I'd been holding my breath but now great pants escape as I pick out the contents.

My diaries.

Lined notebooks neatly covered with the smiling faces of pop idols, posters ripped from the pages of *Smash Hits* to brighten the dull covers of the books. Ten journals, ten summers, a million broken hearts and a million dreams captured between the pages and the one name, over and over again.

The Ghost you keep in your head.

***

*1988

I met a boy today. I was at the fair on the common and he walked past me. He was so fit and looked a bit like Luke Goss, he even had the same haircut. He was with two boys from the village, Lily said I should go and say hello but I didn't. Someone that handsome won't want to talk to me.*

***

I pad around the kitchen wrapped in a large clean towel that I found in the bathroom cupboard, and put music on the ancient radio that sits beside the toaster. Like all the appliances in the house it now looks tired and battered, dents in the metal catching the light but it works and I fiddle with the tuner to find something other than the dreadful local radio station but all I get is static. With a grumpy sigh, I tune it back into Otterleigh FM for a different, yet still annoyingly over bright, presenter to talk happily about the weather, and some nonsense that no one could ever really be interested in.

"You may have heard that the storm is set to last at least two more days," she says and my heart sinks. "So, it's rather apt that we play this classic from The Weather Girls, and you never know ladies, it just might rain men!"

It's hard to stay miserable with such a disco classic filling the room and I throw myself around exuberantly whilst belting out the words at the top of my voice. The rain continues to lash down, beating out a separate rhythm on the window panes, but as I dance and sing and spin around the room, things don't feel quite as bad as they did.

"Nice singing." A voice says behind me and I spin on my bare feet in shock. My towel slips from my body displaying my nakedness to the uninvited guest. Time slows. The clock on the wall ticks with a loud, deliberate clang, each second lasting eons longer that it should. He stares at me from under his hood. I stare at him, seeing nothing but the bearded jaw of a man hidden by his coat. My body is dripping soapy suds onto the floor, while his waxed coat drips water into a puddle at his feet. Drip drip drip. No one moves. There is a thud in my ears, it's slow, thick and booming. Boom. Boom. Boom. Then he moves, briefly, a shift of weight from one foot to the other and time speeds up, the second hand of the clock begins to whizz around and I become painfully, desperately and acutely aware of being very naked in front of the hooded man. Very naked.

I want to die.

I want the ground to open up and swallow me whole.

Or I want to wake up.

This has to be a dream. It has to be. Any minute now I'll wake up.

Any.

Minute.

Now.

But I don't.

Because I am awake.

I am awake and I am still naked.

"Are you going to kill me?" I whisper wrapping my arms around my nakedness.

"What?" He mumbles something else that I don't hear, a string of words splurges from his mouth and he turns abruptly on his wellingtons and disappears out of the door.

I am still naked.

***

CHAPTER TWO

"Naked?"

"Completely and utterly naked Zoe." I say, embarrassment creeping into my tone. My best friend laughs a musical, sunny laugh and I flush a deep crimson. "It's not funny Zo!"

Zoe can't disguise her mirth. She says through gasps of laughter. "What did he do? Ravish you? Pin you down on the kitchen table and take your chastity?"

"You've been reading too many erotic fiction novels Zoe!" I remonstrate. "Of course he didn't, even my husband doesn't want to ravish me on the kitchen table. He legged it, of course! There is literally a hole in the tile where he spun on his wellies so fast…"

"Oh, that's just burst the fantasy bubble." Zoe says glumly. "What did you do?"

"I cried. A lot. Wrapped in my towel obviously!"

"You cried? Oh no, Jessamy, you can't cry down there all alone."

"Yeah I did cry. I seem to be doing it all the time, you'd think it would burn calories, what a design flaw that is! It's the thing I seem to do when I suddenly remember that Lily is dead, Phil needs space and Rachel is hundreds of miles away being young and fabulous. It's then I look at myself and wonder what I'm doing with my life! I'm forty-two and time is ticking."

"Well my dear, sweet friend, you know that I'm here for you, always, whatever decision you make in life, I'm right behind you. As for what's going on right now, I guess it depends how long you give Phil space for and whether you want to be in his space when he decides to come back. Personally, I think he is behaving like a bone fide prick but that's just my opinion…"

I laugh. "Yes, he definitely is being that! He's gone to France apparently. He can't think at home, there is, and I quote, too much of me there. I was going to just go home but..."

"You can come here…"

"I know I can, thank you, and it's a huge help to know that, more so than I can actually put into words." I look out to the garden and sigh deeply. "I owe it to Lily to stay down here for now, she wants the light brought back, and despite it feeling that the sun has been switched off, I have to at least try and do what she has asked."

"Are you ok down there? Do you need help? Shall I come down?

"I don't think you'd get here. The rain is biblical and we've been advised to stay inside so honestly Zoe, I wouldn't want you to even chance it! In the last couple of hours, the water has risen to the door step." I sigh. "It's very strange being back here, you know. Very strange. So much is missing, not just Lily, but the life, in the house…it's gone. Once upon a time you could almost hear it breathing and now everything is so still."

"How long will you be there for?" She asks softly.

"I don't know. As long as it all takes, I suppose. Perhaps it will do me some good to be here, maybe I need some space too, space to think, space to write, my inbox is filled with emails from old dears baying for my blood because they've not had their next fix of hero!"

"It's because you write romance so well and they've only got dribbling, infirm husbands to look at!"

"I can't write romance, it's been too long since there was any!"

"Just think about your hooded stranger, that'll get the juices flowing!"

I laugh. "Now that would kill off my readers!"

"Please come home soon Jess, don't be gone too long." She says quietly. "The coffee shops of Bath will go into administration if you're not here. You are personally responsible for the economic wellbeing of our beautiful city!"

"No pressure then!" I smile. "Please don't worry, it will all work out, whichever way life takes me." I say it more so to convince myself. Looking out at the rain as it continues its incessant hammering on the window, everything seems as far from alright as it can be. The gloom outside seems to be moving in closer, creeping its fingers around the trees and the plants, tapping on the door with the insistence of an unwelcome visitor. "I'm going Zoe, I'm need to put some music on as loudly as I can, I'm sick of listening to the rain!"

"That's my girl! Love you."

"Love you too, Zoe, I'll ring you soon." I put the phone down and lean back in my chair. Yes, I tell myself with forced enthusiasm, it will all work out in the end.

I wake with a jolt from a disturbed sleep. My dream, a strange mix of faces and voices - Phil, the Ghost and the hooded man - sweeping and swirling through my mind, kept me from fully giving into the sleep I so desperately need. I lie in bed looking up at the peeling ceiling until my racing heart slows to its normal beat, wondering fleetingly what Phil is doing now. He is such a creature of habit that if he were at home I could set my watch to his actions, but his being away has thrown everything into the unknown. Across the room the box stares at me from its place on the chair and I glare at it, willing it to magically vanish in a puff of purple smoke. I try to close my ears to the whispers from inside that are tempting me to look, their taunts becoming louder and louder the more I try to ignore them. Surely it can't hurt? Just one look?

One page?
Just one?

1990
There is a dark tunnel through which I am walking. The darkness never seems to end and it seems that I have been walking forever without a hint of the tunnel ending. Occasionally the darkness will become a little lighter but there is no light at the end of my tunnel.

In the past it has seemed as though my journey has ended as the tunnel has been filled with light, but this is not so. The light fades leaving an aroma of memories in the air that I breathe.
I am scared but I cannot turn back for fear of going in to the past with the memories that I want to replay in my mind, so I must carry on.

Maybe I'll walk forever, maybe there will be light and the tunnel will end or maybe I can find a way to climb out.

Well, that was an epic mistake.

I carry the box downstairs and drop it with a thud onto the kitchen table. "Don't look at them again." I mutter crossly. "It does you no good." I shiver as a cold draft engulfs me. "If that's you Lily, you can go away. I told you to burn the bloody diaries…" Angrily I wrench open the fridge finding coffee, milk and the remains of the wine, but

27

nothing edible. "Who puts coffee in the fridge?" I mutter sounding ungrateful and petulant. I switch the coffee machine on and fill up the filter. The machine splutters and spits, sending hot water in my direction so I back away quickly. While the coffee percolates I rummage in the freezer. There's nothing breakfast-like in there so I put a chicken ready meal into the microwave longing for a bacon sandwich.

The weather remains ghastly. The flowers bow their heads against the force of the rain. I can't see the three grand oak trees from here, the mist and gloom obscuring their majestic forms. I turn on the radio to fill the quiet but the presenter is too chirpy for the misery so instead I put some of Lily's soft jazz on the gramophone and turn the volume up as loud as it can go.

The gale outside rattles the windows and pushes against the door, now locked tight against any intruder who may lurk outside. I think about the hooded man. He was prominent in my dream, there was a feeling associated with him that I can't explain, particularly now I'm awake, not fear, no I wasn't scared of him despite asking him if he was going to kill me, but he has intrigued me and somehow, he seems familiar. Yes, I'm intrigued as to why a hooded man was standing in the kitchen on one of the worst nights of the year. And then I remember I was naked.

Naked.

For fuck's sake!

The ping of the microwave offers relief from my mortification. The slop it has cooked looks unappetising but I'm too hungry to care and rip off the film, not bothering with a plate. It tastes better than it looks, at least, and stops the painful rumblings of my empty stomach. Putting my feet up on the spare chair I balance the plastic tray on my stomach and sit staring out the window. This is all mine. It's hard to reconcile that, so used to seeing the house as Lily's, the home that I loved for so long. The house does indeed need a new lease of life, new songs, new stories, new memories to hold onto. It's so tired and run down, in need of a makeover and some brightness. It's the bricks and mortar version of me. Maybe we could do it together, the house and I, be partners in the changes that need to come.

The jazz ends and the house is plunged into silence. I discard the plastic food tray onto the table push myself up and out of the chair to change the record when my phone rings. The shattered screen no longer displays the caller so I take the chance that it will be someone I want to talk to.

It isn't

It's Count Vlad. The vilest of the vile exes.

Again.

My heart sinks.

I've never liked Count Vlad. His name isn't really Count Vlad, it's Count Alexandru Georgescu the Third. He has the strangest, sharpest teeth and palest skin of anyone I've ever met and he has a creepy way of seeming to know exactly what one is thinking, often before it's a complete thought. He lives in a crumbling castle high in the Romanian hills surrounded by a dense, dark forest. Rachel and I went to visit just after he and Lily married, about ten years ago, and we stayed one, very long, night. The howling of the wolves and shrieking tick ticks of the bats were too much to bear and we made our excuses and left the next day never to return. Rachel wanted me to write a novel about him but Bram Stoker already had the monopoly on blood drinking Romanian Counts. Lily wasn't married to him very long and she left him languishing in Romania for a hot-blooded Italian she met on the plane to San Tropez.

"Hello Vla...Alexandru."

"'ave you found ze money Jessamy?"

I sigh. "Not this again. I've told you and the solicitor has told you, there is no money. Her accounts are empty. All that was left was the house..."

"And now you 'ave eet."

"That was her wishes."

"I am 'er huuusband,"

I clench my empty hand into the tightest fist and as calmly as I can manage I reply. "There were three husbands after you, Alex, I'm sorry but her will was very clear. All she had to leave was the house and it had already been signed over to me when I was born. I'm sorry that you are disappointed but there is nothing I can do. Please stop calling me, I can't help you. You will just have to marry another rich lady."

"I am rich..."

"Then you don't need anything from Lily. Goodbye Vlad..."

"Vlad? 'Oo is zis Vlad?"

"Never mind."

I put the phone down. Under the shattered screen, lights twinkle with unread messages, no doubt from the agent I've been resolutely avoiding. I will have to write something soon.

***

I feel out of breath by the time I reach the top of the staircase that leads to the attic and catching sight of myself in the dusty mirror at the end of the hallway makes me feel dismal. Dressed in an oversized jumper and pair of joggers I look like the sad old woman who dressed in the dark. If I close my eyes I can see the small, skinny, gawky kid I once was, the one so desperate to be accepted. I feel a pang that takes my breath away as I think about that girl, me, always with my head in the clouds, always looking for an escape from home life and finding it here, amongst the craziness of Lily's life, hanging out with the local kids on the beach. How different life was in this grand house that stood so proudly at the top of the hill. Lily used to say that the house touched the heavens and we were the goddesses lent to earth.

I wish.

I wish I felt like a goddess, shimmering with an ethereal light, not the lonely, unhappy soul that reflects back at me.

I walk towards the mirror, looking for some clue that I am still here, inside the body I no longer recognise.

I feel so lost.

I turn sideways and glare critically at my reflection. "Well Jessamy," I tell the clone in the mirror, "you've got to sort your shit," and I poke out my tongue and turn away, taking the small right-hand corridor that leads to the attic.

The door is locked. It's painted pale blue and is smaller than the other doors in the house, looking more like the doorway to another world. As I find the key under the window sill and put it in the lock I fearfully wonder what may be lurking in the darkness - vampire, zombie or something more sinister – until I nearly don't go in.

A draft of cold air and a dank, musty smell escapes as I push the door, creaking and groaning, open. There is a murky light, similar to the shade of gloom outside but more threatening somehow, a warning perhaps to leave everything well alone. I keep my back in the door way, shivering as the creepy air wraps itself around me until even counting to fifty doesn't calm my racing heart. I run my hand along the wall in search of the light switch assuming, like the rest of the house that it's a modern square panel. It's not. It's a hanging cord about a foot in front of the wall. I reach out for it, fumbling in the dark, and each time the silken threads of spiders' webs entangle themselves around my fingers I yelp, the sound echoing around the attic.

"Come on Jess." I step fully into the room and wait for the light to warm up. It makes little chinking sounds as the dust on the outside burns while the filament heats up. Once the room is brighter I look around with a sinking heart.

It's filthy.

The dust is inches thick on the surfaces and cobwebs litter the rotting beams and the small, circular windows at either end. Boxes clutter the room, covering every inch of space. This is the first time I've ever been up here. Boxes are balanced upon boxes, cardboard towers that wobble as I move around them. I recall the door always being locked, a different door to the one that sits there now, thicker, rough enough to give me splinters the first time I tried to get in. Did she lock her secret in here, buried in cardboard?

It's there for you to find.

There is so much here. I look around with an ever-sinking heart. This will take weeks, likely months, to sort through. I won't be going home anytime soon and I get a little flicker in my belly. Relief?

Do I feel relieved at being here?

There is some sense of peace being away from the thick, cloying atmosphere of home but being here just entangles me in the past that I've been trying to forget. I shut my eyes tightly. The phrase *out of the chip pan and into the fire* pops into my head, when did it all get so hard?

I shift a couple of boxes to make a pathway and search the loft for the painting. I remember it well. A ghastly modern painting of Queen Victoria painted in heavy dark oils. Lily bought it because she had a brief affair with the artist, Crispin, a curious chap who dyed his hair pillar-box red and had a penchant for silk cravats and smoking jackets. The affair didn't last very long and despite him endlessly showering

Lily with love letters she quickly moved on to husband number five, or maybe six. I was sad to see the end of the affair, I liked Crispin for all his quirky craziness and he was infinitely better than Charles, the investment banker from London, Lily married next, who enjoyed spending his time being serviced by latex-clad ladies in basement clubs.

She didn't ever choose well.

The attic is draughty, a cold wind creeps in between the roof tiles and the ineffective insulation, which makes me shiver. I sit down on a sturdy box, under the light, my chin resting on my knees listening to the pitter-patter of rain on the roof. Occasionally a drop lands on me and I brush it off before resuming my position.

Was it ever Lily's intention for me to go home? She was never Phil's greatest fan, considering him to have a hidden agenda disguised beneath his pretty-boy exterior. I always thought she was suspicious of everyone because of her chaotic and emotion-led life. Perhaps I've been wrong all these years and she saw more about my life than she let on. *There is a new chapter waiting for you but I fear that all you have known will change before you feel ready.*

I don't know if I want 'us' anymore.

Beginning at one end of the attic, ducking to avoid the strands of web that hang from the beams, I search for the painting. Clouds of dust mushrooms up from the floor making me cough dryly as I move boxes and bin liners looking for it. I clear a path through the clutter disturbing the spiders who quickly scurry out of the way, feeling more and more despondent at the monumental task of emptying the loft. She must have stored everything here.

Clambering inelegantly over a large box, I eventually find the portrait hidden in the alcove beside the chimney. Looking at it after all these years, affected by the damp, swollen and cracked, it's more grotesque than I remember. The Queen looks at me forlornly, as though resigned to her fate in the dank, dusty loft and I shudder. It is a truly monstrous portrait that would suit Vlad Manor very well.

"Come on Vic," I say gripping the frame either side and bracing myself to move it. She weighs a ton. It stands as tall as I do and slightly wider with a heavy oak frame that has the green flecks of mould growth dotted on it. I pull a face.

Here goes nothing.

I adopt a squat position, my thighs shaking under the pressure of holding my bulk at an unfamiliar angle, and wiggle the portrait, a centimetre at a time, from its hiding place, sweat running down my face and pooling in the hollow of my throat.

"Gross." I pant, "really you are gross," and then I laugh saying to the portrait, "which one of us am I talking too?"

It's a slow process to move the portrait and it's hot, hard work. I prop it against the wall beside the door. "Right then, Vic, what secrets are you holding?"

With a few expletives, I manage to turn the painting around and lean it against the wall beside the door. Dark brown tape covers the seals but sticky patches either side of the tape suggests it's a new fastening. I find the end and pick at it with my fingernail until enough comes away that I can pull it. As I do the frame slips and crashes loudly to the floor, dislodging another cloud of dust that sticks to my hot, sweaty skin.

"Holy fuck." I shriek leaping back before the weighty frame can crush my foot. The sound echoes around the attic, a booming sound that hurts my ears as it rings around the beams.

Holding my hand to my chest I wait for my heart rate to return to normal before pulling off the remainder of the tape and sticking it to a nearby box.

Find the painting, Jessamy, the one that we hung for the sheer hideousness of it (do you remember?) and when you find it, look closely at it for that's where you'll find my legacy.

"What have you hidden Lily?" I ask out loud whilst lifting the back off and leaning it carefully against the wall.

Beneath the back are thick sheets of newspaper, some dating back as far as the 1970s, and under that…

"Oh my God!"

I sit back heavily onto the floor, taking in heaving breathes of air. I don't notice the dust, nor the coughing, as I stare in shock at the inside of the frame.

Neatly stacked and covering every inch of the five-foot tall frame are bundles upon bundles of twenty-pound notes. There must be hundreds of thousands of pounds here, kept inside a mouldy painting inside a draughty attic room. Oh my God, Lily, what were you thinking?

33

***

I pour a large whisky from the bottle I find on the side table in the morning room. I dislike whiskey ordinarily but this is no ordinary time and it serves a medicinal purpose despite burning my parched throat painfully. I have a bundle of cash down here, bringing it with me in a daze from the attic and I sit staring at it as though I've never seen money before. All that cash, hidden away…anything could have happened to it. I was blissful in my ignorance but now all I can think is *what if something happens.* I was expecting a small legacy, and small would be so much better than this. I didn't ever have Lily pegged as a batty old lady who hid money under the bed, but on reflection this is so much worse. What do I do with it? I can't leave it up in the attic, not now I know it's there and it's not as though I can walk into a bank and hand over a few bin liners of cash, they'd call the police and the vile exes will be lining up to stake their claim. It's as I'm finishing the last drop of whiskey that I suddenly remember that Lily had a safe in the cellar. The solicitor has already done an inventory so if the safe is still there it will be empty of anything valuable and under my shock is the pleasurable thought that none of the vile exes can gain anything further from her. I'll forever wonder why she always chose unsuitable men, there must have been a reason but I suppose now I'll never know.

I pull my fleece on and drain the final drop of whiskey before walking out of the room.

The corridor is really cold and I zip my fleece up against the chill. I stand before the portrait of Lily, looking for an answer, anything that may be a clue to the secrets she held so close. I lightly run my fingers over the brush strokes and the gold signature at the bottom, squinting at it. There is no doubt to me that whoever painted this loved her passionately, they captured her spirit so completely, but as to who it is, I'm none the wiser and the signature gives nothing away. I sigh and push the bolt holding the door shut. It screeches like nails down a blackboard and I grimace before opening the door.

The air that rushes up from the cellar is old and stale and I heave a little at the heaviness of the stagnant blast. Switching on the light I twist my hair up into a band and walk slowly down the wooden steps to the cavern below. I've always disliked the cellar imagining all sorts of horrors held under the house and all because of a summer spent watching scary movies trying to be cool. Those nights I slept curled up with a teddy in Lily's bed too terrified to be alone. All to impress the boys.

One boy.

The boy.

I'm thankful that the light is bright and illuminates even the darkest corner. There are no monsters here, only the ghosts I bring down with me but I can hear them. Being here is a constant reminder of the past, every single corner of the house tells a story and I feel both comforted and frightened. It has all been buried for so many years that to suddenly have a rush of intense pictures and voices seems almost too much to deal with alongside the other chaos in my life. I have the urge to cry until there are no tears left but I fight it, there is no need for more tears. It won't solve anything, nor will it miraculously take life back to the way it was. The cold becomes almost unbearable the lower I go. The cellar, spanning the length of the house, is empty apart from a wall of neatly stacked wines. I'm surprised the exes didn't demand them, if only to drown their sorrows at receiving nothing. Lily always kept a full cellar, impromptu parties happened all the time and she liked to be prepared. Alongside the wine are shelves of boxed glasses and unopened bottles of spirits and mixers. It cheers me slightly that if everything does indeed fall apart I can at least drink myself into the next century. I put a couple of bottles of wine beside the cellar stairs and retrace my steps.

At the very back of the cellar is the safe. It stands on legs about two-foot-high but the box itself is no more than a foot squared. It was once black but over the years the outside has fallen foul to the damp cellar and the black is now more rust coloured. The key hangs behind a pipe which I retrieve and open the safe.

It's no way big enough to safely store the piles of cash upstairs, nor is it secure enough. The door wobbles on the rusted hinges and while it may be ok for smaller items, wads and wads of cash wouldn't fit, nor be safe. I'm going to have to order a new one. A big one, with CIA style security and fire proof to boot. I'm not going to sleep tonight for fear that something will go terribly wrong and the money will be lost.

"God Lily, why didn't you put it somewhere safe?" I groan out loud.

I suppose she did really. No one in their right mind would want to walk out with the portrait but the enormity of what is hidden in the house is more than I feel able to deal with.

At the back of the safe is a small book and a key. I reach in for them and close the safe, waiting for the lock to ching before leaving the cellar, quickly, just in case there is something lurking in the shadows, slamming the bolt across as soon as I'm in the safety of the hallway. For a moment, I stand in front of Lily's painting.

"If you were here Lily," I remonstrate, "I would be going ape shit right about now!" Childishly I poke out my tongue and retreat to the kitchen.

***

Lily's book sits on the kitchen table with the key beside it. I pick the book up, turning it over and over in my hands but I don't open it. Curiosity burns but my heart says, no, wait, wait for the right time.

So, I listen.

Occasionally I hold it tight to my chest, a small embrace, while the tears fall but I don't feel strong enough yet to delve inside.

That's for another day.

Not today.

It takes six trips but I move the money to the cellar and my arms now ache so much that I know what it's like to take on Rocky. The cellar door is padlocked with a spare lock I found under the sink and the key is inside the jar of coffee. I figure anyone breaking in wouldn't think to look there and the most I can do is pray to any God listening that the house stays upright until the safe I've ordered comes.

The rain is relentless.

I've no idea of the time but the darkening sky makes me feel trapped and claustrophobic. It's eerie. A strange blue/grey colour that hangs low over the bay. Some of the flowers have lost their heads and the rest just look miserable. I eat some microwavable slop and nurse a coffee, watching the raindrops fight for space on the window.

I should write.

I can only plead an extension for so long. My agent is merciless and will neither care nor make allowances for Phil having a mid-life crisis or me being down here sad and alone. She is amazing at her job but the downside is she wants blood, every last drop, and the flashing of messages under the cracked screen are likely to be increasingly irate ones from her.

I finish the uninspiring meal and open my laptop, bringing up a blank page and sit staring at it.

"Come on inspiration…hit me." I beg and type *Chapter One.*

I delete Chapter One and write *A story about nothing.*

I delete that and write. *One dark night a stranger came…*

"It's not an autobiography Jessamy!" I laugh and then flush. A stranger saw me naked.

Me.

Naked.

Fuck.

Fuck. Fuck. Fuck.

I pick up one of the diaries and bury my embarrassment in the past.

***

1990
I feel very alone and very unloved and it's a horrible feeling.

An almighty crash above wakes me violently, the diary falling to the floor with a thud. The sky has turned a colour so deep it takes on a strange red glow. I leave the diary on the floor and pull myself up, keeping the blanket wrapped tightly around me. There is a humidity in the air that feels as though it's tightening around me, pushing me lower and lower, weighing down oppressively.

The lights flicker with each boom as I hastily make my way along the corridor to the kitchen. With each bang of thunder, I yelp, my racing heart making the blood flood my brain until I feel dizzy and nauseous. I sit back down at the table, the discarded bottle of whiskey from earlier looks more and more appealing with each boom. My hands shake as I pour a generous measure and look out into the night, clutching my glass tightly between my cold hands. I feel tired. And scared. I've always hated storms but in Bath, surrounded by the honey stone houses, they are less fearsome but down here, all alone, with the shadows and strange noises, this storm feels like it's been sent by an angry God, reigning vengeance down on me.

I think about Phil. He sits at the forefront of my mind and I hear him in every thunder clap. I remember the first storm we had together, curled up on the bed in the tiny flat Zoe and I shared, and he told me he would always look after me, always protect me. How things have changed.

He said he would never hurt me but he has. Being down here alone has made me realise just how much my marriage to him made me feel almost whole.

Almost.

But not quite.

Something has always been missing.

I thought I hid it well, kept everything wrapped up tightly and locked away but misplaced pride and misplaced jealousy has torn my marriage in two.

I have to take the responsibility for that.

The rain lashes down and above me the thunder bangs, followed swiftly by the brightest flash of lightening that covers the sky in a strange silver and illuminates the three oak trees at the end of the garden. They are swaying violently in the wind, their branches reaching out, inviting me to join them in their morbid dance. I watch the sky turning a myriad of colours as the storm rages. It's hypnotic, tantalising the senses, drawing me to it with a magnetic pull.

I push the chair back and walk to the door. The key, as ever, is hanging from the beam. Lily never took security seriously, never believed that anything terrible could happen in this sleepy little town, even with all her money in the attic, she still left the key on show. I reach up for it and place it in the lock, twisting the handle and pushing it harder than necessary. *I'll move the key tomorrow.* The wind whips my hair and steals my breath as I walk out into the storm. What am I doing this for? To be cleansed? To be free? To be struck by lightning and fried in my hideous shoes, the ones Phil bought me for a joke, that I always seem to wear. The door slams behind me and the wind screams making my ears ring. Beneath my feet, the grass is soggy and squelchy making each step harder and harder. The rain soaks through my clothes and the hot, angry tears on my cheeks mingle with the falling water. I'm so angry that I want to scream. So, I do. As the thunder bangs above me so I scream until my throat is sore and my voice is hoarse. The sky lights up the garden and a figure moves towards me, its hand reaching out, the face hidden by the shadows of the storm.

I turn and run. Above me heaven continues its violent call as I race as fast as I can across the sodden ground, losing my shoes to the grip of the earth. I fumble at the door handle, yanking it open and entering the safety of the house, collapsing back down in the chair. It's only when the door opens do I realise with a bone chilling fear, I didn't lock it behind me.

"What the fuck are you doing outside in a storm? You crazy bitch." The figure stands before me in a coat dripping water into a puddle on the floor, his face obscured by an oversized hood and a dark copper beard cut close to his face. I find myself staring at his mouth as it moves, a full mouth, framed by the bristles that cover his jawline. The curses flow from his tongue, the Devonshire accent deepening the angrier he becomes.

I start to laugh.

I can't help it.

Close to hysteria the laughter rings around the room and I grip my stomach, doubling over, unable to take in a full breath as the laughter continues.

"What's so funny." He demands glaring from under his hood. In the dim light I can just about make out the flashing of green eyes, fiery and furious, glaring at me. "What the fuck is so funny?"

Nothing is funny, but I continue to laugh anyway. "You're telling me off for being outside?" I puff out the words between giggles. "Yet you're standing in a puddle of rain water soaked? Don't you think that is a little bit funny?"

"Do I think it's funny?" He hisses at me. "Funny that you're outside in the middle of the worst storm on record?" He takes a step backwards. "No, I don't think it's funny. Not in the slightest. Lily left me instructions…guard you with my life but you seem intent on killing yourself so her concern is wasted…"

"Why do you care?" I retort, shocked by the seething anger of the stranger before me.

"Why?" He rips down his hood and says. "Because I do."

"Jack? Jack Grayson?" I say with surprise, squinting through the dripping rainwater that rolls down my forehead. "Is it you?"

"Who else?"

"Oh my God! I've not seen you since…"

"A long time."

The Jack I remember was skinny with carrot coloured hair but somehow in the last two decades he's morphed into - I look him up and down and almost drool – a tall, broad, copper haired God.

"Stop staring at me." He says huffily. "You're freaking me out."

"Sorry it's just, well, you don't look like the Jack I remember."

He gives me a scathing look and gives my body a quick peruse. "Neither do you." He replies sharply.

I flush and pull my cardigan closer around me. "Was that you the other night?" I ask in a mere whisper looking down at the floor suddenly feeling the sheen of embarrassment wet my skin. "A man came into the house, I was…um…in my towel and…"

"Yes, it was me."

"Oh."

The pause is long and very painful. Jack's smile grows wider and wider the more embarrassment colours my skin.

"There is no need to smile at me quite so gleefully. It's really nothing to smile about."

He starts to speak but a crash above us makes me jump like a scalded cat. Immediately a fork of lightening so brilliant flows from the sky and hits the middle oak tree, Lily's tree. Sparks fly as the wood catches alight. "No…No…No…" I scream as the flames lick the leaves. I tear the door open and watch with sickening terror as the great oak succumbs to the flames, burning from the branches down until the trunk is engulfed in tendrils of orange and yellow. It's captivating and horrifying and transfixing. I'm vaguely aware of Jack making a phone call before he runs back out into the night, his form highlighted by the flashing sky. I swear I can hear the tree screaming in pain and a knife of anguish twists its serrated edge into my belly. I wrap my arms around my middle, holding myself together and slowly sink to the floor. "Oh Lily, I'm sorry, I'm so sorry…"

Time slows. Eventually sirens wail from the end of the driveway and Jack runs back inside to open the gates from the panel beside the fridge. I cross the kitchen to the hallway and watch as the fire engine speeds down the drive, too wide for the wheels to fit, churning up the plants and the grass from the verges in the haste. The sky is inflamed by the storm, the colours switching from black to grey to a hellish lilac so fast that I see spots in front of my eyes. The fire engine slides on the sodden ground, the wheels finding no grip as it passes around the house, scraping against the out building on its way across the lawn.

It's like something from a horror film. The flames grow despite the rain, licking the leaves of the grand oaks either side. It's an enchanting dance, that of life and death, intoxicating yet so fearsome to witness. The firemen pull out the hose and a powerful jet of water erupts in an arch from the nozzle, hitting the tree with force. I tentatively walk out into the rain, my bare feet sinking into the squelchy mud, ducking my head against the icy drops that fall painfully against my skin, pummelling me so hard that I wonder who the sky is angry at. The thunder booms making my ears ring with the sound and the sky immediately turns a hellish silver as the lightening seeks its next victim.

"What the hell are you doing?" Jack grabs my arms and almost pulls me off my feet dragging me back towards the house. The wind grabs his words and whips them up with the leaves it has found on the floor. I have to run to keep up with his stride, too shocked to do anything other than follow his lead.

He bangs the kitchen door open and turns to me with fury. "What the fuck are you doing?" He says again glaring at me. "It's dangerous…"

"If it's so dangerous why are you out there?" I glare back with my hands clenched on my hips. "This is my house, my tree…"

"It'll be your funeral too. Stay here." He pushes me further into the kitchen and turns on his heel, back out into the rain. I watch him run across the lawn, shouting something to the fireman beside the engine. The windows rattle with the force of the wind and I watch as the fire fighters battle to extinguish the tree. Of all the trees, why did it have to be that one? All those summers days spent sitting under that tree, it knows my secrets, my thoughts, it's grown on soil wet with my tears both of sorrow and of laughter. It's the tree that Lily wanted to be scattered under and as the fire rages so I wonder how I can lay her to rest there now.

Occasionally I hear shouts above the wind but the words are indistinguishable in the storm. I sit at the table, fanning the pages of one of my diaries, looking out at the chaos. I don't know what else to do but sit. A raging storm, a raging fire and an equally raging man was not part of the plan.

1988
I don't want to fancy him but I can't help it.

Jack makes me jump. "The fire is out. Don't go out there again, the storm is showing no signs of moving on." His eyes flash as if daring me to argue.

"I won't."

"Good." His hood is down and his face is blackened and sooty with streaks where the rain has fallen onto his skin. He looks wild, hair springing in all directions as wearily he rakes his hands through it. Droplets of rain roll down his forehead and I watch one as it slides down his skin and into his thick eyelashes, eyelashes that frame the brightest green eyes, hypnotic eyes, eyes I don't remember ever being that vibrant. The same eyes that are flashing at me with a simmering anger, it would seem.

Oh shit.

I drag my eyes away from his, flushing slightly. I'm staring for longer than is polite but this manly ruggedness is more captivating that I would like to admit. For God's sake, Jessamy, it's Jack!

Jack.

Jack was never rugged or captivating.

Jack was skinny and gangly and always had spots.

This new version has wrong-footed me somehow, being so very rugged and very captivating and very…

He frowns as though reading my mind and the groove between his eyes deepens.

"Are any of the old gang still here?" I ask giving myself a mental shake.

"Some."

"Who?"

"Orrion, Tori, Rob, Andrea, Debbie…you know about Nate and…"

"Yeah, I do, Debbie told me."

"Oh. I didn't think you came back?"

"Once."

"Oh."

The pause is long and painful. I clear my throat. "Thank you for sorting the fire. I'm amazed the firemen got the truck through."

"I think they took out the outhouse. I'll look tomorrow. Don't go outside until the storm stops. You saw the tree...I don't want Lily haunting me, I've enough shit going on." He pulls the coat hood back up over his sodden hair and abruptly turns from me, striding across the room and out into the night.

It's only after he's gone do I realise I've been sitting in the dark.

CHAPTER THREE

I wake up entangled in bedding that wraps round me like bind weed, with an aching head. I move slowly, stretching one limb at a time, cramp spreading through my stiff joints. I didn't sleep very well, waking over and over from a recurring dream of a hooded man. It wasn't Jack, which makes me feel strangely disappointed, but nor was it Phil or the Ghost. A psychologist would likely have an answer as to why a strange, fearsome man was in my dream but there isn't a valid reason inside my muzzy head.

I replay the events of last night over and over.

Jack.

The tree.

Jack.

The tree.

The total decimation of the majestic oak from a lightning bolt intent on destruction.

Jack saw me naked.

Holy hell, 'hot' Jack saw me naked.

I pull a pillow down over my head as though protecting myself from the squirming embarrassment. There is no one here to hide from but it doesn't matter, if anything I'm hiding from myself.

Fuckity fuck fuck.

He saw me naked from the waist up more times than I can count in my youth, when the taut skin was stretched over my skinny frame, but the skinny me no longer exists and the image he saw was round, soft, slightly droopy and…

I feel sick.

This house is cursed. I am cursed and the sooner I can get out of Otterleigh the better.

There is no point lying here trying to ignore the inevitable so I remove the pillow from my face and sit up. I have to see the damage for myself and the sick feeling returns. I swing my legs over the edge of the bed and stand up. The blood feels as though it's rushing to my head and the room swims in front of my eyes. Collapsing on the floor in a tee-shirt that's far too small would not be the best start to the day. Ignoring the whoozy feeling and my aching body, I rush down the stairs, setting of the alarm in my haste. It takes several attempts to

44

deactivate it, the wailing screech making my ears ring painfully. "Argh shut up, shut up!" I yell above the ringing trying to put my hands over my ears and shut down the system. "Goddamn it! SHUT UP!"

I cross the hallway, the tiles freezing cold under my bare feet, and down the corridor to the kitchen. My heart pounds, dreading what I am going to see when I look out the window.

"Oh...fuck..."

I yank open the door and speed across the lawn, stopping to pick up the muddied shoes half buried in the sodden grass, stolen last night by the storm. I slip my feet into them grimacing as the mud squelches between my toes as I continue down the garden to the oaks. My chest heaves with the exertion and I'm painfully aware of my thighs rubbing together beneath the short tee. The failings of my physique are forgotten as soon as I reach the trees. In the cold light of day, the oak looks far worse than I could ever have imagined. Charred bark is flaking from the trunk and the flames have destroyed all its leaves, leaving the boughs blackened and bare. The swing that used to hang from one of the largest branches is a burnt, mangled mess on the floor, the ropes that held it in place remain hanging but are shrivelled and melted. There is a slight blistering on the oaks that stand either side but they survived the worst of the fire for which I am grateful, not all is lost. I walk around the middle oak, the grandest of the three, reaching out to touch the scorched wood that still feels red hot under my fingers. My chest tightens until breathing becomes painful and the familiar sense of grief returns. Death has its grip on The White House so tightly that I wonder how I can bring the life back. I pick up a handful of burnt leaves and they crumble to dust in my palm. Gone in one moment. Just like that.

Look up Jessamy. A slight wind picks up and rustles in the leaves of the two remaining trees. *Look up.* I'm going mad. I'm hearing things. Sleep deprivation, grief and a marriage in tatters is having a detrimental effect on my mind. I feel a frigid hand grab my arm and I physically jump. I rub my skin trying to get the warmth back, but as I do I have the strangest feeling. "Lily?" I whisper, the scent of her perfume strong in the air.

Look up Jessamy.

"What?"

Look up.

I stand back and look up at the bare tree. High above me nestled in between the blackened branches is a solitary leaf, fluttering in the breeze, holding on so tightly I can almost see its stalk gripping the branch.

Oh, thank you God. The breath I hadn't realised I'd been holding onto escapes with a hiss and my knees buckle beneath me until I'm sitting on the wet ground. One leaf is all it needs. I can do what Lily asked, there is still life in the tree. I feel a bubble in my stomach that erupts in a peel of laughter until I'm snorting and holding onto my stomach as tears roll down my face. I laugh until it hurts then I cry until there are no tears left and my face is a blotchy, dribbly mess. Pulling myself up, I slowly walk back across the grass skirting around the debris from the storm that litters the garden. It saddens me to see the broken branches, fallen leaves and beheaded flowers in the normally immaculate oasis of colour that Lily loved so much. The outhouse has bricks missing and a metallic red stripe along the middle from the fire engine, deep grooves in the grass from the tyres. All in all, the garden is in a very sorry state.

"Good morning Jessamy." The Vicar's cheery voice carries across the garden. "Lots of excitement here last night I see." He gestures to the track marks in the ground. "I saw the fire engines...didn't come over though, my dear, the lightening..."

"I made the mistake of going outside..." I tug at the hem of my tee-shirt feeling the spread of embarrassment across my already red face.

"Jessamy!" The Vicar is doing his best to keep eye contact but he looks as awkward as me.

"I know! I know! The tree wasn't so lucky but I survived." I rub my eyes and yawn widely. "Honestly John, I thought I was coming back to quiet, unassuming village life!"

The Reverend laughs. "Nothing quiet and unassuming here my dear!" He says with a twinkle in his eye, turning to look at the tree. "Have you never heard the phrase, 'it's the quiet ones who are the worst'? A sad ending to a majestic life." He says shading his face with a hand to his brow.

"Yes, I suppose it is." I smile softly. "But at least one leaf survived, perhaps all is not lost."

"Sometimes, something that seems small and insignificant can bring such hope." He reaches for my hand, his warm and dry, calluses rough against my palm. "Go inside, it's cold, you're in your...not very much! I'll come back over later and talk about Lily's scattering. One leaf on a tree is all that's needed, her ashes will make it grand again. I promise."

"Thanks," I say quietly looking at the solitary leaf dancing in the breeze. "I hope so."

***

The two burly men I open the door to, look less than impressed with the location for the new safe. I worry that one, or both, of them will collapse under the weight of it and die in the corridor in their too-tight trousers and holey jumpers that do little to disguise their protruding bellies. They sweat, curse and groan as they move the heavy safe down the cellar steps, shouting profanities as they navigate the small stairway down to the cellar. The furious glances they send in my direction has me hiding in the lounge until they leave. As soon as their van has gone out through the gates I input a new code into the key panel and move the money from the bin bags into the safe. Then I give a huge sigh of relief.

The house could burn to the ground but the money is safe.

Taking advantage of the change in the weather I pull on my boots and my thick woollen coat to walk into town to see if I can get my phone repaired. I feel almost hesitant at going. I have so many memories, fixed and unchanging, wrapped up in this sleepy little Devonshire town that I wonder if I will recognise any of it. I still see it as it was, quaint, unhurried, safe. Yes, it was very safe, a sanctuary from my parents, from school, from unreasonable demands for perfection. I'm not sure I can handle it if anything has changed.

My boots crunch on the shingle as I walk up the long drive to the gate. The front garden looks worse than the rear, with huge welts in the ground from the fire engine and decimated plants thrown to all corners. It will need a miracle to put this garden right again. Fleetingly I wonder what it would look like with creams and greens in the borders, rather than the bright pinks and reds that Lily preferred. More serene, perhaps, a haven of calm, but then I feel guilty and push the thought away. I punch the code into the panel beside the gate and wait for them to clank open. They slam shut behind me and I cross the road and head south, towards the cliff path.

Along the length of the road are terraced houses painted white with thatched roofs, each with rambling roses around the front door and a pristine picket fence. The gardens are uniformed with neat lawns and immaculate beds, or at least they were before the storm, the paths free of weeds, looking like a picture on a biscuit tin. Cars line the roads, pulled up tightly to the kerbs, their mirrors facing inwards, now covered in debris that had been thrown around by the winds. It will take the village a fair amount of time to recover from the storm but so far it seems The White House has had the worst of it.

I follow the road to the end and cross over to walk down the steep, winding path that leads to the beach and beyond to the town. It has been newly paved, the stones bright and light grey, unbroken and complete unlike the old damaged ones that caused many a post-beach party fall. The wooden rail has been replaced with a cold, steel one that has taken a battering from the overhead seagulls, splotches of white excrement dotted along the metal, making it no longer fit for its purpose. There is the feeling that I may fall as I navigate the steps with nothing to hold on to so I take them slowly, moving sideways rather than looking directly down the cliff. I don't remember a similar affliction to the old wooden hand rail but memories have a way of giving the past a rosy glow. My ears sting from the wind that whips up from the beach below and I walk a little faster, pulling up my hood and holding it in place with a cold hand.

The sea is raging. Great, white tipped waves rise from the murky, brown water and crash onto the sand. "It's July." I mutter grimly. "Where is the goddamn sun?" I dip my head lower and continue down the steps, a vivid memory of bright blue sky and five boys encased in neoprene surfing, us girls lying on the beach pretending not to notice them. No cares in the world, the only purpose of life then was to have fun. It looks like an entirely different beach today, angry and vengeful, no one is in the sea and only a solitary person walking a dog can be seen on the sand.

I shrug my head further inside of my hood and shove my hands in my pockets, rubbing my fingers over my palms to warm them up. Winter has come to Otterleigh, smothering the summer weather with an icy embrace. I need some sun, even if just to feel as though life is continuing. It feels dead, empty and hopeless at the moment, my dark mood blackening further each day.

A woman in bright pink sports kit begins to run up the steps, barely breathing as she comes past me. She gives me a questioning look as though she knows me, which I return, searching my memory for a clue as to how I could know her, but she elegantly strides past seemingly unconcerned by the height or number of steps, no sweat marring her skin. I watch her run up the final steps more conscious than ever of the straining buttons of my coat. The woman doesn't look like she'd ever find anything hard work. Even her hair swings neatly. At the top of the steps she does a series of painful looking squats, her perfectly pert little bottom almost touching the floor. She looks at me for a while and descends back down the steps stopping beside me.

She stares at me. "You look really familiar..." She squints, "sorry I don't usually accost strangers but your face...I feel I should know you."

"Likewise." Up close she looks even more familiar, the almond shaped eyes and the rosebud mouth too striking to be common place. "I used to spend my summers here..."

She leans forward and then gasps. "Jessamy? Jessamy Summers?"

"Yes..." I take a step backwards. "Do I know you?"

"I'm Tori, Tori Fielding...Jones now."

"Orrion? I always wondered if you two would get together. Wow, Tori, it's so great to see you...you look..." I search for the right word.

"Thin!" She says triumphantly.

"Well...yes...goodness, I wouldn't have recognised you..." The Tori I remember was always curvy, soft and pre-Raphaelite looking, always suiting the puppy-fat that she carried. The new Tori is lean and strong, defined muscles tight underneath the pink.

"You look...." She eyes me and I squirm under her gaze,

"Fat." I finish for her.

She grins, "I would have said, you look well."

I laugh. "That's the polite way of saying fat."

"Jessamy...I thought you were never going to come back! The last time I saw you…"

"I had to come back because Lily died..."

"I heard, I am so sorry."

"Thanks." I change the subject quickly. "Do you put yourself through this torture daily?"

"Most of the time!" She looks down at the watch on her wrist and it omits a loud beep. "That's my cue to get moving. It's so good to see you Jess, it really is. We often wondered what you were up to, I read some of your books! Are you staying at The White House?"

"Yes, for now…"

"I'll pop by and see you, it would be nice to catch up, I'll bring the others, it would be like old times! Must dash..." and with that her pink lycra'd form races up the steps and along the cliff top path. I feel exhausted just watching her. Perhaps that's what I need. Exercise. *You've let yourself go...used to be so sexy.* I feel a grimace spread across my face and immediately the vision of frothy cappuccino and a slab of carrot cake pops into my mind and stays there.

***

1989
Lily and I went into town. The boys were eating ice cream on the bench outside of the shop. Nate looked so sexy in his leather jacket and jeans. We didn't speak to each other.

Otterleigh looks exactly the same, even under the constant cloud and fine drizzle. Mrs Thornton's teashop is on the corner, still painted a pale blue, with overfull flower pots sitting below the windows. Across the road is the post office, painted red and white, with the same wooden tables and seats on the small courtyard which was where we used to sit to eat our ice creams. I poke my head inside. Apart from the lino being replaced by wooden flooring the lay out is exactly as I remember, even down to the piles of post on the long oak counter. I smile at the lady behind the counter and leave the post office hurrying up the street past the fish and chip shop, the bank and the local shop to Mr Davies' shop. He was the local handyman and if anyone could fix my phone it would be him but I have no idea if he is still around. If he seemed old back then, he'd be ancient now.

The shop sits at the end of the High Street, opposite the tiny village school. The clutter from the windows has gone and the interior looks organised and tidy. I feel my heart sink a little. Not everything stays the same then. The little bell above the door tinkles as I open it. There is a short, balding man about ten years older than me behind the counter looking at something on the worktop through magnified glasses. There is one customer in the shop, his broad shoulders encased in a dark leather jacket that set off his copper hair...oh shit.

"I'll be right with you love." The man in glasses looks up at me briefly.

"No rush." I say hearing a quiver in my voice.

Jack turns around and glances at me through narrowed eyes. I flush awkwardly as his green eyes harden.

"H-h-hello." I stammer aware of a flush on my cheeks. *Be cool Jess.*

He nods curtly and turns back to whatever task is being undertaken. It takes all my willpower not to turn and run.

"Can I help you Miss?" The man asks from behind the counter. I turn as the doorbell chimes, and watch the retreating figure walk across the road. It bothers me that he didn't say goodbye.

"Um, I hope so please." I reply drawing my attention away from the striding figure. I take my hood down and pull my fractured phone from my pocket. "I broke my screen. Is that something you can fix?"

"I can fix anything and everything love." He smiles. "Not called Clever Clive for nothing you know!" He winks. "Are you new in town or on holiday?"

"I'm at The White House..."

"Ah, Lily's niece. I've heard about you! Jessica, isn't it?" Clive asks.

"Jessamy..."

"Ah, that's right! The Vicar said you were coming. The weather isn't being very kind, is it?"

"No, not at all!"

"I was very sad to hear about Lily. She was a big personality in this town." He says softly.

"Did she come here a lot?"

"Not really. Fleeting visits mainly, always lugging a big suitcase that she wouldn't let anyone help her with. We all wondered what was in it. She said it was the dismembered remains of her vile exes! It wasn't until this past year that she came back and stayed. She didn't come into town so much then and the house was a lot quieter. I guess her illness had a lot to do with that. I watched over the house for a time, you know, repairs and maintenance, well she was hardly ever there. I had to stop when I took over the shop when my dad, Don Dixon, died…"

"Died? I'm so sorry. I remember him very well. Such a kind man…"

"Yes, he was. Mum moved to Weymouth to be near her sister and I took the shop on."

"It's very tidy!" I grin. "It didn't used to be!"

"Ah, my dad was a hoarder but he knew where everything was. Like a crazy talent or something, I suppose everyone has one."

"I suppose they do."

He reaches for my phone. "What do you do?" Clive asks rummaging under the counter. He remerges with a small package from which he takes a phone screen. "What's your special talent?"

"I write. Books. Romance mainly."

"Nice. My wife reads a lot of books." Clive falls silent as he concentrates on the phone and I walk across to the window. It's begun to rain again. Outside a lady struggles with a small child and an umbrella intent on turning itself inside out.

"Where does Jack live?" I ask as nonchalantly as I can manage.

"Jack Grayson? He owns the farm, or runs it, I'm not quite sure which. The ladies all go a little gaga for him…they seem to like his moodiness. Personally, I think it's a little rude that he doesn't really speak…"

"I knew him when I was younger but he seems to know Lily better than I thought." I'm fishing but Clive doesn't seem to notice

"He helped her a lot with the house and garden after I had to stop. He spent time with her, towards the end, not every day but it was well known around town that he'd go around and make her a large gin and tonic. The nurse used to get so cross but as he said, there wasn't a lot of time left so a gin wouldn't hurt and he'd take her out to the oak tree and sit with her for a little while. No one knows why, perhaps she reminded him of someone or more likely he reminded her." Clive shrugs. "It's a sad world when we question motives don't you think?"

52

"Is he married." Clive gives me a questioning look and I arrange my face to look as innocent as possible.

"Yes, to a local girl, but if village gossip is anything to go by, he won't be for much longer."

"Oh?"

"Ah, you know what gossip is like, always wrong." Clive smooths a plastic backed cover over the new screen and hands me the phone. "Voila!" He says. "As good as new. Try not to drop it again! You need a better cover, one that goes all the way around. I don't sell them but you can get them on eBay."

"Thank you!" I turn the phone on and the device begins to beep with unread messages and voicemails.

"I don't have a phone." Clive comments ringing 40.00 into the till. "I like not being accessible. The wife knows where I am, I couldn't deal with all the beeping."

I laugh. "You know, Clive, sometimes I turn my phone off!"

He gives me a wide smile. "Forty pounds please love."

I hand over a couple of Lily's notes. "Thanks Clive." I put the phone in my pocket. "Oh, one more thing."

"Yes?" He asks putting the credit receipt in his till and shutting the drawer.

"Are there any personal trainers in the village?"

"Any what?" Clive asks incredulously. "What's one of those?"

"Never mind, I'll google it!" I pull the door and the little bell chimes. "Thank you, Clive, no doubt I'll be back in with something else I've managed to break."

"It'll keep me in business if your phone was anything to go by! Go careful in this weather."

I nod. "I will."

***

I sit nursing a cappuccino in Mrs Thornton's tea shop with bags of shopping balancing against my legs. Now that I can read my text messages, I wish I'd left the screen cracked. Mostly the messages consist of *'where the hell is the first draft'* shirty texts from my Agent whose calls I have avoided pointedly for the last three weeks. As it stands my first draft consists of '*His eyes were the deepest green…*' and not much more. The advance cheque is sitting in my business account untouched. Some are from Rachel checking on my welfare and the final message, a short one from Phil. '*I'm leaving for France. I'll ring when I'm back.*'

"Yeah, yeah whatever." I say crossly to the phone. I get a strange look from the old man sitting on the next table. He's reading the local newspaper, a pot of tea in front of him. I give him a faint smile and flick to Facebook, scrolling quickly through the various posts, most of which boast of fabulous lives. I wonder how much of the 'fabulous' is true. I thought my life was pretty fabulous and I got that horribly wrong.

The café door swings open bringing with it a draft of icy wind. I look up and lock eyes with Jack, his face set in a grimace. I give him a slight smile and drag my eyes away willing my thudding heart to slow down. This is ridiculous. I'm married…sort of…it's Jack. Jack! Skinny, carrot haired Jack. With a wedding ring and a wife. I pretend to be busy with my phone but I no longer see the statuses on Facebook, the words all blurring into grey, because I am too conscious of where he is.

For fucks sake Jessamy, it's Jack.

"Hello." He says pulling out the opposite chair and sitting down.

"Hi."

"You ok?" Jack asks picking up the menu and looking at it.

"All good."

"The tree?"

"Has a leaf."

"Does it?"

"Yeah." The pause is long. I'm so conscious of my straggly hair and too-tight sweater.

Jack appears to want to say something but instead says, "see you," and as quick as a flash he's out the door and crossing the road towards the post office.

I watch him go and sigh. This is all too crazy. This village turns normal people crazy.

I need to leave.

Maybe.

***

1988

I had a really weird dream last night. Debbie, Jack and Nate and I were hand gliding and we crashed. Nate took my hand and his was really warm. I feel really confused.

"We have entrusted our sister Lilian to God's mercy, and we now commit her mortal remains to the ground: Earth to earth, ashes to ashes, dust to dust. In sure and certain hope of the resurrection to eternal life through our Lord Jesus Christ, who will transform our frail bodies that they may be conformed to his glorious body, who died, was buried and rose again for us. To him be glory forever, Amen."

The urn weighs heavy in my hand. The vicar and I are standing under the burnt tree, the one remaining leaf blowing haphazardly in the wind, held on by hope and not much else. I watch it spinning and flapping in the storm that has not given up its grip on the weather, and we shiver, huddled under umbrellas. It's not the ideal day to scatter her under the tree and the way the wind is whipping around us it's likely she'll be scattered over Dorset too.

John finishes his speech and takes the urn from my hands. Upon it he draws the sign of the cross and whispers something I can't hear. His face twists in pain and it's too raw to witness so I avert my gaze, giving him the privacy of his grief. He loved her. He always had loved her. Lily inspired love, she needed to be adored, revered almost, to be the first thought in a lover's head. She achieved it all. They all loved her, wanted her, craved and desired her, but it was never enough. Something was always missing.

John hands the urn back to me and I twist the top off. Is this really all we become, our beings reduced to nothing but ash? I bring the urn to my lips and give it a kiss. "I love you Lily. I miss you so much but I'll see you on the other side, have the martini ready for me." The wind picks up leaves and petals, debris from the unending bad weather and twists it into a spiral that moves upwards and scatters beyond the trees. It feels poignant. I walk around the trunk and slowly tip the ashes from the urn around the base. The rain dampens them into the ground and I feel a sense of something, relief perhaps or peace, that she will remain here, kept still by the rain.

"Life will come from her." John whispers, "this tree will be glorious again. You mark my words."

"I hope so." I say wiping stray tears from my eyes. "Thank you for this, for being here, for not saying no. It was so right and you know, I could feel her here."

"So could I, my dear, so could I."

John pats my arm and leaves me beside the tree. I run my hand up the charred bark, "look after her." I whisper to it and lean against the trunk, letting my tears flow. These are the last tears, there can be no more. I'm conscious of someone standing beside me and a hand reaching out for mine. It's a warm palm, large, strong, holding mine in a comfortingly tight grip. I say nothing. I know who it is and I'm grateful for the kindness.

The same kindness I knew a long time ago.

We stand in silence, my eyes are closed but the tears escape from under my lashes, rolling softly down my cheeks. I don't sob. I don't cry. I am letting it all go. Lily's wishes were met, the tree kept its promise and I feel a sense of calm beneath the grief. Jack's hand squeezes mine before letting go. I hear him leave, the air around me cools but I remain leaning against the tree until I can no longer bear the chill.

***

The lamps give a warm glow to the morning room. I love this room, it's small and snug with squashy cream sofas that one can get lost in. A pathetic looking fire is trying to burn in the grate, sending sparks up the chimney rather than igniting the kindling. I lit it for comfort but now I'm thinking that eating my way through a mammoth bar of chocolate would have worked so much better.

The plants in here look sorry for themselves, wilted and browning so I add generous amounts of water to each one and hope they survive. On the mantle is Lily's urn filled with cream roses and one bright orange lily that the florist in town delivered not long ago. It feels the right tribute to her, she always loved cream roses and with the absence of a grave on which to lay flowers, turning her urn into a vase feels like the next best thing. I thought today was going to be the hardest day I've ever had to deal with but actually there was none of the agonising pain I've experienced since she died. It has been peaceful. Calm. Quiet. I've had the strongest sense that she has been with me, her hand on my arm, her spirit enveloping me in a warm, safe embrace.

She is here.

She said she would be and she is.

Her book, taken from the small safe in the cellar, is on the table in front of me. I wonder about opening it but have so far hesitated. *All my secrets are there for you to find.*

I pick up the book and hold it tightly to my chest. I wonder if there are some things that should remain unknown. With my free hand, I pick up the wine glass from the coffee table and raise it to the urn. "Rest in peace, Lily." I have a sip and open the book.

21st June 1952
Dear Diary.
I saw a boy today.

I was walking through the town with Prudence, who lives next door, when he came out from the post office. Prudence nudged me hard as he passed us and he grinned the widest grin when he saw what she did. He was the most handsome boy I've ever seen, with bright red hair and sparkling eyes.

I got home and Ruby wanted to know what caused such frivolity. We didn't tell her and she pulled such a face, as though she had eaten something sour, which made us laugh so much she went and told Mother we were being unkind. Mother was furious and sent Prudence home and me to my bedroom where I have been ever since.

I wonder who he is? I've not seen him before. I hope he's here to stay.
Lily.

3rd May 1953
He says he loves me.
The Summer holidays can't come soon enough.
Lily

9th July 1953
He wants to marry me.
I'm so happy.
I think I'll be happy forever.
Lily

The rest of the pages have been ripped from the book.
Who was he?
I lie back on the sofa. Lily didn't ever speak of a boy from the village nor did she ever talk of coming here before she bought The White House, the year I was born. Yet, the content of the journal feels significant but with it comes unending questions for which I have no answers. They must be here.
The answers.
Are here.
Somewhere.

***

9th August 1991
Debbie, Andrea and I watched Dick Tracy this evening and Nate turned up. He sat reading Asterix cos Dick Tracy was pissing him off. He bought me a Cadburys crème egg. I'll be sixteen in 31mins.

I find a box of videos under my bed. They're dusty and most are missing cases and labels. With the absence of anything to watch on TV I carry the box down and pick one at random.
The rain is coming down heavily again and the light grey sky has turned dark and menacing. I curl up on the sofa, under the large red blanket that is always draped over the back of it and put the tape into the machine. It has a blank label and the grinding noise from the video recorder doesn't sound too good but despite a wobbly start *Dick Tracy* starts and I'm fifteen again.
The film ends and I stand up, stretching out my limbs one by one and crossing the room to switch off the video. It makes a loud groan and spits out the video keeping some of the tape behind. "Bugger." I pull the tape from the machine but Dick Tracy has met a gruesome end and I have to pull hard to free the crinkled tape from the spools. "That's

the end of that then." I leave the rest of the videos piled up neatly and head to the kitchen in search of food.

Day has turned to night. The storm picks up and the wind begins to howl again, banging against the window like a crazed ghoul until the rain comes, drowning out the screaming spirits intent on coming in.

From somewhere nearby there is a loud, deep bang and the sound of something very large splintering. The lights flicker, crack and go out. It's pitch black. I stand up, knocking my knee against the underside of the table. "Ouch, fuck, ouch." I yelp and rub my smarting joint. It's a limpy walk across the kitchen. I bang into the Aga and stub my toe, swallowing rapidly to quell the nausea that increases as the pain in my foot takes hold. "Bloody, bloody, bloody ow!" I howl between exaggerated gasps of breath. "Ow! Fuck! Ow!"

"No need to swear." Jack's voice comes from somewhere near the door.

"What do you want?" I hiss in his direction, rubbing my toe and my knee. "Why are you here?"

"A tree broke power cables when it fell. I came to check if you were alright."

"Do I look al-bloody-right?" I seethe.

"I don't know, I can't see you."

"Funny."

"As long as you're still alive that'll do for me." The kitchen door bangs closed and the room is suddenly silent again. I rummage blindly in the kitchen cupboard for a torch that works, remembering a little too late I left the big one in the attic. A small one, with a pathetic beam, works and I limp very painfully back to the table and shine the light to find my phone. I feel isolated in the stormy blackness but a link to the outside world would make this darkness bearable.

"Hi Mum." Rachel sounds bright and breezy. "Are you ok?"

"We've just had a power cut and I think I've broken my toe. How do I know?"

"Why? What did you do?"

"Walked into the Aga." I mutter pulling off my sock and shining the light at the swollen mass my big toe has become. "My toe is massive and red and walking is excruciating."

"You'll need MIU or A&E Mum," Rachel says patiently.

"I'm not really feeling inclined to go out. The weather has blown up again. Can't you do anything?"

"I can't do anything over the phone. If you're not going to go to hospital then take some paracetamol and bind it tightly. If the swelling goes down, you'll be ok, if it doesn't then it could be broken. Keep it raised." She pauses. "Should you be there on your own? I've seen the Devon weather reports. It's going to flood…"

"The house is high, Rach, I'll be fine."

"Why not ring Dad, ask him to come down?"

"He's in France…"

"Oh yeah, he did say. Look Mum, I know things aren't great but he does love you." She says kindly.

"Did he tell you that?"

"Well not in so many words but I know he does. He's just having a mid-life crisis. People do. It's a very real thing. Perhaps he'll buy a Ferrari and get everything out of his system." She laughs and I smile. "It will all be ok Mum, really it will. Are you sure you're ok? I can't do much from London but I can get you the A&E number."

"I'll be fine Rachel. I'd rather not go out. I'll bind it up once the lights are back on and see how it is tomorrow. Thanks babe. I love you Rachel."

"Love you too Mum. I'll ring you in the morning. Bye."

"Bye darling."

The silence is too loud. It rings in my ears but with no electricity I can't even put the radio on. I don't like it, being sat here in the blackness on my own. The house creaks and groans while the wind taps at the windows. Sounds that could send a person mad. It's at this moment, in the darkest black I could ever imagine that I feel completely alone, until I notice the crème egg on the work top.

**

The swelling on my toe has gone down and in its place, is a dark purple and red bruise. Walking is no less painful but somehow I managed to sleep deeply and I feel less pathetic this morning. The new day has brought yet more rain but the wind has subsided and the strange fog that enveloped the garden yesterday has retreated to where it came from. The electricity is still off so I boil a pan of water on the Aga to make coffee and once it's boiled I stand in the window, my hands wrapped around the mug.

I think of Phil and suddenly I want to speak with him, want his quiet reassurance that everything will be alright. I reach for my phone and scroll through for his number. Perhaps it's not too late, perhaps the past can be buried finally and we can move on from this blip that has taken over our lives.

Is that what you want Jess?

"Hello Jess." His soft voice echoes down the line.

"Hi."

"You ok?"

"Yeah, I was just thinking about you. I wanted to check you've arrived safely and that you're ok?" There is a long, uncomfortable pause.

"I'm fine Jessamy."

There's a noise in the background and I swear I hear a woman's voice.

"Is someone there with you?" I ask straining to hear.

"No." He answers quickly and sharply but I know he's lying to me. It hangs in the air and a desperate sadness comes over me.

"I don't believe you." I say unhappily. He doesn't say anything but the clock in the kitchen seems to tick louder and louder the longer the silence goes on. "Phil..?"

"Bye Jess." The phone clicks and the line goes dead. I twist my fingers together and lean my forehead against them. My heart beats a slow, dull beat and the bitter taste of anger swells and rises until it's all I can taste. He's lied to me. So much of his behaviour recently has been so out of character that I no longer feel that I know my husband.

CHAPTER FOUR

I lean against the damaged tree and watch the clouds through the bare branches, fluffy and white dotting the blue sky, drifting lazily on the faint breeze. It's a peaceful scene, so different to the weather of late and it lifts my spirits a little. The solitary leaf flutters joyfully on the puffs of summer air and its little dance brings a smile to my face.

Until Phil pops into my head and my moment of peace is lost.

He lied to me.

I know he did.

Just as he knows I lied to him for all these years.

What is worse? Lying to protect the other person or lying to protect oneself?

Have I done both?

I wriggle further up the trunk until I'm sitting upright and the house comes into view. If my marriage is to be saved the house cannot be part of my future, that much is clear, but whether Phil and I have a future is looking more and more unlikely. The longer we are apart the harder it will be to fix anything or want to fix it.

I thought change came subtly, quietly so one didn't notice, not like this, so abruptly with the force of an atom bomb that fractures everything in sight. I want the voice that is whispering, *you know the answer Jess* to stop talking for a while.

Closing my eyes, I send a wish out on the summer breeze, a wish for the answer to come, for guidance, for a quick peek into the future and to know that everything will be ok. The slamming of the side gate interrupts my conversation with the divine and I open an eye to see Jack striding purposefully across the lawn towards the house. Watching him cross the grass gives me a strange bubbly feeling in my belly.

I don't know why.

It's Jack!

***

1989
I had an argument with Mum on the phone this morning and she threatened to send me to boarding school AND summer school.

"Hi." I say finding him in the kitchen.

"Hi." Jack replies. "I was looking for you."

"Oh?"

"I've got someone coming to look at the outhouse this morning. We're due another storm…"

"Another one?" I interrupt. "Surely there can't be any rain left?"

Jack furrows his brow and gives me a withering look. "Do you not listen to the news Jess?"

"Not usually, too depressing."

He shakes his head and continues. "As I was saying, I've got someone coming this morning, I'm not happy that the outhouse is still structurally sound after the fire engine hit it so I want to make sure, before…" He stares at me. "…the next storm comes."

I search my mind for something to say but I'm saved by the ringing phone. The relief is temporary. *Oh hell.*

"Hello Mum." I say answering the call and bracing myself for the expected tirade. Jack opens the back door and walks through it, letting it close behind him with a bang.

"Have you phoned the estate agents Jessamy?" Not even a hello, that's a new low for her. Without pausing for a breath, she continues. "The house can't sit there festering while you dilly-dally." Her tone is so sharp it could cut glass. I can picture her, sitting on the Chippendale in the study, lips pursed so tightly they disappear, her bone thin face filled with displeasure at having to speak to me. I often think how much she looks like Cruella de Ville from the Disney cartoon, angular and devoid of warmth. I cannot ever remember a time she gave me a hug or ever seeing any semblance of affection between her and my Dad. Dad is less angular but slim and has always retained the air of feeling more important than he is. Now retired from their careers as Judges at the High Court, they rattle around their large West London home avoiding each other as much as possible.

"Not yet..."

"Oh, for goodness sake Jessamy, you can't just sit on it. Why Lillian left the house to you is astounding really, given Grandma is still alive, and the poor husbands, all that money and they get nothing..."

"Lily's accounts were empty..."

"You can't expect me to believe she left nothing. Lilian was a big spender but even she couldn't spend everything she accumulated. It must be there somewhere Jessamy. Grandma and I have had poor Alexandru on the phone, almost destitute, and he's a Count. He could lose the home that has been in his family for generations. She gained millions from him, millions. You must look for it. Stop wasting time in that backwater, find the money and then get back home. You have a husband Jessamy, you've been there for too long as it is. When I think of poor Phil home all alone while you're down there doing goodness knows what." Mum squawks loudly.

Behind me the door bangs softly and I hear footsteps. I would turn around but it's far easier to lay my forehead on the counter and close my eyes.

"Poor Phil is in France Mum..." As soon as the words leave my mouth I wish I could take them back. I hear Mum take a sharp intake of breath and I steel myself for what is to come.

"He's in France? Without you? What have you done this time Jessamy?"

"What have I..." I squeeze my eyes shut a little tighter. "Always you blame me." I whisper, my voice breaking. "Always. Has it not occurred to you that maybe Phil going to France without me is not my fault? That perhaps it's down to him?"

"He would never go without you..."

I jolt my head up and make a fist with my spare hand that I slam down on the counter. "Well he has, Mum. He left me down here all on my own and went to France. Does that make you feel happy? Is that 'poor Phil' enough for you..."

"There is no need to take that tone with me."

I twist my hair through my hands and take a deep breath. "Perhaps you could give me a little credit for not always..."

"Credit?" Mum interrupts at high speed. "You want credit? For what? For your husband being in France without you or perhaps you'd like me to congratulate you on throwing away your education and career for a one-night stand with some hillbilly from Devon who didn't even give you a backwards glance..."

"Oh my God. Seriously Mum, you're dumping that on me again?"

"I don't have time for this Jessamy, you need to get the house on the market and let poor Alexandru have some money before his castle crumbles around his ears. I've no doubt that Lillian has stashed money there somewhere and you need to find it. Grandma had to the pay for the funeral and the memorial..."

"Grandma was her sister..."

"It doesn't mean she was responsible for her. Lillian should have left provisions for her death."

"Oh, for God's sake Mum, she's family, we are responsible for her."

"Family? Lillian was nothing but an embarrassment, hardly surprising given her past."

"What do you mean? Her past?"

"Nothing dear, only you may find your precious Lily isn't what you thought." Mum sounds almost giddy.

"What does that mean?" I snap. "Lily was the only person in this crappy family who ever gave two hoots about me."

Mum laughs mirthlessly. "Because you are both the same. Now sell the house and let that poor man have his money."

"It's my house Mother, I will do what I see fit." I slam the phone down and wrap my arms around myself. "Evil, evil, evil witch." I mutter between clenched teeth and promptly burst into angry tears. I turn around rubbing my blotchy face, Jack is standing beside the door looking uncomfortable. I feel my cheeks redden. ""Did you hear that?" I mumble and blow my nose on a piece of kitchen roll. "Sorry…that's embarrassing. My Mum...well let's just say, she makes Darth Vader look like a pussycat." I give him a weak smile.

"She wants you to sell the house?"

"Yes."

"Are you going to?"

"I don't know."

Jack shifts from one leg to the other and looks as though he's searching for something to say. "Joe is here." He says finally.

"Joe?"

"Joe who is looking at the outhouse." Jack draws in a sharp breath and grimaces. "I'll be outside."

The door slams behind him.

***

I sit alone for an inordinately long time.

The venom in my mother's words weigh down on me. She's a bitter, twisted woman for whom nothing would ever be good enough, particularly me. I've been a continual disappointment to her and my father, never doing anything that they deemed worthy so perhaps the time has come that I stop hoping for their approval. It won't come now. It's hard to see them as anything other than two peas in the same vindictive pod.

I put my cardigan on and slip my feet into my shoes, leaving the warmth of the kitchen for the garden. Jack is standing in front of the outhouse, a tall, balding man wearing a luminous jacket with him. Jack gives me a cursory glance through narrowed eyes but the other man makes up for his lack of enthusiasm.

"Jessamy I presume?" He says extending a large, calloused hand.

"Yes." I reply taking his hand and cringing at the rough, sandpaper skin that encases my palm.

"Lily talked of you often." He says. "I'm Joe, Lily may have mentioned me?"

"Hi Joe." I look between the two men. "Thanks for coming out at short notice. You knew Lily?"

"I did some maintenance work for her, rebuilt walls, built the outhouses and the summer house. Jack here keeps it all tidy but I do all the manual stuff!"

Jack gives Joe a cuff on the arm. "Joe doesn't build anything. He directs the builders."

I smile widely. "Is that right Joe?"

"Guilty as charged." He says laughing, holding up his hands in surrender. "She was a good egg, your Lily. Only ever used local tradesmen even if they were more expensive. The autumn that she commissioned all the outbuildings to be rebuilt gave the locals their very grandest Christmas. It's not a wealthy town, times have been tough and if it were not for the tourists I think it would be a very sorry place to be. Lily kept a lot of people going. She was spending her 'ill gained money' as she termed it."

"Was she here a lot?"

"Not really." He says echoing what Clive in the hardware shop said. "More so in the last few years. She paid some of us to keep an eye on the place, keep it clean and still standing but only at the end was she here more often. I did wonder when we'd meet you. So, Jack here," he nods at Jack, "wants me to sort the wall of this outhouse but honestly pet, the damage means it would have to be rebuilt completely. It wasn't designed to take on a fire engine in a storm. I could take it down and get you a good price for the bricks. The local builder is always on the hunt for this stone for the extensions the out-of-towners insist on." Joe grimaces.

"Not keen?" I ask grinning. Jack makes a grunting noise and mutters something under his breath.

"They push the prices up so the town youngsters have to move out. They come down here in their huge cars, speeding down the lanes and scaring the livestock with their big engines but the flip side is that it keeps the locals employed. The big city types love to bring their hoity-toity friends to the town and play Lord of the Manor. In the summer months, they are always in the local pubs, in wellies and wax jackets that have never seen a field, having a pie and a pint. It makes them feel 'down with the serfs'" he wraps the words in air quotes, "and the locals charge them accordingly." He winks. "It's win-win really."

"They keep you in a job." Jack says grumpily.

"They do. But it doesn't mean I have to like the buggers." Joe says good naturedly. "I'll sort this and sell the bricks. What do you think you may want in its place? A hot tub?"

"I've no idea." I say. "I'm unsure yet what to do with the house. My life is in Bath…"

"You're going to sell then?" Joe asks a beaming grin spreading across his face. "I know someone who would love this house. He's a developer, good one too, mostly retirement apartments and would jump at the chance to get his hands on this place. Obviously," he comments his eyes scanning the house, "a big extension would be needed but that's ok because my cousin is the planning officer…would you give me first refusal?"

"I…uh…I…look Joe…"

"I'd get you a very good price."

"I'm sure you would but…"

"Give it some thought. Right Jack, I'll get the labour sorted and be in touch. Bye Jessamy, lovely to meet you." Joe saunters around the side of the house and out of view.

"Did that just happen?" I ask astounded looking Jack.

"Yes." Jack replies gruffly.

"They want to turn this beautiful house into apartments for old people?"

"The minute you sell." Jack says bristling. "I don't trust that Joe as far as I can throw him..." He mutters something inaudibly and picks up the large spade leaning against the outhouse and stalks off towards the flower beds.

"Jack?" I call. He turns his head and fixes me with his green-eyed gaze.

"What?"

"Look...I...I'm not sure about your pay. For the gardening...Lily didn't say anything...well I didn't know...so...um...can you tell me what I need to arrange please? For all the work you're doing?" I find myself shrinking under his narrowing gaze. The green eyes flash darker.

"You don't."

"I don't?"

"No." He says turning from me.

"Oh." I watch him stamping the spade into the earth. "Why?"

"I had an arrangement with Lily."

"What arrangement?" I ask, trying and failing not to look at his tight, firm arse as he bends over the flower bed.

"That is none of your business." He snaps not looking at me. I stare at his backside a little while longer and with a sigh I retreat into the house.

***

1990

Nate is seeing Debbie and it hurts so much. I don't know why, maybe it's just cos she got him and I didn't. I went shopping with Tori. She wanted to cheer me up. I bought a gorgeous picture of an angel above a perfect earth. I like the idea that someone is watching over me.

I walk slowly up the stairs. To imagine this beautiful property as apartments, its soul ripped out, churns my stomach. There is no way I can ever allow that outcome to be the house's fate. I slide my fingers up the varnished bannister, somehow, whatever happens, I have to keep this house safe.

My soul is here.

I cross the landing to my bedroom and take the key from the drawer in the bedside table, turning it over in my hand. It's an unusual looking key, a triangular shape and the strangest colour of green. Of course, it may be that sitting in a rusty safe in a damp cellar has tarnished it and I scrape my nail along the surface, breaking the nail and doing nothing to the green. It's obviously a key of significance but there is no lock downstairs that I can see, for which it would fit. I leave my room and walk down the landing hesitating outside of Lily's room. If there was any place for a strange lock for the strange key it would be in there but going in seems a monumental task for which I don't quite feel able to achieve.

I grip the key in my fist and hold it against my chest. "You could have just told me the secrets Lily." A cold chill lifts the hairs on the back of my neck. "You twisted woman." I laugh slightly nervously. I must admit feeling her here, the peculiar coldness that occasionally touches my skin and the important secret she kept hidden is comforting. I never really believed in life after death or ghosts and spirits but right now the idea that her spirit is here makes life a little less bleak. I reach out for the door handle, my heart hammering so hard in my chest I swear it's going to explode from my rib cage. I turn it slowly, my mouth so dry I can barely swallow and push the door open.

Lily's room overlooks the garden. Four windows stand floor to ceiling and the sunlight streams in. I cross the room quickly and open the windows, to me the air in here has the smell of illness and death but likely it's all in my head. The huge four poster bed sits against the inside wall, red silk draped from its carved oak posts. In front of one window is a chaise longue, the feet carved in the same pattern as the poster bed and upholstered in the same deep, rich red. The walls are pale gold, painted the same colour as the morning sun. A heavy oak dressing table sits on the far wall, above it is a small square window from which one can see the sea. On the dressing table is a photo of Lily laughing, holding a cigarette with her black hair swept up in a chignon. Next to that is a photo of Phil and I on our wedding day and the first photo of Rachel, taken just after her birth, perfectly pink and swaddled in a soft white blanket. I pick it up. It could be yesterday. I run my finger over the photo, tracing the line of her closed eyes, the thick black lashes touching her cheek and the rosebud mouth a deep pink colour. She was a beautiful baby, her face a perfect replica and even now it takes my breath away every time I see her.

She is the image of him.

The Ghost you keep in your head.

It's so still in here. There is a thin layer of dust covering the surfaces but the room is too tidy, too empty. I should be tripping over discarded shoes and clothes, not walking around hazard free. I put the key in my pocket and sit down on the bed. I don't know where to look for a lock to fit this key. Perhaps I'm making too much of the key, perhaps it's just a random key. But, if it were random then why was it locked in the safe? I fall backwards onto the bed and look up at the carvings. All roses. Beautifully detailed and exquisitely crafted, the flowers are so delicate looking but made from such strong, dark wood, that the fragility is an illusion. I've never noticed before how many roses are wrapped around the posts, on the bedding and in the hand painted stencils around the top of the walls.

"Why the roses?" I ask out loud to the empty room. Sighing I pull myself up and climb down from the bed looking, briefly, underneath to see if there are any locked drawers I didn't know existed. The under space is empty except for a forgotten sock so I try the ensuite and lastly the dressing room.

The dressing room is bright with rows upon rows of rails holding clothes from every era, and a shelving unit built into the wall houses Lily's shoes, handbags and hats, Beside the shelves are the drawers that are filled with her jewellery and accessories. I used to lose myself in here for hours when I was younger, playing dress up with the feathers and furs, the sparkling costume jewellery that Lily favoured, pretending to be someone of great importance. The furs are now shrouded in garment bags so I open one, taking out the wrap from within and holding it against my face, inhaling the scent. It's the epitome of a glamourous age, the beautifully soft fur that has no place in today's world. I don't know what to do with them, they are unwearable but too stunning to throw away. I zip the wrap back up and hang it beside the others.

None of the drawers have locks so I leave the dressing room, closing the door behind me, feeling more puzzled than ever.

***

"Rachel? Oh my God, what are you doing here?" I pull my daughter to me and squash her into a tight embrace.

"Argh Mum, you're suffocating me!" She says wriggling loose from my arms. "Surprise!"

"Surprise? It's the best surprise ever? How did you get here?"

"I took a train, then a bus to the town then I had to walk up here. Apparently, there are no taxis in this town! I'm knackered."

"I bet you are, it's a fair old walk up those steps."

"Guess what…"

"What?"

"He's gay." Rachel's face falls.

"Who's gay?"

"Juan."

"Oh."

"Yeah, big bloody 'oh'. Still, the limb amputation was a good learning experience although I did have to swallow my own sick as the saw started cutting through the bone. Amputation isn't my kind of medicine. Anyway Mum, are you going to let me in or leave me standing on the doorstep while you look as though you've never seen me before?" Rachel grins.

I stand back. "Come on in Rach!"

"Thanks."

Rachel walks into the hallway. "I had no idea the house was like this. It's gorgeous."

"Isn't it just."

"And massive!"

"It is that. It feels enormous rattling around here on my own. I'm so pleased you're here. How long are you staying for?"

"A couple of days. Maybe a week. I don't know. Long enough to see you, not long enough that you get me helping."

"Oh, my dear girl, you've come at the wrong time to avoid helping! I've an attic to clear and you're just the med student to help me do that."

"Oh fuck."

"Yep, you should have phoned instead." I laugh and link arms with her. "Come on Rach, cheer up!"

"And there I was thinking you'd be so pleased to see me we'd spend our days drinking wine and eating fish and chips!"

"You know what thought did Rachel!" I grin at her.

"Don't I just."

***

"Oh, good God alive…" Rachel takes a step backwards and leans against the wall. An enormous spider, lazing on its web just above her head, stretches out a leg and I grab her arm.

"You need to move before a spider takes up residence in your hair!" I laugh as she rubs her hair down, leaping from foot to foot dramatically. "It's not in your hair, it's happily in its web, just looking at you…"

"I bloody hate spiders. Hate them." She wails. "Honestly, Mum, I hate them. You need to get a cat."

"A cat? Why?"

"Cats eat spiders, it's survival of the fittest and the cat always wins." Rachel wraps her arms around herself. "I bet there's hundreds in here…"

"Thousands…all waiting for you!" I giggle. "Don't worry Rach, I'll save you. Now, can we please start? I'm not sure where we'll start, but start we will!" I eye her edging closer to the door. "Or I'll start and you'll…"

"Go and spy on your gardener whilst pretending to work on my assignment?" Rachel suggests. She saw Jack yesterday and hasn't stopped talking about him. It makes me feel strange, jealous almost, more aware than ever of how much I feel invisible next to her youthful beauty.

"No! You can go down and make coffee and bring those biscuits up with you?" I pat my belly. "A girl can't work on a nearly empty stomach!"

"Not that awful instant?" Rachel groans.

"Tea then! Anything I can dunk my biscuits in." I move a couple of the boxes to the side to make a small walkway. I cannot even imagine what Lily has stored up here. Decades worth of items she likely had no need for. I pray that there is nothing further of immense value hidden up here but after the money I remain unconvinced. Rachel grimaces at the unending pile of boxes and disappears through the small blue door to make the tea.

I walk slowly through the attic, moving more and more boxes to create a path. This is going to take forever to sort.

Will I ever be going home?

***

Rachel and I sit drinking strong tea from a bright red teapot, the crumbly chocolate biscuits tempting me from the plastic plate perched on top of a dusty box.

"Are you planning to start this anytime soon Mum?" Rachel asks nodding at a box. "We've been up here for an hour!"

"I know! I'm stalling because...well...I feel a little afraid. Once it's gone, it's gone and that's it. No coming back from gone is there."

"No there isn't but this is just stuff. It's not Lily and keeping it won't bring her back, as much as I wish it would." Rachel's voice breaks. "I miss her so much Mum, I miss her ringing on a Sunday evening, I miss her coming to see me like she always did when she was in town, I miss hearing her stories...it's nice to be here though, in her house, I can feel her here, it may sound a little crazy but I can."

I smile gently at Rachel as she gnaws down on her lip to keep her sadness at bay. "I feel her here too Rach, all the time. She hasn't gone anywhere yet, I don't think it's her time to go."

"Do you think she's here to make sure you're ok?"

"Yes." I reply simply. "Yes, I do. It's not a great time at the moment and I keep feeling her hand on my arm, like she wants me to know that she's here for as long as I need her to be."

"I think it's because of Dad."

"Dad?"

"Yeah, I think she wants to make sure you're alright, whether you and Dad stay together or not." She breaks a biscuit in half. "Do you know that I've been phoning him and he's not once answered the phone. Not once. I know you and he weren't getting on well but he promised he wouldn't be weird with me..."

"I think Dad needs to sort things out in his own way Rachel. It's not about you, it's never been about you. It's me he's resentful of and I kind of understand it all. He loves you, he loved you the minute he met you, even though you were covered in chicken pox and screaming your head off. Let him have his space for now, when you reach your forties you'll understand that it's a peculiar time of life, rather like your teens, less puberty of course, but the same amount of confusion. It's probably why it's called a midlife crisis."

"You're ok with him being away and being odd and basically being shit to you?"

"No. But I have my own issues, it's what happens. Nothing is ever plain sailing Rachel, as much as I wish that your life will always be sweet and rosy, it's just the way it is. If you don't have bad times how will you ever know when it's good?" Rachel nibbles her biscuit. A coldness wraps around my wrist and I put my tea cup down. *Thanks Lily, for being here with me.* "Ok," I say suddenly motivated, "let's start."

"What's the plan?"

"Move the boxes downstairs and go through each one I guess." I look around the room. "There's not enough light, or space, up here to see anything." I pick up the box closest to me. "No time like the present hey?"

Rachel follows me down the attic stairs and into one of the guest bedrooms. The sunlight floods in making a spot in the middle of the whitewashed floorboards.

"I should be outside topping up my tan." Rachel moans.

"Rachel, I'll make a deal with you." I say picking at a corner of the yellowing tape holding the box shut. "Help without moaning and I'll treat you and Phoebe to an all-expenses paid holiday to the sun, wherever you want to go. It's on me." I pull the tape which makes a loud screechy sound and crumple it into a ball. "Here goes nothing."

"All expenses paid? How? Have you sold a kidney or something?"

"I've a little cash put away," I don't look at Rachel as the lie rolls off my tongue. "You deserve a treat, so why not spend my cash on you and my beloved Goddaughter?"

"I'll not say no!" She grins. "Thanks Mum, that would be amazing. You're amazing!"

"Funny what the promise of cash does!" I laugh as she throws a crumpled roll of tape at me. I open the box. "Oh." I'm not sure what I was expecting to find but a box full of old cheque books and receipts was not it. "Well that's not exciting. Who keeps used cheque books?" I mark the box with a black pen 'BIN'. "What's in yours?"

Rachel tears the tape off and lifts the lid. She yelps when a family of small spiders' scurry down the side of the cardboard and take off across the floor. "Bloody spiders." She says shivering looking inside the box. "It's a tea set." Rachel lifts a cup out of the box and turns it over. "Royal Daulton, very nice." She passes the cup to me. "Worth something I'd imagine."

"It's so pretty, look at the artistry." I say. "I went to Royal Daulton once. My friend moved to Stoke years ago, she was a young mum like Zoe and me, but very together and very glamourous. She would rather have picked off her own fingernails than gone out in a charity shop tracksuit like we would. We saved for months for a night out in Bristol and when we were out she met a footballer from up there and went off with him the very next day. He went on the team coach, she went on the National Express with Gabriella, her daughter. She came back months later dressed up to the nines in designer clothes from shops in Manchester and a massive diamond ring, gave everything from the flat to the charity shops and that was that." I scratch my neck. "I forget who he played for, I don't think it was the team in the stripes, it may have been the other one, the one Robbie Williams always went on about. You were about two when we went to stay. We tried to be cultural and visit all the potteries but we made it to Royal Doulton and then spent the afternoon in the pub. I did buy a plate from the seconds shop, I used it every teatime! Zoe was most put out that I didn't get her one, but I was so broke back then that one was all I could afford. Perhaps I'll send the tea set onto her! Make up for the lack of plate twenty-odd years ago!"

"Do you hear from you friend now? The footballer's wife?"

"Sometimes. She left the Stoke chap after about five years for a player from Spain. Don't you remember that we used to get copies of Hola! through the post. She sent them if she was in it but she's had a lot of surgery and doesn't look so much like she used too." I screw up my face. "I often wonder if there is something to be said for Botox."

"How would anyone know how you were feeling if your face didn't move?" She sets her face straight. "Hello I'm happy."

I giggle. "You're right!" I look at the cup. "I'm going to keep it. What else is in the box?"

"A sugar bowl and some side plates."

"Afternoon tea sorted then! I wonder if there is a cake stand?"

"Why would you want a cake stand Mum? You can't cook! Do you remember that birthday cake you made for my eighteenth? It was rock hard! Granny broke her tooth."

"Yes, I remember that well. Mum didn't let me forget it, either! I did sometimes feel a little sense of satisfaction!"

"Mum!"

"Yes?" I ask in an innocent tone.

"You're so bad!"

"Perhaps!"

***

By lunchtime we've made little progress. The boxes seem to reproduce at the same rate that we unpack them. The spare room is littered with mouse eaten cardboard and ancient newspaper. Lily has accumulated so much pottery, most of which is ghastly and is now sitting in one corner ready for the charity shop.

"I'm going to find some bin bags." I declare standing up and stretching my back out. "Now that I can no longer see the floor I think it may be time to start bagging! How can anyone collect so much crap and leave it packed up?" I pick up a twisted vase with demons on the side. "I wonder if she bought this when she was married to Count Vlad. Looks like something Dracula would have, doesn't it?"

"Count Vlad? Is he still alive?" Rachel says reaching out her hand. "Give me a hand Mum, my back is killing me!"

"Unfortunately."

"I told you he was immortal." Rachel shivers. "I really didn't like him. He just seemed to pop up all the time, in random places, like he'd just walked through the wall or something."

"Sadly, he is still going, and now he has Granny chasing me for the money she assumes I have."

"So, where is it?"

"Where is what?"

"The money?"

"What money Rachel?" I ask innocently.

Rachel laughs. "I'm not daft Mum, but I shall thank Lily for my all-expenses paid holiday to the sun. Is there a budget?"

"Nope!"

"Hawaii here I come!"

***

I put the wrapped parcels of fish and chips down on the kitchen table and Rachel attacks hers with enthusiasm. They smell delicious, covered liberally with salt and vinegar and washed down with ice cold soda from cans. We both sit facing the garden, the few days of sunshine having made all the difference to the pitiful looking flowers. They now stand with their heads high, proudly surveying their domain.

"It's so lovely here, how can anything be wrong with the world when there is this to look at?"

"It won't stay like this though Rachel, a storm is forecast. You may want to be safely back in London before it hits…" I fall silent. Now that Rachel is here I want her to stay, the idea of being alone again is depressing.

"Mum?"

"Hmm?"

"Do you ever think about my real Dad?"

I look across at her. She looks thoughtful, her blue eyes focused on somewhere else. "Sometimes. Why?"

"I just wondered." She says, popping a vinegary chip into her mouth. "I think about him sometimes, wonder if he'd like me, if there was anything about me that was like him, you know. More so now since Dad has gone all weird…"

"Rachel, he would love you, of course he would. As to whether you are like him…" I reach for her hand. "There is much of you that is him, it's quite breath taking sometimes." She waits for me to say more. "It's not just how you look, your face and his face are identical, right down to the shape of your eyes and the way you smile, but some of your mannerisms are exactly how I remember his. Rachel, it is ok to think about him, really it is and you mustn't think otherwise."

"I feel like I'm betraying Dad though."

"You're not. Honestly darling, you're not. Dad would never want you to feel guilty about thinking about your real dad. Dad loves you, you're still his little girl, what is happening now is about he and I, not you. It's never been about you or where you came from." The lie rolls easily from my tongue. "Dad just needs some space from me and actually, I think I needed space from him."

"Will you stay together?"

"I don't know."

"Do you want to?"

"I don't know," I whisper. Her face twists in pain and I give her hand a squeeze. "I'm sorry Rachel, don't get upset, it may all be ok, if we want it enough."

"When is he coming back?"

"I don't know."

"Mum?"

"Yeah?"

"Isn't life shit sometimes?"

"It sure is."

***

1989

Debbie, Andrea, Jo and I went to the sports centre to play badminton. Jack said I looked very sexy in my cycling shorts and he liked it when I bent over. I told him that I did not fancy him but he kept following me around being silly. We all went outside and it was so cold so he said he would warm me up. Andrea started flirting with him and sticking her boobs out so he forgot about me. I wonder when I will get boobs.

"Oh my God!" I discard the tissue paper in a heap on the floor, a layer of dust rising as I chuck the box lid beside it. Coughing I wipe the grime off the front of the frame and turn it to show Rachel. "My fourteenth birthday, look at us. Can you believe that it was ever ok to wear hooded tops and cycling shorts, with no bike in sight? What did we look like?" I laugh. "We thought we were so cool…God, can you imagine?"

Rachel takes the frame from me. "Well, no. I can't imagine why you would ever think that! How did you ever pull anyone dressed like that?"

I reach into the box and take out another tissue wrapped bundle. "What was wrong with looking like a wannabe of Olivia Newton John in her 'physical' days!" I laugh loudly. "One of the boys I was friends with reckoned I looked fit dressed like that…" I tail off as Jack pops into my head, not as he is now, but the skinny, carrot haired Jack of the past. I remember him telling me how fit I looked and how I laughed, not to be unkind but because no one had ever told me I was fit. I remember his face falling and the horrible guilty feeling I had for days afterwards. I push the memory from my mind.

"Oh. What's this?" I drop the tissue on top of the paper previously discarded and hold three hardback books in my hands. "Oh goodness, these are my stories. I had no idea she kept them." I stroke the covers and raise them to my face, taking a big breath in and smelling the leather. "Lily gave me the books. She got them at a souk in Marrakesh during one of her holidays. I was fourteen or fifteen I think. The colours have faded," I comment looking at the books now lying in my lap. "They were such rich colours, bold and bright, and I remember how strongly they smelt of leather." I sniff one. "Now it smells like old paper."

"What stories did you write then Mum?" Rachel asks, emptying a box of material swatches. "Why would she keep squares of material?" I take one from her.

"My stories? Always love stories, boy meets girl, boy always loved girl, always immune to the glamourous friends' charms!" I laugh. "Sadly, not the same story as in real life. Listen to this…*I walk through the park. The wind whispers your name and the birds sing their songs for you. You are like the beautiful treasure that I cannot own. At night,*

79

the stars' twinkle, winking at my dreams while the moon lights up your window. I can feel you near me, your lips caressing mine. But your dreams are not intertwined with mine for you dream of another but I still love you. How dramatic I was!" I run the material through my hands and tell Rachel, "Lily wanted to redecorate the morning room. She wanted something more vibrant but, in the end, she settled for creams, the same colours as the roses she always had. I'm glad she didn't go for any of these, they are pretty vile, aren't they?"

"Gross." Rachel comments closing the box. "One for the bin I think." She looks behind us at the steadily growing pile of junk. "What say we do one more box each and call it a day. My arse is killing me from sitting on this floor and I cannot breathe in anymore dust."

"Good idea! It must be nearly gin o'clock." I say glancing at my watch. "Somewhere in the world at least."

I pick up a box an arms-reach in front of me. It's small and tatty, with a faded produce label on the side. The tape holding the flaps closed has disintegrated and breaks apart with ease. My heart hammers painfully in my chest and I feel almost faint. It's a very strong feeling that inside this box is something of huge significance.

"Mum are you alright?" Rachel asks reaching for my arm. "You've gone really pale."

"I don't know." I whisper pulling the flaps open. "I've the strangest feeling about this box."

My hands tremble so violently that Rachel takes the box from me and opens it up. "What is it?" I ask.

"Probably nothing." She takes out a small folded blanket. It may have been white once but age has turned it a blotchy yellow colour. Rachel passes it to me and I take it, bringing it up to my face, but the stale, musty smell of it makes me gag. I put it gently onto the floor and reach for the next item, a small red box, faded with age, inside of which is a delicate cross and chain, tarnished and blackened but perhaps silver underneath the discolour. I take it from the box and hold it across my palm. An intricate design is engraved onto the surface of the cross, delicate swirls and the smallest roses and on the back, the words, *Because of Love.*

"It's beautiful." I say holding it up. "I've never seen it before. All Lily's jewellery was kept in her dressing room. Why is this up here in a box? Is there anything else in there? Any clue to what these things mean?"

"No, nothing else, just those two things."

I look at the blanket and the necklace. My heart speeds up and with it comes the realisation that these two items are significant. "Come on Rachel," I say to prevent any questions from my daughter. "I owe you a very large drink."

We walk down the stairs in silence, the box weighty in my hands. My body aches but I can't stop thinking that I may have uncovered the first piece of the puzzle.

CHAPTER FIVE

It takes me two solid weeks to clear the attic. Rachel disappeared back to London after a week with as many 'exotic holiday' brochures as she could carry and the house was plunged back into silence. The only thing to keep me occupied in the empty house was to clear out Lily's stock pile of randomly saved items. The interesting items I kept, the less interesting are packed ready for the charity shop and the ornaments of very questionable taste are in a big box ready for shipping to Vlad Manor. I pack these with a twisted smile on my face. It's highly unlikely even Count Vlad will appreciate them but as he is the husband I disliked the most it gives me a juvenile pleasure to send them onto him. I should be more mature, just send them to the charity shop with the rest and let them sort out what will sell, but to me, this is the same as blowing one huge raspberry and so I keep packing.

The boxes weigh a ton. I struggle out to the car with them, my arms feeling as though they will be ripped from their sockets at any moment. Huffing and puffing with the exertion I somehow manage to manoeuvre all of them but the car suspension groans under the weight and something makes a snapping noise that I ignore. I wipe my face with the sleeve of my shirt and lock the house up before getting into the car and driving the short distance to town.

It's a lovely day. The bright, blue sky sits in the heavens for as far as I can see and the sun, beaming yellow against the blue, spreads its rays across the houses turning the honey stone a rose colour. I drive slowly down the main street and find a space outside of the charity shop. I pop my head inside and ask for a trolley.

"How much do you have?" The lady behind the counter asks incredulously.

"Lots and lots." I grin as her face falls. "I won't be offended if none of it is any good, I've been sorting my Aunt's loft and honestly, I don't want to keep any of it but I'm not convinced that anyone else will want it either."

"Let me come out and help." She says turning off the till and pocketing the key. "You're from the big house on the hill, aren't you?"

"Yes, how did you know?"

"A new face offering me an aunt's loot doesn't take much working out!" She smiles. "You've sparked my interest now!" She comes outside and looks in the boot. "Golly, there is a lot. Don't you want to keep any of it?"

"I've kept some bits, some is being shipped to Romania and the rest is in here. It could be good for business, probably worth quite a bit, my Aunt didn't do anything by halves. It's all been gathering dust in the attic for years I expect, but some of it…well let's just say it will need a unique taste!"

"I can do miracle displays." She says patting my arm, "it will all sell!"

"You've not seen it yet!" I grin.

"Your Aunt was famous around here, it will sell and sell well."

"I hope so. I hope it makes lots of money for you." I fall silent and she pats my arm again.

"Let's unpack your boot and give your car tyres a reprieve," she says. "Otherwise you'll be driving back up there with flats."

The woman goes back into the shop and brings out two wheeled trolleys. Between us we load the trolleys and groaning with the weight we push them into the stock room of the shop.

"My goodness," she says, "that's more exercise than I've had in months." She fans her face and opens one of the boxes. "Oh." She comments her face falling a little.

"Sorry, I told you, it will take a special kind of taste to appreciate. If you don't want some of it just let me know and I'll take it somewhere where no one knows me!"

The woman laughs. "If I put up a sign saying this was Lily Summers' stuff, it will sell like hot cakes. She was an enigma around here. If she was in town the sales of hairspray and red lipstick shot up, she made the beige women of this town sit up and take notice, someone had to, the boring lot that they are. I liked her very much, no one threw a party like Lily Summers. I was sorry to hear she had died."

"Thank you."

"How are you coping in that big house all alone?"

"I've been keeping very busy." I tell her.

"I bet you have!" She smiles. "it's a big house, lots to sort I'd imagine."

I'm distracted by a copper head walking past the window. My belly flutters and I will it to be still but regardless I find myself by the door looking out. Jack is standing at the cash machine, a dark-haired woman beside him, her hands on her hips, defensive. His face is dark, closed and broodingly handsome but I keep well back so he doesn't see me. The woman turns around, her face like thunder, and I take a sharp breath in.

Andrea.

1989
This morning I phoned Andrea cos it was her birthday. She told me that she got off with Jack and that she's going out with him. She also told me that the music was put on on purpose so me and Nate would dance. Jo kissed Nate but Andrea told me that he doesn't fancy her. I bet he does. She's pretty and thin. Andrea said she was going to phone him to find out if he liked me but I couldn't phone back because I was going out with Lily.

I feel blindsided.

Clive said Jack was married to a local girl. In a town as small as this one, with locals who stay here from birth to death, it makes sense but somehow, I feel winded anyway.

You're being ridiculous Jessamy.

I know, but words of wisdom don't help at times like this.

I also feel a little guilty.

Andrea was my friend once, most of the time a good friend, and I've been having dreams about her husband…

This town is nothing but trouble.

The woman is talking to me as she takes out a few items from the top box and I half turn, out of politeness rather than interest, and try to focus on what she is saying.

"You're right about the taste but honestly, Dear, I have no doubt that the crazy folk in this town will snap everything up. Can I advertise them as being Lily's?"

"Do whatever you need to do to sell them and make as much money for the cancer charity as you can." I reply distractedly, paying more attention to the interaction between Jack and Andrea. Her hands are on her hips and her face set firm. She used to light the room, but whatever has happened between her and Jack, or perhaps just the passing of the years, has taken the glow from her. She looks furious but, from my new vantage point behind the mannequin in the window, her eyes have such sadness in them that I feel my stomach twist.

The woman is still talking to me, not noticing my lack of response. I move from the shop window and say, "thank you for taking it all. I must go but I really hope it does well for you." I bid her goodbye and leave the shop, keeping my head down and walking away from where Andrea and Jack have been. I don't dare look to see if they are still there, instead I hurry down towards Mrs Thornton's tea room. I'm neither hungry, nor thirsty, but the car is right beside Jack and Andrea and I don't feel now is the time to say 'hello'. I hesitate outside before crossing the road to the Post Office where I buy an ice cream. It's as good as I remember, a thick, creamy chocolate ice with a flake that I nibble on my way to the beach.

It's busy with holiday makers, day trippers and locals making the most of the perfect day, a rainbow of beach towels covering the sand. Beach huts line the pathway, their wooden slats painted pastel colours, and just beyond them is the small cabin that sells inexpensive food and drinks. From them I buy a coffee and take it and my ice cream to a shaded spot below the rust coloured cliff. I mull over a plot, tapping notes out onto my phone, unconsciously describing my hero as auburn haired, then consciously changing the hair colour to chestnut. *Focus Jessamy.* The ice cream drips down my arm as the story takes shape, until a brave seagull swoops and takes it from my hand. "Oy!" I yell, knocking over my coffee as I stand up, my phone forgotten as I watch my stolen ice cream disappear. "Bloody bastard sea gull, I hope you drown." I seethe.

"That's not very environmentally focused." A voice says behind me and I turn to see Jack, a short distance from me, standing on the path that leads up the cliff.

"Bloody thing stole my ice cream." I moan, wiping my hand on a tissue I find in the pocket of my jacket.

"It's ok, you've kept the bit of it that is around your mouth." He says with no hint of humour. I flush and use the tissue to wipe my mouth.

"Is it gone?" I ask.

"Yeah."

"Do you always have to be around at the times when I look my absolute worst?" I mutter, licking my finger and running it around my mouth just to be sure.

"Why would you care?" He asks.

"I don't." I snap. "I was just commenting. Where's Andrea anyway? I was going to stop by and say hello."

"Don't bother." He replies sharply and without speaking further he begins to climb the steps up the cliff. I watch him briefly, his posture rigid, and sigh. The Jack in my diaries is now a man and I don't know this version, he's unfamiliar. The Jack who was my friend, my reliable Saturday night snog when Nate was off with someone else, the one who walked me home when I was tipsy and held my hair back when I was sick, is a grown up. I look down at the rings that adorn my wedding finger. I'm grown up.

I have a husband.

I think.

***

I sweep the attic. Now empty of boxes it's a huge space with colossal wooden beams holding the roof in place. I open the windows at either end and a light breeze drifts in, disturbing the piles of dust. It takes me a while to fill bin bags with the sweepings, the small dustpan is not suitable for the mounds I've swept but it keeps me busy and that's a good thing. I tried phoning Phil earlier. I had no intention of doing so and even as my fingers sought out his number, I still didn't plan on dialling but somehow the call button was pressed and I listened to the foreign dialling tone ring until the phone cut out. Now I'm imagining all sorts and I wish I'd just left things as they were.

I wish I'd left him to his space.

I don't even know what I would have said if he'd answered. 'Hi', maybe, or, 'how are you' or perhaps even something like, 'are you having a nice time', but as I waited for him to pick up I had the sense that it would be a stilted and unnatural conversation, both of us scrabbling around in our heads to find something to say. I should not have called.

I switched off my phone afterwards because I don't know what I'd say if he rang back.

I can hear the voices up here, the hushed whispers, the ghostly murmurs of memories and I shut them out by turning up the little tape player as loud as it will go and singing along to Wham!. Just for something to fill the time, I scrub the attic floor with a small wire brush I find under the kitchen sink and the swishing sound drowns out the whispers. It's hot, sweaty work. Perspiration pours from me, giving the remaining dust somewhere to settle, but I don't stop until I've washed every floor board, traipsing up and down for more and more soapy water until they gleam like new.

My back and arms are screaming with the exertion of more exercise than I've done in years. My hair sticks to my face and every inch of exposed skin is caked in dust. Despite the filthy state of me I do feel a proud sense of achievement at the spotless attic. "Well, Vic," I say to the hideous portrait, "you're all that remains and you're off to a new home soon." I feel almost sorry for the portrait, having to spend all of eternity in a mouldy castle in Romania that I blow her a kiss.

Moving from the alcove to the far window I look out beyond the trees to the deep blue horizon line where the sky meets the ocean. The water sparkles like diamonds under the bright sun and I watch, transfixed, as the lazy sea glints as it drifts towards the shore. This could be a perfect place to read and to write. Despite its size, the house doesn't have a library, Lily never had the time or the inclination to read, and there would be nowhere for me to store my vast collection of books. This room would be ideal.

I can envisage oak bookshelves lining the walls, groaning under the weight of the literature I've amassed, most of which is in boxes in the loft at home, and my handmade desk, a gift from Lily when I began my writing career, would be the right height to sit under the window that looks across the garden to the sea. I can just imagine the floorboards sanded and varnished and an easy chair beside the chimney breast, for those moments I sit and plan. It would be the dream room for a writer, bright and airy, the large windows letting in the ocean air, and the everchanging picture beyond providing inspiration in the moments when the words don't come.

I feel a bubble of excitement in my belly until I think about going home and the bubble bursts.

"For fucks sake Jessamy." I mutter to myself. "Of all the times…" I pick up the brush and the bucket of now brown water and stomp down the attic stairs, pausing to close the door behind me. "How to spoil a perfect daydream."

I continue down the stairs and cross the hallway to the corridor that leads to the kitchen. The bucket is heavy and the water omits a stale smell from the dirt that floats on top and I groan when I slop some of the brown liquid down my leg. "Bloody hell." I rub the small puddle on the floor with my socked foot and empty the bucket down the utility room sink, putting the brush in the bin. A knock on the door startles me and I turn around to see Jack opening the kitchen door.

"Shit." I groan. "Shit, shit, shit."

"Looking good." He comments closing it behind him.

'Every sodding time' I think gloomily and then say. "I knew you were coming, made an effort..."

Jack's eyes narrow until they are mere slits. "Joe has just called. He wants the bricks, offering a fair price for them, so it's up to you what you want to do..."

"I'll keep them for now."

"Fine."

"Is Andrea home?" I ask.

"I've no idea."

"Oh."

He seems to relent. "She may be. Why?"

"I just wanted to catch up with her, it's been a long time."

"How did you know I was married to her?"

"I told you I saw you both in town but I didn't think it was the right time to say hello."

"There isn't ever a right time these days. I'll tell her to come over...when I see her." He lets the door swing closed but he pauses outside. I wait. He takes his phone from the pocket in his jacket and looks at it with a frown. I push the door and step outside.

"Jack? Is everything ok?"

He laughs mirthlessly. "Tip top." He says. I retreat into the house.

Now feels like a very good time for a gin and tonic.

***

"What do you want?" Jack asks grumpily swinging open the farm house door. He looks really pissed off, a dark flush on his cheeks clashes with the copper colour of his cropped beard. He also looks really sexy and I am aware of biting down hard on my lower lip rather than tell him exactly what is zooming around my head. *Think of Phil, think of Phil.*

"What a nice greeting. Do you welcome everyone that way?" I say lightly, releasing my smarting lip from the iron clench of my top teeth.

"I save it for special people." He stands glaring at me but I hold his gaze, almost challenging him to say something more. He doesn't.

"I'm so glad I'm special." I retort forcing a smile onto my face. "I wondered if Andrea was home…"

"She's not."

"Will she be back soon?"

"I've no idea." I swear I hear the words *and I don't really care* but his mouth doesn't appear to move.

"Oh." I shift from foot to foot. "Well, if she is, perhaps she'd like to come around for a drink? It would be nice to see her."

"Would it?" He asks folding his arms over his chest. "Really? When you didn't get in touch with anyone when you left here?"

"Jack…"

"What?"

"There were circumstances…"

"You hurt a lot of people Jessamy, Andrea was one of them…"

"I didn't mean to, it was a hard time…"

Jack seems to relent slightly and says, "sorry, you caught me at a bad time. If…when…Andrea comes home I'll tell here you were here."

"Jack, is everything alright?"

"Tip top." He closes the door and I stand for a few moments staring at the dark green paintwork before sighing deeply and retracing my steps across the yard to the gate that joins the garden. Perhaps I'm not the only one with a problematic personal life, Jack's strange answers to my questions makes me think that all is not rosy in his world either and I'm surprised at how reassuring that is.

It shouldn't be

But it is.

You fancy Jack

Don't be silly
Jessamy...
Shut up.

***

I cross the kitchen and walk out into the garden.

The air is fresh and clean with the scents of flowers floating on the gentle breeze. Not yet warm enough now to clear the evening chill, I shiver as I walk over the wet grass. My flipflops are no barrier to the damp but rather than go back to the house, I continue towards the vegetable beds. At the back is a new archway covered in roses of pink. The ivy is wrapped around the iron work almost covering it completely and either side of the arch are beds of cream flowers, honeysuckles and daisies. The floral scent is delicious, and within the flowers come the sound of satisfied buzzing bees hard at work. I walk under the arch reaching up to gently stroke the delicate leaves of the flowers. More roses.

The bench has gone, replaced by a small circular wooden table and two chairs. In the centre of the table is a candle holder, a large glass vase sitting on the top of a pewter stand, the metal twisted into roses and petals and inside the vase are the remnants of a candle, now burnt down to a flat circular shape with a blackened wick in the middle. It's filled with water, probably due to the storms and on the top a few leaves float round in a lazy circle, moved by the breeze.

I wonder how many times Lily sat here, during her final months, embraced by this calmness, surrounded by the beauty of the garden and the soft scents of the flowers. It could be a million miles away from anywhere, it's safe and comforting but if I listen closely enough I can hear the whispers, my name being called from a time long ago.

1990

The most amazing thing happened. Lily called up to me while I was listening to Madonna to say that Nate was here. Heart beating I went down stairs and there he was looking lush. He goes, are you coming out? I asked Lily but she said it was too late but that we could sit in the garden. Lily said, he's got an earring and I said, he's got two! Lily said, so that's Nate. She said he seemed interested in me. That is so odd because I'm not exactly God's gift to men. Lily said to let him do the running. I will. I wonder if he'll come down tomorrow.

"Jessamy?"

I wake up with a jolt, painfully aware of drool pooling in the corner of my mouth.

"What?" I ask squinting through the night. My gin glass is lying beside me and my hair is wet with the contents. I wriggle up to sitting, smoothing my wet hair down with a grimace and wiping the moisture from my lips. "What do you want?"

"Is Andrea here?"

"No. Was she supposed to be?"

Jack sits down beside me on the damp grass. His profile is lit by the small lights that dot around the secret garden. "She said she was coming to see you..."

"Is everything ok?"

He takes a deep breath in. "Not really."

"Oh."

"The worst part is that I no longer care." Jack sighs loudly. "That's the worst thing."

"Is there anything I can do...help in any way? Although my relationship guidance is likely to be questionable at the moment."

"Nope." Jack says abruptly, "you are the last person who could help."

"Do you always have to be rude to me?" I snap. "Every time I see you, you're rude or standoffish. You don't have to come here Jack, you don't have to make conversation with me if you'd rather not, I can stay out of your way."

"Whatever." He says moodily. "Do whatever you want."

He stands up, brushing the damp grass from his bottom, a bottom that is perfectly encased in tight denim, a bottom that I cannot stop staring at."

"Are you checking me out?" Jack asks catching me.

"No." I retort far too quickly. A small smile lifts the edges of his lips.

"Yes, you were."

"Bugger off Jack." I say blushing a deep red, thankful that the night is too dark for him to see. "Bugger off with your delusions."

"Oh whatever." He says calmly and leaves me alone in the glade with the improper thoughts that I should know better than to have.

1989
I told Nate there was no way I fancied him. He doesn't believe me.

***

"Hello Jess."

"Phil." I bang my head painfully against the edge of the kitchen cupboard as I turn around sharply. There is an audible intake of air that I think may be mine, but it can't be, I'm not breathing. Phil looks exhausted. His time away in France clearly wasn't as perhaps he had hoped. His hair looks slightly greyer and his middle softer. It's like looking at a stranger. "I wasn't expecting you."

"I can see that." He nods at my appearance.

"I've been sorting..." I shake my head and dust falls onto my shoulders. I must look a fright, dirty and dishevelled. "There is a lot of sorting, Lily seemed to keep everything…" The atmosphere is cold and clogging. I feel as though I cannot get my breath. "It's been harder work than I thought." There is a long, awkward silence, only the clock ticking so loudly I want to rip it off the wall, fills the emptiness.

"Oh. Right." He rakes his hands through his hair. "I suppose I should have phoned but I've just got back and came straight here."

"Did you have a nice time?" I ask nervously. This is a man I've been with for two decades and he feels like a stranger. Already. He's looking at me like he's never seen me before.

He shrugs.

"Are you hungry? I can make you something…not sure what, my shopping skills have been letting me down somewhat." Phil doesn't say anything, just watches me get plates and cutlery, placing them on the table, then taking various random food stuffs from the fridge. He pulls a face as he sees what I am putting out. "Won't you sit down?" I say pulling out my chair at the table. He appears not to hear me.

"I didn't realise the house was so big." Phil comments walking around the room. "And the garden. You always made it sound so small."

"Perhaps because Lily and I were only ever in four rooms." I smile. "Mainly in here so we could look out over the garden."

"I thought you would be able to see the sea from here. I could hear it as I pulled up."

"It's at the bottom of the cliff which is behind the trees over there. You can see the bay from the bedrooms, if it's not raining."

"Has it been raining then?"

"Yeah."

There is a long, uncomfortable silence. Phil looks at the pictures that hang from the stone wall at the far end of the kitchen. "Most of these are by you." He laughs. "She was quite the fan!"

I giggle. "It was a modern art phase I went through when I was about sixteen. I went to an art gallery and figured if they could do it so could I! I was misguided but Lily liked those. We spent the whole summer drinking gin and tonic and painting as flamboyant a painting as we could manage. It was disastrous but so much fun!" I smile and then my face creases up with grief. "It is very strange being here without her."

"What are you going to do with the house?" Phil asks.

"I don't know." I say honestly as I cross the room to switch the coffee maker on. It bubbles and hisses as the moisture on the hot plate heats up. "I guess it all depends on what happens to us. You're here, that must be a good sign." As I say the words I'm not convinced I mean them. Since I've been here there has been no need to apologise for anything and I've not had the suffocating feelings that I've been letting anyone down. I've begun to find a peace I didn't realise I was lacking and now that Phil is here I feel the old anxieties beginning to surface.

"Yeah, I am." He looks at me and sadness flits across his face. "I never thought we'd get to this, Jess, I thought it would be forever, but this is my fault, I'm sorry..."

"I'm responsible too." I interrupt. The aroma of percolated coffee, normally so enticing, is making me feel nauseous. I slop the liquid into two mugs and stir in milk and sugar. I can't remember if Phil even takes sugar. What is happening to us?

"No, it's not. This is all down to me and I'm happy to accept the responsibility... well not happy but, you know..." He tails off. The clock ticks loudly and the tap begins to drip in time. I reach across to turn the tap off and resist the urge to throw something at the clock.

"I know." I say quietly, not daring to look at him.

There is a knock at the kitchen door and immediately it bangs open and Jack walks in. I'm so used to him just walking into the kitchen that it's only now that it occurs to me how strange it would seem to Phil. Jack stops abruptly when he sees that another man is standing in the room.

"Sorry," he says, "I should have waited before coming in."

"It's ok." I mutter. "Phil, this is Jack, Jack is an old friend. Jack this is Phil…"

"Jessamy's husband." Phil interrupts possessively. Jack's eyes narrow and he seems to stand straighter, shoulders squared. Phil mirrors the action but it isn't as threatening on his slim frame.

"Uh, can I help you Jack?" I ask suddenly feeling that a whole new can of worms has just opened.

Jack is glowering at me and I'm suddenly reminded of another pair of flashing eyes, blue, rather than green, and the colour of the sea. "The outhouse is being demolished today, remember? They will be here shortly and you'll need to move your cars for them to fit the skip in front of the house. It will take a couple of days. You just need to decide what you want me to do with the space…and the bricks, there's a lot that can be done with them if you don't let Joe have them."

"I don't want him to have them…"

"Fine." Jack says curtly and leaves the room, slamming the door behind him.

Phil is glaring at Jack's retreating back. "Who's he?"

"Jack? He is someone I used to know from the summers with Lily. He was one of the group I hung out with. He lives next door, been helping with the garden and he looked after Lily when she was ill, although I still don't know why."

Phil's eyes narrow as he turns to me. "Nice looking bloke."

"I've not noticed." I reply flushing. This is not going at all well.

"Is there somewhere we can go to talk? I don't want to be here."

"Then why did you come?" I ask sharply.

"To see you. But this house…I don't want to be in the house Jessamy."

"Don't you think you're being a little dramatic? It's just a house."

"Please don't insult me." He glares at me and I feel the burn from his hard eyes.

"Let's walk to town then…"

"What's this?" Phil interrupts picking up a diary from the table.

"Research for my next book." I smile nervously. *Please don't open it.* "I'm working on a new idea and the house is full of research." I take the diary from him and put it into the box on the floor. "I'll just get my bag."

***

Phil doesn't say a lot on our walk down the cliff steps. He is usually full of chatter, commenting and pointing out something that has caught his eye. Today he is sullen, withdrawing further and further into himself the more steps we take.

I sigh. Phil glances at me briefly and I give him a small smile that he doesn't return. From lovers to strangers in such a brief time, how quickly life can change, no warning, no notice, no chance to stop the impact or at least prepare for the explosion that hits so fast. Despite Phil's insistence that this is his doing, I have to take my fair share of blame. He wouldn't be struggling like this if it wasn't for me.

"Phil?" I ask tentatively.

"Hmmm?" He takes a glasses case from his pocket, a new one, sleek black, one I've not seen before and opens it, putting on the sunglasses contained within. Phil puts the case back in his pocket and keeps his hand inside, shoving the other in the far pocket. I wonder if it's to avoid contact with me.

"Do you like the view?" It wasn't what I was planning on asking but my mind is blank.

"It's lovely."

We walk in uncomfortable silence. Phil clenches and unclenches his hands over and over, his demeanour tight like a coil. He holds himself so rigid that if a powerful gust of wind hit him he'd likely snap in two.

I reach for his hand.

He pulls his away.

"Don't Jess."

"Phil..."

"Don't..."

"I was just going to ask if you want to walk across the beach?"

The teenagers frolicking draws my attention. Their laughter is carried by the breeze and it brings back a memory so strong that I close my eyes against it.

1989

This morning on the beach Nate came up to me and said that loads of people have told him I fancy him. I hit him! Then said what would you do about it if I did, and he walked off. I wondered what I had done but he came back later on and took my hand. We walked across the beach to the wall and he said 'well' and I said, 'well what?' He said, are you going to go out with me. Then Debbie came over and we couldn't talk anymore.

"Jessamy are you listening to me?" Phil says crossly. I open my eyes to find him glowering at me, his brown eyes flashing with ill-disguised anger. "Where were you? Happily drifting through the past with your ghost?"

"Oh, for God's sake Phil. You are referring endlessly to a part of my life that ended twenty-four years ago. Can't you let it go? You are sending me insane with this obsession you have. Seriously, you have to stop going over and over things that cannot be changed. I'm not going to apologise for loving someone a million years ago, it happened and it's over. Over. You have to let it go. I can't go on like this Phil, your jealousy is tearing everything apart."

"Perhaps I don't want to let it go. Perhaps I just want to let this..." He gestures aggressively between us. "...go! Perhaps I've had enough of being second fucking fiddle in your tragic love story. Perhaps I've had enough of never being good enough, never being loved enough, never meeting your ridiculous expectations or getting anywhere near the pedestal to knock him off...perhaps I've had enough of being married to a woman who just doesn't give a shit that she has just let herself go…"

I grip my head painfully between my hands as spots appear one by one in front of my eyes. I feel a rage so black, deep within my belly, that I don't dare speak, too frightened of the words that will erupt from me that I will never be able to take back. I faintly hear him saying my name and the vitriolic words that spill from him as though the dam has been broken. How long has he sat on these feelings? Letting them fester until all I hear is regret and loathing and bitterness. The bond that held us together is now so frayed that it is about to pull apart, the strands of rope no longer able to be wound back together. I know that my marriage is over.

I take a deep breath and push the anger as far down as it will go. "Phil..."

We are standing alongside the teenagers. They look at us. I can see myself through their eyes, I've been sat where they're sat watching people like me and thinking that old seemed so far away. How does it flit so quickly from then to now? I scan their faces until one makes my breath catch in my throat.

It cannot be.

The boy's face.

It's impossible.

Impossible.

"Jessamy will you stop staring at that kid, you are going to freak him out." Phil speaks harshly as he looks around at the young group. "They'll call the police on you..."

"Don't be silly Phil..." My voice sounds so distant, ghostly, but I cannot drag my eyes from the boy. His face is so familiar, so instantly recognisable that I could be fourteen again, looking at the face I remember, one so like this boy that my head begins to spin.

Phil takes my arm and leads me back the way we came. His grip is tight on my limb and it hurts. I almost struggle to keep up with his furious strides pulling my arm back but his clasp tightens.

"Phil..." I wrench my arm from his. "Phil. Stop. Just stop. This is terrible. Terrible. We've never been like this...."

"I made a mistake coming here." He rakes his hands through his hair until it sticks out in all directions. "I don't want to be here."

"Here with me or here in Otterleigh?"

"Here with you." He whispers, his face gripped by a pain that doesn't relinquish its hold. "I don't want to be with you...I've..."

"You were away with someone else, weren't you?" I knew I'd heard a woman in the background, I knew it wasn't my mind playing tricks on me.

"Yes." He turns from me and walks onto the path that leads from the beach to the town. Strangely I wonder if he has any idea where he is going and I watch him for a moment before hurrying after him.

"Who? Who is she?"

"Jess...don't do this."

"I want to know. I have a right to know if there is someone else in my marriage."

"It hurts, doesn't it? To have someone else inside of something so precious." Phil hisses at me.

"You bastard." I push him as hard as I can but only succeed in jarring my shoulder. An older woman walks past, hesitating as she sees the interaction between Phil and me. He's holding himself as if he's ready to attack, his handsome face red and furious. Her face is soft, kind and there is a familiarity that I cannot place. My heart thuds painfully in my chest and her eyes meet mine. *I know you. Why do I know you?* I drag my gaze from her as Phil continues his verbal assault.

"I'm a bastard, am I?" He laughs without mirth, a strange sound that could come from inside the gates of hell. "Me? The man who gave you everything. Everything, Jessamy, and for what? What have I gained from it? A child that's not mine and a barren wife..."

I slap his face.

The sound echoes around the cliffs and I watch as his cheek whitens from the impact of my hand. He raises his arm as if to strike me back and the woman moves closer, close enough for me to read the concern in her violet eyes.

Even the teenagers stop what they're doing and look at us.

I feel open, exposed and so lost that there is no way back to the path I was on.

"I don't know who you are," I whisper as fat tears roll down my cheeks. "Barren wife? I asked that we go for tests, I would have done anything to give you a baby. Anything."

He turns from me. "She's pregnant Jess, the problem wasn't me." He sounds almost victorious. His bow has fired the final poisoned arrow hitting the target and sending venom through me, vein by vein until I can't breathe. Pregnant? I hear a strange choking noise, a bubbly gasp of someone burning from the inside out.

It's me.

"Go away." I whisper, my throat closing over. I grip my neck but I can't get the breath in, my heart slows until I feel so dizzy I may collapse here on the ground. "Go away and don't come back."

"Jess…Jess?" Phil reaches down for me, the anger on his face replaced by regret. "Oh Jess, I'm so sorry, so sorry, it wasn't supposed to be like this, I wasn't going to tell you…"

"That makes it, better does it? That you weren't going to tell me? An affair, a baby…Who are you? Where did my husband go? He was good and kind, you…you are nothing but a low life, Phil." I look around me. The woman has retreated slightly but she stands watching, her handbag gripped in front of her as though she is preparing to hit him with it. "You lied to me, after all these years. I can't believe you lied. I trusted you with my life and you made someone else pregnant." I take a big breath in. I can feel it filling my lungs, the light of that one breath bringing warmth to my blood. "Just go, Phil, get out of Otterleigh, this is my place and I don't want your poison spoiling any part of it. Lily was right about you…" I flex my fingers, the blood flowing again to them, tingling as they come back to life. "Go to your other woman Phil. She is welcome to you."

"Jess…"

"Send everything that is mine down here, I'm never going back to Bath." I turn on my heels and break into a jog towards the high street. My legs burn in protest but I won't stop, there's no going back, the only way is forward.

***

I find myself back on the beach. I walked up and down the small high street for an hour hoping to find the woman, to understand how she seems so known to me, yet I have no recollection of ever meeting her before. She gave no hint that she knew me but I cannot shake off the familiarity and now I'm sitting on the sand trying to make sense of what has happened this afternoon.

The boy, so like Nate that it was as though I was looking at the person I once knew. There cannot be any other explanation other than he's the child of a family member, Nate's little sister perhaps, although she'd be in her late thirties now. I should have tried to find Nate's family, should have looked harder. Rachel should have had the chance to know them but now I wonder if it's too late? I did try a couple of times when social media came along but it was half hearted. Should I look now? Would Rachel want to know?

And Phil. I can't link the person I know to the person who was here today. My marriage is over. Already I can hear Mum's voice, the shrill *I told you so*, Grandma's sneer *You'll never amount to anything now, foolish girl.* Dad's voice, loud and disdainful, *You little slut…*

***

CHAPTER SIX

1990

I wish I was confident. Debbie says really mean things to me like, I get all the boys and you don't. I know she says it when we're messing around but it really hurts and any minute now I'm going to start bawling my eyes out. Perhaps I need to lose half a stone and maybe someone will like me.

I feel...I don't know how I feel exactly because I can't see beyond the red mist that swirls in front of my eyes like a poisonous fog. There is a strange cycle of emotions blighting me this morning – from rejection to relief, to thank God Lily left me the house, to what the fuck do I do now, to blinding anger.

The anger is beating all the other feelings into submission.

I'm so angry.

I'm angry at myself, that I failed Phil and blew a massive, irreparable hole in my marriage because I just couldn't feel the way I should. I'm angry that Phil failed me, that he found happiness with someone else. I'm angry that it wasn't good enough to make things work. I'm angry that I gave twenty years of my life to someone who could hit me round the face with his perfect mistress and her working reproductive system.

The anger is rotting my insides and I have a foul taste in my mouth.

It tastes like decay.

I storm up the stairs to the attic and wrench the door open, slamming it back on its hinges. Despite scrubbing the room until the brush wore out it still has a musty smell about it made worse by the heat of the day. I'm bombarded by the flies that have taken sanctuary up here. They buzz around my head until I flap my arms and they fly off landing high on the beams. The portrait of Queen Victoria leans against the wall and I turn it around until she's facing me, looking forlorn, and I stare back at her with a look that mirrors hers. Once she caused much merriment, the grotesque image of the queen, old and bloated, but now she just looks lost. She looks like I feel, discarded and unwanted, her face not fitting, her body not giving pleasure anymore, the slender figure of youth giving way to the thick set of age. She reminds me of me and I can no longer bear to have her in the house.

"You have to go." I tell her sharply. "Sorry, Vic, but you have to go."

She's pregnant, Jess, the problem wasn't me.

I grab the corners of the frame in a surge of rage, and twist it back and forth towards the door.

Where it jams.

Stuck.

Goddamn it.

"Goddamn it!" I screech and kick at the frame, splintering the doorframe. The portrait refuses to budge and I lever myself against a standing beam and push with my feet. "Arrrrrrrrrgh." I heave sounding a little like Rocky as I use all the strength I possess to push it. The final kick dislodges the frame and the portrait tumbles towards the attic stairs. I run after it and somehow manage to prevent it from slamming against the bedroom door at the bottom of the steps. I put my weight behind it and slowly, painfully slowly, move it along the corridor, past the spare rooms, my room, past Lily's to the main staircase. I'm sweating so much I can hardly see as the perspiration flows from my forehead and down my face. I use my shoulder to wipe away as much of it as I can but as I'm shaking under the exertion it's a pointless effort.

At the top of the stairs I relax. Nearly there.

"Oh SHIT."

I relax too much and let go. The portrait falls forward and crashes through the bannister to the floor below.

Tentatively I creep to check for damage, hardly daring to open my eyes as I peep beyond the mangled and broken bannisters to the destroyed portrait that has hit the black and white tiles at the bottom of the stairs. I take care not to stand on any splintered wood as I race down the stairs, my heart pounding, praying that the antique tiles survived the landing. "Oh, thank God." I sigh relieved as all that has broken is the frame of the portrait. "Count Vlad is just going to have to reframe you at Vlad Manor." I tell the unhappy monarch. "Stop looking at me like that, I feel as shit as you do."

"Are you alright?" Jack comes speeding across the hall. "I heard a smash…"

"I accidentally threw the painting down the stairs!" I giggle nervously. "It got stuck…"

"Shit, woman, I thought it was you falling." He says pale under the auburn stubble that covers his jaw.

"Nope. Just the Queen…" He glares at me and I cower under the flashing green stare. "Why are you still here anyway?"

"The workmen are just leaving."

"Oh yeah, I forgot about them."

"So, if you're not dead I'll go back to them."

I twirl with my arms out. "Still alive."

He makes a harrumph noise and crosses the hallway back to the kitchen, slamming the door behind him.

"Anyone would think he actually wants me dead." I mutter to the portrait. "Now, what I am going to do with you?"

I pull at the frame, managing to free some of the portrait from the fractured wood but the rest remains held fast. Scattered across the floor are broken fragments from the fall that I begin to sweep towards me until a nasty splinter stops me.

"Fuuuuuuuuuuuuuuuuuck." I wail loudly. "Can this day get any worse. God, are you listening to me? What more are you going to send my way?"

I stomp off to the kitchen, sucking my throbbing finger. I hunt through all the cupboards for anything that would take the splinter out of my finger but only find a plaster in the first aid box. In the drawer alongside the fridge, in amongst the clutter of pens and takeaway leaflets I find a sewing kit branded with The Ritz, likely from one of Lily's many trysts. Pouring a tot of whisky into a bowl I lie the needle in it for a few minutes and turn my finger back and forth. The splinter is in deep and already I feel the pain of removing it.

"No one has died from a splinter." I mutter.

"I think you'll find they have. They rot and go septic." Jack says behind me. "Let me see." He pulls his gardening gloves off and washes his hands in the sink. I sit down at the table and hold out my hand. My wedding ring glints in the light and I wrench it off my finger discarding it on the table. There is no point wearing it now.

If Jack notices the absence of the gold band he doesn't comment as he picks up my hand and studies my finger. For a man who works outside a lot his hands are very smooth, soft, warm…a tingle travels up my spine and sends my brain into a spin. It's the closest I've been to him in decades and he smells…earthy, manly, musky…I feel faint.

It's the splinter.

The splinter.

Not Jack.

The splinter.

His head is bowed as he runs his thumb over my finger.

It burns.

My heart races.

In his other hand is the needle. "Brace yourself." He says. "It's in deep."

"Have you done this before?"

"Only on cows."

"Oh." I giggle nervously wondering if he's telling me the truth. He flicks his green gaze up and I feel trapped like a deer in headlights. I can't take my eyes from his, they're hypnotic, dazzling like the brightest light…A strange look crosses his face and he pulls his eyes from mine and turns his attention to my finger.

I feel funny.

It's the splinter.

It's Jack.

It's the splinter.

Jessamy!

Shut up.

A cold hand links its fingers with mine and I close my eyes at the sharp pain of the needle piercing my skin. I clench my fist and feel the coldness grip tighter. Ow. It's hurts. A sharp, intense pain and then, just like that it's all over, a plaster encases my finger and Jack says. "All done."

"Thank you."

"Welcome."

The pause is long. I'm looking at him and he's looking at me and no one moves. No one speaks. Just the gentle ticking of the clock. Tick, tock, tick, tock. His hand is still holding mine, hot now where it was warm before, his skin burning my skin but I don't want him to let go.

I like my hand in his.

Little slut.

You'll never amount to anything.

Used to be so sexy.

His wedding ring is missing. Without thinking I reach out my index finger and trace the band of white skin at the bottom of his ring finger. He watches me silently.

What are you doing Jess?

I can hear his breath deepening. He's looking at me and I'm looking at him and the anger I've been feeling so darkly seems to evaporate the longer I look into his eyes.

Were they always so green?

"Your ring?" I whisper.

He looks down at his hand. "I don't need it."

"Oh." I'm not sure what he means. My mind feels jumbled, uncoordinated, the longer he holds my hand in his the more all the anger seems to fade. Somehow everything seems ok. "I don't need mine either."

"Oh?" He asks in barely a whisper.

I have the urge to kiss him. His mouth is captivating, I don't remember it being so full, so curved or so enticing. He moves slightly, shifting from one leg to the other and confusion masks his face. *No, I think, please don't be confused. I'm not confused.*

"Jack?"

"Jess?" He groans, almost like he's in pain and I take the smallest step closer, hardly breathing, unsure what to do, unsure of anything except the strong pull I feel to him.

"Yeah?" My words are almost inaudible, he moves a step closer to me until we are merely a few inches apart. His fingers tighten around my hand and I entwine them with my own. My heart thuds loudly in my ears and the scent of him is making me feel dizzy. I long to close my eyes, to give into this moment but I can't drag my eyes from his glittering green gaze. We're under a spell. I'm under a spell. I feel a cold hand on my arm guiding me forward so I take a final step. I'm so close now I can feel his sweet breath on my forehead.

"Jack…" I murmur.

Jack lowers his head and I close my eyes, waiting for the kiss that I know is coming.

Then my phone rings.

The shrill tone is deafening in the silent kitchen. Jack leaps backwards like a scalded cat while my heart pounds with shock. The trance is broken. Whatever moment we were having has been splintered like the broken frame and the speed in which Jack moved means we are unlikely to have that moment again.

I feel mortified.

He's looking at me with horror on his face. Without speaking he chucks the plaster wrapper onto the table and leaves the kitchen, the door swinging heavily behind him.

I watch him go, wishing he'd stay, longing to ask him to stay.

It's Jack.

What am I thinking?

I pick up my phone and look at the missed call. Pressing the recall button, I lay my head on my forearms longing to be someone other than me.

"Hi Zoe." I say bursting into tears.

***

1989

I wonder if there is anything I can do to make myself prettier.

I hold the hammer in my hand. On the floor is the portrait and the frame that has become my nemesis. Right now, I no longer care if the portrait survives but one way or another the frame is coming off.

Victoria looks up at me.

Sad.

Fat.

Old.

The mirror across the hallway shows a reflection that matches and I flick between the two images, sickened by both. *Used to be so sexy.*

Jack's face. The shock on his face.

The broken spell.

From somewhere deep below comes an almighty rage and I start battering the frame with the hammer. Shards of broken wood fly around the hallway, some hitting me, others getting lodged in my hair as animal noises erupt from me as I pound the wood. A stream of tears flow with abandon down my cheeks, spotting the floor as I continue my assault on the frame until it becomes nothing more than fragments of wood. I fling the hammer at the mirror where it shatters the glass and the reflection is more grotesque.

I'm not looking any more.

Used to be so sexy.

Let yourself go.

The tears are hot, angry, resentful. I'm better than this, I should not be feeling this way and the tears of desolation are not directed at Phil, the anger is mine, this is about me. He deserves to be happy, he's a good man. I hate myself for the resentment I feel that he has finally found what he has been looking for all these years but more, I hate myself for how mortified I feel after the moment with Jack. Once he would have kissed me, would have said all the things a shy, unconfident girl longed to hear, but I don't look like her anymore and he will see what I see. Deep down, I am still that girl who needed somewhere to feel safe, needed a home to belong.

I am still her.

I just don't look like her.

Strong arms wrap around my torso and I crumple against the figure, sobbing until there are no tears left to cry. No one speaks. Not him. Not me. He holds me for an age, at least, if feels like it and his strong, warm body is both comforting and disturbing against mine.

We are so still.

His heart is beating fast against my back.

I don't think I'm breathing anymore.

I don't know what to do and without meaning too, I relax.

Behind me Jack tenses, his arms pinning mine and then, in a flash, he's gone and I'm cold.

What is happening?

Something?

Or nothing?

I listen for the whispers but none come. It's quiet again. The house falls back into its slumber and I remain on the floor curled up in a ball. It's dark outside and there is faint tapping of rain.

I'm so tired.

Tired and lost.

So lost.

There is a crossroads and I don't know which road I am meant to take.

There is no one here to guide me and each way is unlit.

I struggle to my feet, my bones aching from being on the floor, and take a painful step into the unknown.

***

1991

Debbie asked me if I still fancied Nate because I was spending a lot of time with him. I said no.

"Would you look at him." Zoe breathes admiringly at Jack working in the garden. "Would you look at those muscles and that tan and...his bottom is like a ripe peach..." She flicks cigarette ash out over the patio. "I mean...Jess, don't you just want to grab him and do naughty things with him..." She raises her glass of gin and tonic to her lips. The ice cubes clink against the glass and I watch as the bubbles rise up and pop against her pink painted lips.

I risk a glance at Jack. He has his back to us and I watch transfixed at the muscles in his back rippling as he works on the shrubbery, cutting back branches and trimming the overgrowth. I shift in my seat.

Zoe turns her attention to me. "How do you get anything done?"

I attempt blasé. "Oh, it's just Jack." *Just Jack? Who are you kidding Jess?* "I snogged him loads when we were younger. Mostly because Nate was never interested in me."

"Did you?" She breathes. "Did he look like that? Look at those biceps..."

"He was skinny then and his hair was more carrot! He really wasn't hot then!"

"Well he is now! I could stare at him all day, bending over the flower bed with his fabulous bottom all tight and...oh! I'll be dreaming about him for weeks!"

I laugh. Zoe is in the perfect relationship with a perfect man and the perfect mother to three perfect children. Phoebe, who was born on the same day as Rachel and eighteen-year-old twins, Alice and Ava. Not only does she have the perfect family, perfect husband and perfect

108

life but she also has the most successful events company in the South West.

I'd be jealous of her if she wasn't my very best friend. I met her at a cooking class for teenage mums in London, both of us sent there as part of the Young Parent Health Programme. She was living in a grotty bedsit in a hideous hostel in the west of the city sharing the dire facilities with drug addicts and alcoholics, and while they didn't seem to notice the extreme squalor, Zoe did and she feared for her unborn baby having to live in a place like that. She couldn't go home either. Her family were dysfunctional and her father was so physically abusive and beat her so badly she was hospitalised twice. She's never been back. Shortly after we met we moved to Bath and Zoe wiped her history, changing her last name so no one could find her and she went to night school, vowing to never be as pathetic and useless a mother as her own.

We were best friends from the moment we met. Similarly terrified at the prospect of being teenage single mums, both with parents to whom we were an embarrassment and a failure (I still shudder now when I think of the reaction my parents had when I said I was dropping out of Oxford to have a baby). Zoe had a shock of purple hair and matching purple lipstick on that first day, the smallest of bumps encased in a skin-tight Guns and Roses tee-shirt. I was already swollen and immense despite spending my days vomiting. Lily lent us a deposit for a tiny flat in Oldfield Park and we worked various jobs saving as much as we could for the babies when they came along. They were happy times. Zoe breezed through labour, barely breaking a sweat and by the time Rachel decided to make an appearance I'd been in labour for three days and had burst every blood vessel in my face. Zoe sat holding my hand, looking serene whilst breastfeeding her happy, contented little baby, as I screamed and groaned and wailed my way through an agonising birth, finally producing a plump, red faced angry daughter who refused to be soothed by anyone other than Lily. I wanted to call her Satana, after the devil himself, but eventually, during one long night when Zoe and I paced the rooms taking it in terms to rock grumpy babies, and watching an episode of 'Friends' we decided on Phoebe and Rachel.

We were dirt poor.

I wasn't used to it, coming from a background where wealth was the only thing in life that mattered but we managed in our tiny flat, working opposite shifts, determined to not be a victim of the teenage mum mould. It was a happy time.

I don't think I've ever been that happy since.

"Jess?"

"Yeah."

"What are you thinking about? You've got a faraway look in your eye! Are you thinking about your hot, brooding gardener?"

"Actually, I was thinking about our time in the flat in Bath."

"Ah, good times." She grins. "I often look back and wonder how we managed on our meagre money."

"Because we weren't going to fail Zoe. Can you imagine how awful it would have been to have proved everyone right?"

"My dad would have gloated." Zoe shudders and crunches an ice cube in her teeth. "Not that I would have ever let him within ten miles of Phoebs. I'd have killed him first."

"Wouldn't you like to see him just once just to say, 'fuck you, I'm amazing,'?" I ask her. She thinks for a moment, flicking her cigarette into a plant pot.

"I'd love to rock up in my sports car, with my designer clothes and my fabulous, amazing children to the squalor pit that he lives in and show him that I've made it and I'm so much better than him." She pauses again. "Except I'm still scared he'd be able to knock me back down, make me believe again that I'm worthless and nothing, that I'm unwanted and a burden and all those things he used to say after downing litres of the cheap cider he drank. I will forever wish I had the kind of parents who were proud of me, who bigged up all the silly little nothing things I did, but if I had those parents I wouldn't have ended up in my life, and I'd not swap what I have for anything. Not one thing. I'm not talking about the business or the expensive lifestyle that we have, I'm talking about the kids and Ben and the amazing times we've had.

None of the happiest memories I have of this life, the one I got for myself, have anything to do with the money I've earned, all of them were free. The times we were living off baked beans in our little flat, drinking a can of lager between us and laughing over nothing, or the trips out with the kids to the beach…I'd never swap that, not for the greatest parents in the world."

"Nor would I." I say picking up my glass and swilling the liquid around. "The last time Mum rang it was to tell me to sell the house because poor Count Vlad was broke. Like I should care! It's only because he's a Count that Mum is even interested, she's never met the man!"

"So where is the money..." Zoe silences me with a look. "Don't tell me there isn't any, because my daughter has been spending time looking at the world's most expensive holidays which, apparently, you are paying for. Lily would never have left you with nothing."

"Her accounts were empty Zoe!" I say laughing as she raises an eyebrow. "Lily left me a fortune, she hid it all in the attic, like a dotty old bird so the vile exes couldn't get hold of it! Can you imagine how badly I slept the night I found it all, particularly after all the storms! It's now a bomb-proof safe in the cellar as I figured my parents are highly unlikely to turn up and demand to look in every cupboard! I've not counted it but I've guessed that there is enough not have to write another word ever again! Grandma is going nuts apparently, because she had to pay for the memorial and no one believes that Lily died poor. Can you imagine being that callous about your sister?"

"How did you end up so lovely with a family like yours?" Zoe stubs out her cigarette and joins me at the patio table. "So why do you think your hot gardener has done so much for Lily?" She unscrews the bottle and pours a generous measure of gin into our glasses.

"I've no idea." I hiccup. "It's a mystery that he won't share! He's always here and when I mention paying him for what he does he poo-poo's it like it's nothing."

"Perhaps you need to pay him in kind?" Zoe giggles. "I would. I'd be out there in my smallest smalls to tempt him, like Eve and Adam and the apple..."

"The apple wasn't a sex thing..."

"Ha, as if...a tropical garden, naked bodies...you can't tell me they weren't at it like rabbits!"

"You'll be struck by a lightning bolt..."

"Ziiiiiiiing!" Zoe laughs skipping across the lawn to retrieve her cigarette packet from the kitchen table. "Bring on the lightning bolt!" She says coming back outside.

"You are truly shocking. Get thee to a convent..."

"Can you imagine anything worse! Imagine not being able to spend the day happily staring at your hot gardener!" Zoe sits down and lights up another cigarette.

"I don't stare…"

"I've caught you plenty of times!" She says her blue eyes narrowing as she blows out a plume of smoke. "And I do not believe, for one moment, that you have not looked at him and had improper thoughts once."

"Maybe once."

"Once!" She shrieks. "I don't believe you. Not in the slightest. You fancy him, it's as obvious as being struck by the heavenly lightning bolt." Jack looks up at her from across the garden, his eyes briefly flicking to me. I feel the deep flush flood my cheeks and look down at my glass. "The question is, what are you going to do about it?"

"Zoe!" I stammer. "Will you shush. Please. He'll hear you"

"If you're that bothered then I've obviously hit a nerve!" Zoe grins. "So…tell all?"

"There is nothing to tell!" I say not meeting her eyes but shrinking under her scrutiny. "Now will you stop it you evil bitch. Now pour me some tonic and let's get so drunk that I forget that my husband has left me for a woman with working ovaries!"

***

The house is empty.

Silent.

Zoe and her raucous laughter is on the train heading back to Bath, her hangover very likely as hideous and debilitating as mine.

I feel sick.

The waves of nausea are so violent I've taken to wandering around the house with an empty bin for company. It's been washed out with disinfectant four times in the past hour.

All I can taste is stale gin which no amount of teeth-brushing will get rid of. I need a bath but I'm so cold, my body adopting the freezing shakes and shudders as it tries to combat the amount of poison in my system. I've not had a hangover like this since my twenty-first birthday party.

There is reason.

Hangovers are the work of the devil.

And if hangovers are the work of the devil, so gin is the juice of the devil. And should I ever have the misfortune to meet the devil, I'll hit him, because it's bound to be a him, over the head with a bottle of the evil liquid.

I burp.

Then I vomit.

"Nice." Jack's voice cuts through the quiet.

"What do you want." I ask, retching over the bin. "Can you go away? I don't need witnesses to my affliction."

"The self-inflicted affliction?" He comments dryly. I'd like to hit him but I'm still face down in the bin. I think it's making me feel worse, the smell of Dettol and vomit is a disgusting mix and I retch a few more times, painfully aware of Jack's ill-disguised mirth.

"I suppose you've never been hungover?" I huff, lifting my head and wiping my mouth with a piece of the tissue in my dressing gown pocket.

"Not like you." He says, his mouth curling up into a smirk. "I've seen you look rough in my time Jessamy but today is particularly special!"

"If you're only here to taunt me then go away, back to whichever hole you've crawled from. I'm going to bed. Let yourself out."

I walk on shaky legs from the morning room and up the stairs. The higher I go, the more dizzy and wretched I feel. I don't want to think about the empty bottles littering the work surfaces, nor the congealing cartons of Chinese food from the next town that we had delivered at some point. I found noodles and a piece of chicken in my hair this morning, as I woke, stiff and uncomfortable, from an inebriated sleep, with my head on the kitchen table. Classy.

"Very classy." I mutter as a lank tendril sticks to my cheek.

My phone roars to life from the depths of my tissue filled pocket. "Hi Zoe." I say, my throat hoarse.

"I've just thrown up all over the train." She wheezes then coughs productively. "Everywhere. I had to lie to the cleaner and say I've got a stomach bug. I'm so embarrassed. Everyone had to move and there weren't enough seats as it was. I'm in the passageway, with dark glasses on. I think I may die."

"I've been sick too."

"You have? Well that makes me feel a little better."

"I've got a bruise on my knee. Do you have any idea how I got it?"

"Not a clue. I don't even remember getting into the taxi this morning. I've got my pyjamas under my clothes. I'm gross."

"You are!"

"Not as gross as you, flirting down the phone to Jack in the middle of the night..."

"WHAT?" I screech, the sound hurting my raw throat. "What? What did I do? When? WHEN?"

"I dared you. It came back to me a moment ago. You rang him."

"No! No! No, I didn't. I couldn't have. Oh my God, what did I say?"

"I don't remember exactly but I'm sure it was about how fit he was as a grown up and why was he missing his wedding ring..."

I promptly throw up in the bin.

***

1989

Nate and I were at each other's throats. He hates me and I hate him. We've established that but Lily says he fancies me, but I know he doesn't. He was angry because I called him a 'shithead' to his face but I walked off before he could say anything to me.

"I understand I phoned you last night." I mutter, a flush of deep red covering my chest and face. Jack is staring at me with an unreadable expression in his eyes. He looks less than impressed. If I didn't feel so goddamn hideous I would be feeling less than impressed with me too.

Right now, I want to be hit by a lightning bolt and frazzled to an ashy crisp on the flagstones.

Come on God, do your worst.

Or best.

He says nothing for an age. It could be as little as ten seconds but with the death march going through my head it could be hours. He looks at the bin, positioned between us like a barrier, a barrier that I wish could take this acute embarrassment away.

This bloody house is nothing but trouble.

"Yes." Jack finally says. "Yes, you did."

"Oh…shit…What…um…what did I say? Did I say anything…?"

"You don't remember?" Jack asks, humour creeping into his tone. "Any of it?"

"No." I hang my head. "Nothing. I remember nothing beyond the second glass of gin."

"So, you don't remember ringing me at midnight because the ground was eating you, or at one am because you wanted Marlborough Lights and chips?"

"Chips? I thought we had Chinese food…"

"You did. You slept in it."

"How do you know that?"

"Because you were incoherent and rather than have you vomiting yourself to death in your sleep I came to check on you. You were face down in your chow mein and your friend was snoring on the rug…"

"I want to die."

"Feel free." He glowers at me. "If you keep smoking then it's likely you will."

"Oh, shut up. I don't smoke…not in years."

He takes my hand and a fiery tendril wraps around my arm. I grip the bin, swallowing the waves of nausea as Jack leads me out of the kitchen door to the potted plant beside it. It's filled with discarded cigarette butts. I can't even hazard a guess at how many but it explains the bruised feelings my lungs have experienced all morning. The taste of gin fills my mouth and I retch.

"Can you not look." I whimper from inside the bin.

"You don't smoke?"

"No." I say meekly staring at the plant pot. "Not usually. No wonder I feel so bad." I lean against the wall and hold the bin over my face.

He says. "When Lily talked about you, which was a lot, she always said what a ray of sunshine you were…" I raise my head and stick my green filmed tongue out at him. "That's attractive."

"Why are you always here when I look or feel my absolute worst?"

"You've asked me that before."

"You've not ever answered. Do you plan it? Oh, I bet today is a good day to see Jessamy look like road kill."

"I've seen better looking road kill."

"Were you always this mean to me?"

"You wouldn't have noticed if I had been." Jack says putting on his gardening gloves and picking the cigarette butts out of the plant pot and putting them into a box.

"I just remember you being nice."

"Is that all you remember about me?"

"I remember lots about you Jack." I tell him honestly. He studies my face.

"Do you?" It sounds more like a rhetorical question, one that I'm not sure I have the right answer for. "I wonder if you remember things the way I do."

"Meaning?"

"It doesn't matter."

"Yes, it does."

"No, Jessamy, it doesn't. Forget I said anything." His face clouds over and he says crossly. "Next time use an ash tray. Lily chose this rose to grow up and over the door. She would be really pissed off if she knew you used it for your nicotine habit."

"What do you know about what Lily would feel?" I ask sharply, suddenly feeling defensive. He's looking at me and glowering, a look I am getting more and more used to.

"Lily and I were close…"

"You can't have been that close, she never mentioned you."

Jack chucks the box down on the paving slab and hisses. "When did you become such a bitch, Jessamy?"

The smell of stale cigarettes wafts past me and I retch over and over in the bin. When I finally pull my head out of it, Jack has gone.

***

CHAPTER SEVEN

1989

We were playing kiss chase on the beach. Nate caught me but didn't kiss me. He must think I'm an ugly dog.

It's been one of those days.

The kind where after an hour of being awake you sincerely hope the day is over.

Except it's not over.

I'm standing in the kitchen, watching the coffee maker slowly drip coffee into the pot, plip, plop, plip, plop, while Mum screeches my failings at me down the phone. I'm not really listening, I've heard it all before, but I'm wishing for the ability to be able to step back in time and to have not told her about Phil. Of course, it's all my fault, he would be with me if I cared about my appearance, had a proper job, had not selfishly rushed to Devon when Lily died and on she goes.

I've bitten my tongue so much in the past ten minutes I can taste blood in my mouth.

She moves onto Count Vlad and I begin softly banging my head against the counter. Bang, bang, bang, bang, in time with the plip-plops of the coffee machine.

"No Mum," I sigh, "I'm not selling the house."

She prattles on, the icy tone dripping frost into my ear.

"No Mum," I say slightly firmer, "there isn't any money."

She doesn't believe me.

I no longer care.

"Mum." I snap angrily. "I've just about had enough of the way you treat me. I don't deserve it. I'm a good person, I try hard and regardless of what you may think, I've done well for myself. Things with Phil didn't work out, but it doesn't mean that it's all my fault. We both made mistakes and we both stopped trying, so stop blaming me. I will not let you put me down anymore, I don't want to hear it and honestly, there is nothing more you can say that will upset me, not any longer. I'm finished with trying to win your approval, I'm not going to get it and I don't actually want it. Not anymore. Please don't ring me until you can be civil and if I have to wait until hell freezes over, then so be it."

I don't wait for an answer. I just hang up.

Pouring a large mug of coffee and adding an extra sugar for the hell of it, I cross the kitchen to the table and sit looking out over the empty garden.

I've not seen Jack for a week and during my waking hours I feel terrible for what I said to him about Lily. He was obviously important to her, he was here at the end and just because she didn't tell me about him, doesn't make that any less true. Why I said it, I don't know, perhaps because I needed to be the most important person to someone and that had always been Lily and, if I'm honest, I feel a little pushed out by her closeness to Jack, particularly because she kept it secret. During sleep it's Jack, rather than my ghost, who dominates my dreams. The 'moments' we had replay over and over leaving me bereft when I wake. I wonder now if it all was just a dream, that there was no near-kiss, no strong arms around me when I needed them, no gorgeous bottom to stare at when I should be writing. Perhaps it was all just an illusion my mind conjured up to protect me from life falling apart.

The solicitors letter from Phil sits on the table. Irreconcilable differences apparently. No mention of his new life, no mention of my inability to be the perfect wife, just those two meaningless words shouting out from the page. I'm not sure what I was expecting, the finger of blame pointed in my direction perhaps, or a list of where I went wrong, but I should know better. Phil wouldn't do that. He's a better person than that. I always thought that when people divorced, it was with one side blaming the other but this is a clean ending, just the two words used when no one wants to give a reason of blame, because maybe no one person is to blame for this. Lily gave me a way out, Phil's new baby gave him a way out and that, to me, seems the kindest way for things to end. Both of us with a hopeful future.

I wish him a happy future, the lovely man with whom I shared my life. I will keep the memories safe and forget the final meeting, the angry, hurting man who yelled at me on the beach. "Be happy Phil." I whisper.

I'm not sure what my future will bring but if I could wish for the perfect life, it would be to just feel whole, complete, to know who I am and to recognise the person who looks back at me in the mirror. I want to love with my whole being and to be loved in return, to feel enough and to feel good enough and to be enough.

My thoughts drift to Jack and I scan the garden again, just in case.

It remains empty.

"Arrrrrrgh." I bang my head painfully on the kitchen table. My agent has been on my case and I've still nothing to send her. She's threatening to take my advance back. Apparently, she can. I think about all the cash in the cellar and wonder if I even care about being a writer anymore. It's done me well, made me enough money to support Rachel but I don't know if I want to write slushy romance anymore. Particularly now there is no romance in my life. There is very little to take inspiration from.

I push all thoughts of Jack from my mind and open my laptop searching for personal trainers in the area. "It's now or never, Jess." I say as brightly as I can manage scrolling through the endless listings.

The first trainer I like the look of is a smiley woman in a bra top and leggings. She doesn't answer the phone and I hang up before I can leave a garbled voicemail. The second, a very good-looking man called Mark, who has big biceps and thighs like a rugby player, assuming the photograph on his website is him, picks up. He has a deep voice with a slight Devonshire accent and speaks enthusiastically about his job and the miracles he can perform. I hear myself asking him to take me on and he agrees to come to the house in the morning.

"Be warned though Jessamy, I may sound nice but it's all an illusion, I used to be in the marines!"

"Don't you think you could have told me that before? You're going to kill me!"

He laughs. "What doesn't kill you makes you stronger Jessamy, and by the time I've finished with you, you'll be strong enough to take on a lion!"

I laugh nervously and wish I'd left a message on the nice lady's answering machine.

"See you in the morning, ok?" He prompts as though daring me to change my mind.

"Yeah…ok…"

"Don't sound so nervous." Mark says, "you'll have a great time."

I'm not convinced and as I hang up the phone I wonder if remaining a biscuit eating couch potato isn't such a bad thing.

***

I knock on the door and wait nervously but there are no sounds coming from inside Jack's house. A trio of horse heads look over the stable doors curiously at me as I stand, swaying from foot to foot, chewing nervously on the inside of my cheek. It hurts but stops me from running away as fast as my flip flops will carry me.

I knock again but give up when the door stays shut and walk across the farm yard and out of the gate that leads onto the lane. I wanted to apologise, to explain why I was so mean but I do feel slightly relieved that he's not in. I'm not sure I could focus on much with his green eyes glinting at me and my apology would likely come out incoherently.

For goodness sake, it's Jack!

I should not have these crazy feelings for Jack, I never did in the past, and it's hardly the best time to have a ridiculous crush on someone. It's just a figment of my imagination, thought up to calm the storm.

Yes, that's what it is.

Storm calming.

I cross over the road and take the steps down to the beach. I scan the sand for the boy I saw but wonder if the likeness was as I thought. This town is doing strange things to my mind and in all likelihood, it was a memory resurfacing to save me from the venom of Phil's words.

It feels like I'm trying to convince myself.

I walk up to the shops and buy what I need to replenish the fridge and walk further up the high street to Mrs Thornton's. If I'm employing a personal trainer, then I may as well have one final slab of cake before he puts me on whatever hellish diet is currently fashionable amongst the fabulously fit. The little bell tinkles as I open the door and the girl behind the counter looks up with a welcoming smile. I take a seat in the window and watch the world go by. They say, whoever 'they' are, you should never go back, that it's a good idea to leave the past lying sleeping in the sun, but I'm not sure I agree with them. I did once, when I ran from Otterleigh without a backwards glance, but now, now I feel sure 'here' is where I should be, that everything is coming together somehow to show me the way.

I thought the pain would worsen the longer I stay in the house but I'm finding peace from being here. I still feel Lily's absence keenly, particularly when I wake up in the mornings and for a split second I'm a teenager again, waiting for her to call up the stairs that breakfast is ready. It's at those times where my heart sinks and the tears come and the world feels achingly lonely but the rest of the time, it is beginning to feel like home. I'm bracing myself for clearing out her room, a task I've been able to put off with the immense job of emptying the attic, but now that's done there are no longer any excuses for keeping her room as it is. I suppose it will become my room. Eventually.

One day.

The waitress puts my order down on the table and I thank her, picking up sachets of sugar to add to the coffee. Tori runs past the window but by the time I reach the door she's vanished in a puff of multi coloured lycra. I have so many questions but perhaps asking a slim, toned vision whilst I'm tucking into the world's biggest brownie is not the right time. I hold the door for a woman coming in and return to my seat, stirring my coffee while I mull over the past month. So many questions.

"Hello." I look up to find the lady from the beach standing in front of me.

"Hello." I reply smiling.

"I'm glad I've run into you." She says shrugging off her jacket. "I thought about coming up to see you, to make sure you were ok after the beach but my son said it probably wasn't the best idea…"

"Your son?"

"Jack."

"Jack Grayson?" I feel a flush spread across my cheeks and hope vehemently that she doesn't notice.

"Yes!" She smiles. "May I join you?"

I fiddle with the froth on my coffee, stirring it into peaks. I nod. "Please do."

She pulls out a chair and sits down, placing her handbag on the floor.

"Quite the weapon you have there!" I gesture at the bag. "I thought my husband was going to have to have it surgically removed!"

"It was tempting, but I like the bag. Forgive me, I don't wish to pry, but now I've seen you, I just want to know that you're ok, it looked quite heated…"

Embarrassment floods my face. "What a spectacle we must have looked. I'm mortified about it, we've never been that couple, you know, the ones that argues for all to see. We never really argued, actually, until now!"

"Did he hurt you?"

"Not physically." I pick up my coffee cup and take a sip. It's too sweet. "He came to tell me our marriage was over. I was expecting it, we'd both been in denial about the state of things for such a long time but we drifted along until one affair and one ghost killed what was left of us."

"Ghost? Are there such things?"

"My first love, mostly unrequited but jealousy is a funny thing."

"The affair?"

"His."

"Oh." She picks up the menu and peruses it.

"I'm Jessamy by the way."

"I'm Jenny. I know of you Jessamy. I heard your name a lot once upon a time. Jack…"

"Really?" I perk up and contort my face to hide the grin.

"So, what do you do then Jessamy?" She asks accepting a pot of tea from the waitress. Her features are strangely familiar but as much as I look I can't see anything of Jack in her face.

"I write romance novels."

"Oh…not what I was expecting!"

"Really?" I cringe. "Oh God, what were you expecting?"

"I don't know, a nurse perhaps or a teacher…you have that air about you."

"Not space princess then?"

Jenny laughs. "No, but perhaps one day!" She looks a little self-conscious. "Have I got something on my face?"

"No. Why?"

"You keep staring at me!"

"Oh! Goodness. Sorry. It's just you look really familiar."

Jenny's face closes over and I wonder if I've just offended her. "Do I?"

"Yes."

"Perhaps because of Jack?"

"Maybe." Only I know it's not that. I change the subject. "How long has Jack been at the farm?"

"Not long." Jenny leans back in her chair and smiles proudly. "He's always wanted to work on the land, even when everyone else upped sticks and went to university. His dad was forever on at him to go to college, get a business qualification but Jack was adamant he was going to learn things the hard way. He was always happy gardening and doing odd jobs around town and did very well out of it. He came into some money just before the farm went up for sale ..." for a moment Jenny's face hardens, "so he decided to spend what he had on the farm. I thought he was mad but it has worked out for him." She smiles at me. "He's a very determined boy!"

"Jack has been a big help with the garden, I wasn't born with green fingers and if it were left to me it would be a complete mess."

"He's a good lad, always happy to help, perhaps sometimes it's a little misplaced, but he likes being busy. He has the time now, he put so much into the farm, working all hours but it's almost running itself now."

"How did he know Lily? He seems very fond of her."

"He was." Jenny's lips form a thin line and her eyes flash. "He spent more time than he should have over there."

"What do you mean?"

"Every day he was there, at her beck and call. Just a little strange." I don't like her tone and I feel my hackles rising. As if she senses the atmosphere change she refills her tea cup and changes the subject. "What about you. I understand you inherited the house? Are you staying?"

"It looks like it. I can't go back to Bath, there's no home to go back to, so Lily leaving me the house has been a lifeline. It gives Rachel and I somewhere to call home and I think it will be the right place for us eventually."

"Rachel?"

"My daughter. She's training to be a doctor in London, thankfully she inherited her father's brain…"

"And what about your ghost? Is he still around?"

"No, he's gone. Long gone. I hadn't realised how much being here would sort things out in my mind, and give me space to breath, despite the sadness. A new chapter beckons. I just need to close the book on the last one."

"Very profound."

I giggle. "Isn't it just, perhaps the Vicar is finally rubbing off on me!"

"John?"

"The one and only." I pause to eat some brownie. "Is Jack away?"

"I don't think so, why?"

"I knocked on the farmhouse earlier, there was no answer. I was hoping to see Andrea…" I'm snooping and I am pretty sure my face is full of guilt. Jenny says nothing, her face setting firm.

"You'll be hoping for a long time." She finally says stirring her tea.

"Oh."

Jenny sighs. "A marriage that should never have happened."

"Like mine then?"

A strange look flashes over her face. "Perhaps. The curse of the first love…" She says almost absentmindedly. I ask no more questions about Jack. I try not to stare at Jenny but I cannot figure out how she is so familiar when I've never met her before and I'm sure I'm looking more intently than is polite. We talk lightly, about nothing of consequence, but I find myself warming to her and wishing I'd had a mother just like her.

***

1988

Debbie came over. We went to the beach then back to mine. Not a lot happened. Listening to Kylie Minogue. It's ok. Michael Jackson is better.

I stream music from my phone because the silence in the room is too much to bear. It feels so empty in here and so cold that I have to return to my room for a jumper. I wonder if it's too soon to be doing this, that Lily's personal effects should be here a little while longer but the cold hand on the small of my back pushes me forward.

Are they in here Lily? The secrets you said were held by the eaves? Will I find what you wanted me to know in here?

I hope so.

I've been mulling and mulling over the blanket and the cross that Rachel and I found. Why would she have them in a tattered box the attic? All I can conclude is that it was a gift for someone that she forgot to hand over, Lily was notoriously forgetful. But even so…something is nagging at me and I can't piece it together.

I turn the volume up on my phone and the bright, happy sounds of a nineties boyband fills the emptiness. I take one look out of the window, just in case Jack has reappeared but the garden, basking in the evening sun, remains still. *Go to him, Jessamy.*

I ignore the voices and cross the room to Lily's cupboard. I'm expecting clothes, I find more boxes.

"Oh, great."

Despite my misgivings, the boxes take little time to empty. Mostly books and video cassettes of the classics. I remember rainy days curled up on the sofas in the morning room, drinking rich hot chocolate into which we dunked endless biscuits, sitting under blankets and watching Audrey Hepburn and Marilyn Monroe films over and over.

Good times.

Happy times.

I stack some of the videos to keep and everything else gets re-boxed for the charity shop. It takes a couple of trips up and down the stairs to load the car until there are only three boxes left. These are a different size to the storage boxes and the first one is particularly heavy. I can't lift it and have to push against the cupboard with my legs to pull it out. My arms shake with the exertion and I feel the strain through every part of my body.

"Jeez Jessamy, what a weed." I groan as I pull. How Lily managed to get this box into the cupboard beats me. I feel exhausted when it's finally freed and lie back on the floor taking some deep breaths.

"Ok, Lily, let's see what you have for me." I pull at the tape and the lid comes apart. Inside are photo albums. Lily's whole life, weddings, parties, holidays…husbands and lovers, friends and the jet set, Rachel and me. In each picture Lily has a wide smile on her bright lips, always in fashionable attire, always with immaculate raven hair, a long cigarette holder in her hand with a burning cigarette at the end of it. It's how I remember her, larger than life and laughing and I hold one of

125

the albums close to my chest, hugging it tightly, shutting my eyes against the wave of emotions that bring a lump to my throat. I don't want to be doing this, going through her things, having to decide what to keep and what bin and what to give away.

You will hear me amongst the spirits.
My arm is cold.
Be brave, darling girl, be brave.

***

I take a mug of hot coffee and the biscuit tin up to the bedroom. Popping a biscuit whole into my mouth I chew loudly as I peel the tape from the smaller second box. "Letters?" I lift one out of the box. It's addressed to Lily at a street across the town. My heart thuds as I open the fragile envelope and take out the letter. The paper is very thin, once white or cream it's now turned a sepia colour but the red and white of the airmail logo posted in Australia is still clear. Carefully I take the letter from the envelope and open it. It's so frail I'm scared it will tear in my shaking hands.

Dearest Lily
I miss you.
All I've thought about for the past six weeks on board is you.
We docked late last night in Sidney and were taken to boarding houses. There are so many boys. We are being sent to farms tomorrow for work so I will write again as soon as I have a fixed address. Patience will send on the letters to you.
I will come back for you.
I love you
Jimmy

My dearest Lily
I'm sorry it has been so long since my last letter. We travelled by train to Leongatha and I've been working on a farm for the past month without a day off but today I finally have the chance to go to the town so I can send this.
I've been worrying you'd think I've forgotten about you. Which would be impossible darling Lily.

126

The farm is so big with land as far as you can so we've all had to learn to ride the horses. It was terrifying at first but now I spend my days riding over the land checking on the sheep and mending whatever may need repair. I share a room with four others in one of the outbuildings that have been turned into dorms. The chaps I share with are all from Devon and very jolly. It's very dry, the earth is a reddish colour, rather like Devon rocks. My face is very brown now and we have to wear hats with corks dangling from them to keep the flies away. The water tastes funny but I drink so much of it I'm getting used to it now. Just a quick letter my love, the postman is already here.

You'd like it here, the sun always shines.

I love you

Jimmy

So many letters, so much love spilling from the pages, the black, spiky scrawl declaring endless heartfelt declarations of love. The unusual writing is so familiar that I know I've seen it somewhere before but I can't think where. I feel saddened that I didn't know Jimmy existed and it surprises me that Lily kept him hidden deep given the depth of his love for her. Is he the secret she wanted me to find? I find such a pull to the letters that I don't notice the evening passing me by. I read them all and I find comfort in the loving words, that despite all the bad marriages and bad lovers there was one person who loved her so completely. I stretch and yawn, moving from the floor to the unmade bed, stiff and aching. I lie down on my front, pulling a pillow under my chin and open the final letters.

Darling Lily

I think of you often and wonder how you are feeling. It must be nearly time now and I wish I could be there to hold your hand. Patience said your governess is unkind and that your condition does not endear you to her but I've had word from my parents today and for the first time since we found out, I feel excited. My parents are looking at passage to Australia in June. They will bring you too but you must see them as soon as you can. They will help you Lily, they will look after you on the boat. They no longer feel that the right decision was made and they want to make up for their part in our separation.

Please come darling, I will wait for word.
I love you.
Jimmy

Darling Lily.
My parents have arrived without you.
Mother told me what happened.
My darling girl I am coming home for you. Together we will get her back. Do you remember when we said how we'd live in The White House and watch our children play under the trees? I can build you a white house here, Lily. We can plant the trees and watch them grow.
I am getting the next boat to England and I will find you.
I love you
Jimmy.

Dear Lily
It's with the heaviest of hearts that I write to you. There was as accident in Sidney. Jimmy was running for the boat and was hit by a bus. He didn't survive.
Oh Lily, Jimmy has gone.
I'm so sorry to tell you.
I hope you take comfort from knowing he loved you so much.
You are in our thoughts
Love Patience.

He died.

I wasn't expecting that. My own memories speak to me, voices that whisper. '...there was an accident...surfing...no pain...he didn't suffer.' Just like that. A life over. A past mirroring a past.

Two women, two ghosts.

I feel so much anguish that the cold hand resting on my shoulder is no comfort.

All I can do is cry.

***

I wake up cold. The sun has not yet risen fully and the sky is a vivid pink with the soft rays of colour falling through the huge windows onto the wooden floor. I move slowly, my limbs struggling to work properly in the chill, until I am sitting, the letters scattered around me on the bed. I pick one up and turn it over in my hand.

The writing.

Where have I seen the writing?

I sigh. "Come on Lily, give me a clue." I fold the letters back into their envelopes and carry them down the stairs to the kitchen. Putting the coffee on to percolate I sit down at the table and spread the envelopes out. I've seen the writing before, I'm sure of it, somewhere in the house, it's unusual, spiky, heavy printed...*Go to the portrait Jessamy.*

A coldness surrounds me and I shiver as though someone has just walked over my grave. Pushing my chair backwards I take one of the letters along the corridor to the lounge and stop in front of Lily's portrait. I stand before it for a long time barely able to breath.

The writing in the letters and the shape of the signature on the painting are identical.

Did Jimmy paint this, Lily?

The coldness wraps itself around me until I take the portrait from the wall and carry it back to the kitchen. Fresh tape has been applied to the back, smaller than the previous tape which has left a sticky residue. My heart beats at a thousand miles an hour as I carefully peel off the backing, lifting the wooden board once the tape is off. Underneath is a worn photograph of Lily, about the same age as in the portrait, beside her is a handsome young man, similar age perhaps, with a wide smile and bright eyes. They look so happy, blissfully so. He is gazing at her with such love on his face that I feel the smarting of tears behind my eyes. I can't believe he died. The photo has faded with time and the colours have blended together but there is an innocence to the photo, the first love perhaps, but the way they are looking at each other in that captured moment is unmistakeable.

"He was so handsome, your Jimmy." I whisper to the cold air. Wiping my eyes, I walk back to the kitchen with the portrait and the photo and prop them against the window. I tingle with an excitement that is indescribable. Despite earlier misgivings about snooping into Lily's past I now believe without question that she left them for me to find, perhaps to lay to rest the ghost who obviously followed her.

Perhaps she wanted the world to know that she had that one love, the perfect love that was never forgotten, never let go of and for her, the one that no other man could measure up to.

* * *

1989

We went to see Indiana Jones at the Last Crusade. We sat near the front and the boys sat behind us and kept throwing peanuts at us. The man who runs the cinema threatened to throw us out.

The next box is for me.

It's a plain brown storage box with a removable lid, obviously new and bought specifically for this. I know it's for me because Lily has scrawled JESSAMY on it in giant letters in her swirly handwriting. I trace the letters, my finger squeaking against the cardboard, then lift the lid.

Inside is a shoebox sized box, aqua blue in colour with painted papier mache fish across the lid. I recognise the box, it's one I bought at the summer fair when I was fifteen, for my keepsakes. The contents are wrapped in little parcels in the same tissue paper as the boxes of diaries in my wardrobe. *What are you trying to tell me Lily?* Inside the first parcel is a white and pink spotted gift box, the same size as a tub of butter. I open the lid and look inside. "Oh, my goodness." Theatre tickets for the summer show, Grease I think it was that year, at the pavilion, cinema tickets for the little cinema in Sidmouth and the choices of films bring a smile to my face. *'Three men and a Little Lady,' 'Indiana Jones and the Last Crusade' 'Ghost', 'Dirty Dancing'* and for every single one comes a memory so powerful I can feel it alive in the room. Faces, moments, feelings…it's overwhelming how much I remember, where I was sitting, what I was eating, who I was sharing a drink with…He was always there. My ghost.

1991

Went to see Three Men and a Little Lady. The film was brilliant but the whole night was a disaster. Nate had his hair cut and he's sex. I was really quiet and Nate asked me kindly what was wrong. I said nothing. He said, I bet I can make you laugh. I said quietly, it's your face, it cracks me up. Nate will never want me. He'll only love the person his friends will accept.

The next parcel is larger. "A photo album Lily?" I ask the empty room. "Why?" I feel the cold nudge and I open the book. "Oh my God!"

The young faces of our teenage selves look up at me from the photos, laughing and smiling. There is a loud intake of breath as I look through the pictures, strange feelings and memories flashing through my mind as I study each one, tracing the lines of Nate's face, his smile beaming in the captured moment. How could someone so beautiful be gone? I remember every moment, what he was doing, who he was talking to, whether he was being nice to me that day. I feel sad for my younger self, that so much happiness was placed on the actions of another.

Next, I find some cassette tapes. I grin. I've not listened to these in years,

1989

Nate walked me home. He came in to get some tapes. Lily went out to a party. I told him the only reason I got off with Jack was because I didn't think he liked me in the same way as I liked him. He asked if I liked him and I said no. But I do. I wanted to say yes but he wants to give Debbie one more chance. He acted like he fancied me though so fingers crossed. He said I was a good friend to have. After he left I listened to Faith, Like a Virgin and Electric Youth.

Underneath the tapes are copies of Lady Chatterley's Lover and Pride and Prejudice. Brand new books that I lift out and flick through curiously. Why, Lily?

And then I find the letter.

Dear Jessamy.

I'm speaking from beyond the grave!

By now I'm hoping you found the money and the letters…if you haven't, what on earth have you been doing child? You are a few steps closer to learning more. It does give me a twisted pleasure that I've left

clues rather than telling you all in my first letter. But, dear girl, there is a reason, and all will be clear...

I put this box together because it's what you need to know, about your life. Re-read your diaries and look closely. (Yes, I read them, and honestly Jessamy words fail me...before you pull a face, I was a weak, old and infirm lady with not a lot else to do...)

Look at the contents of this box again and again and again. Look at the books, the photos and put on the tapes. Go back and see Jessamy, I mean, really see. Look past Nate at what else was there, open your eyes.

Remember I said about a new future. The past may hold the key.
I love you
Lily xx

I feel winded and squeeze my eyes tightly shut. The hand that holds the letter is shaking so much that the paper makes a flapping noise. What do you mean Lily? What do you mean?

So many questions that have no answers. What do I need to see? What if it's just too dark to see?

***

CHAPTER EIGHT

1991
I think my boobs have grown.

I'm going to die.

I can't breathe and my heart is pounding painfully in my chest.

If there is a hell, then this is it.

On this beach, under a big fiery sun and a clear blue sky, is my hell.

"Come on Jessamy, get up. Get moving. I want ten more crunches."

"You are a sick, sick sadist." I gasp from my position, flat on my back.

"I've been called worse!" Mark says standing over me with his arms outstretched, palms facing me. "Come on, ten more. You're not going to tone that middle lying there looking half dead…"

"You've killed me."

"We have only been going fifteen minutes! You have another forty-five to get through and if you don't start moving I'll make you run all the way home."

"You wouldn't!"

"Don't find out!"

I groan loudly and struggle up to hit his hands. He counts out, "ten, nine, eight, seven…"

My stomach muscles, buried under twenty years of biscuit consumption, scream and complain almost as loudly as I do. The man is a masochist. He is one of the most handsome men I have ever seen with tight muscles and a perfect bottom but underneath the Thor-like exterior lies a black heart, vicious and cruel.

"Arrrrrrgh." I holler as I complete the ten and collapse back onto the sand, my entire body crying in pain.

There are three teenage girls walking along the beach, a few metres from where I lie in a crumpled heap. Their blonde hair swings like glossy curtains and they carry their shoes, having rolled their jeans up to show tanned, shapely ankles. They look over at me and a mask of sympathy sets on their faces. I know what they are thinking. The same thing I would have thought thirty years ago, '*I'm never going to look like that'* and they watch with interest as Mark puts me through my paces. He preens for them, flexing his muscles as they giggle and flick their hair with flirtatious fluttering of their eyelashes. At what point in time did teenage girls become so confident and immaculate? Gone are the days of garish blue eyeshadow and orange foundation, in its place are contoured cheeks and eyes framed with perfect black flicks.

Mark glances over at them and then proceeds to demonstrate press ups, his strong body rippling as he does them. The girls enjoy the display of manliness but don't disguise their giggles as I endeavour to do one. "Come on Jessamy!" He encourages, "you can do it. No pain no gain."

"Fuck off." I grimace under my breath as the sweat flows down my back, my arms shaking so violently with exertion that I collapse onto the sand, the grains sticking to my face. "Eeeugh, yuck." I complain spitting out sand that's worked its way into my mouth. "You really are vicious Mark!"

He laughs and pulls me up. "This is your first time Jessamy, it will get easier I promise."

"It better."

"You will need to get a better sports bra, those bad boys need support and lots of it."

I cross my arms across my chest. "Do you mind?" I sulk. "It took me thirty years to grow them."

"Say goodbye to them. Get a proper sports bra before your next session otherwise you'll damage the muscles and they'll droop into your socks!"

The rest of the session is equally painful and my audience appears to enjoy both my discomfort and the continued flexing by Mark of his muscles. He's built like a tank, solid and broad shouldered with no excess flesh anywhere.

"I'll see you on Wednesday, Jessamy." He says walking me up to the front door. My legs are about to give way, the cliff path being the final killer activity of the day. "I'll email you a diet plan to follow, be warned, it's strict, biscuits are entirely off the menu."

"They would be!" I moan. "Is there any crap on the plan?"

"The occasional glass of red wine…"

"Occasional? How occasional do you mean? Like every day?" I ask hopefully.

134

"No, I mean one glass once a week…" He grins impishly at me. "You don't need it!"

"I'm a writer…"

"Which means you write, not drink!"

"It goes hand in hand. Some of my best writing has been under the influence." I smile. "It's ok, I don't think I need red wine more than once a week. Now white wine…"

"Is off the menu! There are no health benefits to white wine…"

"You're just mean!"

He laughs. "Perhaps, but when you're a couple of stone lighter and don't have dehydrated skin you'll thank me!"

"What's wrong with my skin?" I ask crossly. "I thought I looked pretty good for my age, apart from the spare tyre."

"Your skin is tired, dull and dry. How you treat yourself shows on your skin. If you live off sugar and cups of tea, coupled with white wine by the barrel and disordered sleep patterns your face will tell the tale."

"So, you're saying I'm a wreck?"

"Pretty much." He says cheerfully. "But not for much longer. By the time I've finished with you, you'll look fifteen years younger. I'm the best money you've ever spent!"

I make a noise that sounds something like 'hurrrrmph' and Mark laughs. "You have to trust me Jess, I'm the most amazing thing to happen to you!" My hands tremble uncontrollably as I try to get the key in the lock. He takes it from me and opens the door. "Lots of water today and an early night, you may feel a little achy in the morning, remember, it's just the fat screaming, you'll be lean machine in no time!"

**

"Honestly Zoe the man is a sadist. A sadist, I tell you! I've got aches where I didn't know I could ache!" I grumble to Zoe after the second hideous session with Mark. "He's got me on a no carb diet with a banned list that includes white wine. No white wine? What the fuck is that all about? Apparently, I am only allowed to drink one glass of red wine once or twice a week, no more, and I don't like red wine. I

135

can have raw or ninety percent chocolate, no dairy milk daim and blah blah blah…He is Satan in shorts."

"So, you fancy him then?" She laughs down the line.

I poke my tongue out at the phone. "No, I do not fancy him Zoe." I say firmly. "You can't fancy someone so evil as he."

"Change trainers then." Zoe says impishly.

"I can't do that, I've paid him upfront for four times a week. Four! For the whole of eternity and all because my crappy husband told me I've let myself go…"

"Nearly ex-husband"

"Don't remind me!" I tell her stroppily. "I got a letter from his solicitor about irreconcilable differences and shared blame. Quite honestly Zoe, I've had enough with husbands, but I'm pretty attached to my chins and I'm wondering if I really need to lose them! I could just take down the mirrors, then I can't see the rest of me!"

"Jess…"

"I know what you're going to say but denial has been a happy place to be and I should be staying there, not running up steps with my breasts giving me black eyes."

"Aw poor Jessamy." Zoe says laughing. "Down there all alone in that big house, with a hot personal trainer and a hot gardener…"

I laugh. "They may be hot but the gardener has vanished and the trainer is the son of Lilith."

"What do you mean, vanished?"

"I've not seen him since my horrible hangover."

"Oh."

"I know. It's a big oh."

"Did you not go around to say sorry for being an evil, vomiting bitch."

"Yeah, he wasn't in."

"Did you go back?"

"No."

"Why?"

"Because I'm chicken shit and because he's always so grumpy and stand off-ish with me."

"Perhaps he fancies you?"

"Oh my God Zoe, how can you spout such shit with a straight face?"

"How do you know my face is straight…"

"Even Phil didn't fancy me and he was supposed to. I'm fat, old and barren. Doesn't make me much of catch, does it?"

"My darling friend, before you go all melancholy on me and have me reaching for the gin, please go and take a good look in the mirror. You are gorgeous."

I cross the room to the mirror on the far wall. "My face is chubby and my chins have their own personalities."

"A little bit of chub doesn't make you any less gorgeous. Be nice to yourself Jess, you're alone down there, don't let your inner voice tell you anything other than good stuff."

I grunt.

"Did you just grunt?" Zoe asks giggling. "Oh my God, you're a Neanderthal."

I nod at my reflection. Bright red and sweaty with matted hair. "That's the look I'm going for right now."

"How's the book coming along?

"It's not. At least, not the story my agent wants."

"Tell me more…"

"Lily had a secret. A ghost if you like, something she kept hidden from everyone. I found some letters and the portrait in the hallway had a photo behind the frame…"

"Secret? What secret?"

"I don't yet know exactly. I found letters and a photo of a boy, Jimmy. They had a love affair, here, in the village. Every summer her family came to Otterleigh on holiday from London and she must have met him here. And they fell in love. Lily must have been mid-teens when he ended up going to Australia although I get the feeling from his letters that he didn't want to go. They mostly implied he was sent. Unwilling. The last letter said he was coming back for them, but I don't know who he meant by *them*. His parents were planning to take Lily but something happened and she didn't go. Zoe, he died."

"He died?"

"Yeah. On the way to the boat. You should read his letters Zoe, so much love. She must have really loved him too."

"How do you know that?"

"Because she kept it all." I pick up the photo. "And because of how she looked at him. You can't fake that, even in a photo." I squint at the picture. "He was really handsome, strong looking…such a shame. I've got the rest of Lily's room to clear out, I'm hoping there are some more answers in there somewhere…"

"I can't wait to find out!" Zoe chimes, her voice dancing.

"You're such a gossip!"

"I know! But my life is all work, work, work and mundane to-do lists that get longer by the day. I really thought when the twins went to university that Ben and I would have more time, but we have less. It wouldn't surprise me if he was bonking his goddamn secretary, she's all he talks about."

I laugh. Zoe's husband adores her, suffocating at times, but he still looks at her with the same doe-eyed look that he did when they first met.

"I have to go Jessamy, I've got a client coming in and I need my wits in one piece, this woman is a nightmare, she makes your mother look like a purring pussy cat. Ring me as soon as you find out anything more, and Jess…"

"Yeah?"

"You really need to make up with your hot gardener…you never know, I could be right and he could bonk you in the flower beds!"

"Oh, shut up!" I grin. "How did I end up with you as my friend?"

"The Gods were smiling at you that day!" She replies breezily. "Love you Jess, speak soon."

"Bye Zoe." I listen as the line goes dead and place my phone on the kitchen counter.

***

"What do you want?" Jack asks crossly opening the door. I try to speak but my mouth is suddenly dryer than the Sahara. Jack is wearing nothing but a towel, droplets of water running down his torso.

His very strong, muscular torso.

"Well?" He demands impatiently.

I cough to clear my throat and focus, instead, on a picture behind him. "I came to apologise." It's a pitiful apology, barely audible as my tongue swells considerably in my mouth. "For what I said about Lily. It was out of order and really unfair and I'm sorry."

138

"Thanks."

I feel so awkward. He's looking at me as though I should be saying more but I'm completely tongue tied.

"Did you want anything else, Jessamy?"

"No…not really." I can think of plenty but clearly by the way Jack is glaring at me, my pathetic crush is wholly one sided and I'm wishing the ground would swallow me up. "I met your Mum yesterday."

"And?"

"And nothing, I was just saying."

"Right."

"Fuck it." I mutter and turn away sharply, nearly sending myself dizzy. "I just came to say sorry, I've done that, have a nice life."

I walk as upright as I can across the farm yard. I've no idea if he's still in the doorway, half naked and looking glorious, but I won't give him the satisfaction of turning back round, nor limping while my muscles scream at me.

As soon as I reach The White House I wrench open the door and slam it shut behind me. "Asshole. Utter, utter asshole." I seethe, crossing the kitchen and out to the hallway. My calves ache and I flex them until I cramp up painfully and I hobble my way to the bathroom pausing every now and again to rub a body part that twinges.

I pour most of the white musk bubbles into the bath and nearly gag on the smell. How was this ever my favourite?

As soon as the bath is near to overflowing, I climb and sink down into the bubbles, closing my nose to the smell as I feel the tension begin to dissolve in the hot water. I hold my breath and sink under the water. It feels so safe under here that I could stay here all day, cleansing in the warmth until I'm grasped by the wrist and dragged upwards.

"Holy shit." I splutter, inhaling a lungful water. Acutely aware of my nakedness I wrap my arms around my body, shielding as much of it as I can. Thankfully the bubbles protect most of my modesty. "Are you trying to kill me?" I shriek at Jack who is looking shell-shocked. "I mean really, what are you doing in here. I'm in the bath. Oh my God, can you turn your back or get me a towel or something. Jesus. Close your eyes!" I shriek like a banshee. "Close your eyes!"

A towel lands unceremoniously on me and immediately becomes water logged. I pull it over my body and stand up, dripping and covered in bubbles. The towel is heavy and awkward to keep wrapped around me but I hold it in a death grip and glare at Jack.

"I mean really why are you in here. I'm in the bath. Naked. Is that what you do, stare at women in the bath…" I can hear myself getting louder and more hysterical the longer I rant. Jack appears to have recovered from his shock and is now glaring at me.

"I couldn't give a shit if you are naked or not, it's not like it's the first time! I thought you'd drowned. I was calling and calling you and there was no response. I did knock…"

"Well I didn't hear you."

"Probably because you were under the goddamn water. I didn't know you were in here and trust me, if I knew you were I would not have come in. Seeing you naked isn't on my list of priorities." I watch as he rakes his hand through his hair. "I'm sorry I came in. Honestly, I thought you were dead. I saw the letter from the solicitor and…I thought you topped yourself. I didn't read it, just a glance. Shit…I promised Lily I'd do what I could to make sure you were safe and I thought you were dead."

"How did you know her?"

"I just did."

"There has to be more to it than that."

"Think what you like. I'm going downstairs. Perhaps you should get dressed."

I tighten my arms around my chest. "Perhaps I'll just finish my bath. Why are you here anyway?"

"I was rude earlier, I came to say sorry." He grins. "I wasn't expecting a full frontal for my efforts! Again!"

"Fuck off!" I say trying not to smile, gesturing towards the door. "If you don't mind…"

He turns sharply on his heel and crosses the bathroom, his boots hard on the floor. He pauses for a moment then says. "She talked about you all the time."

"Who?"

"Lily. She said she always hoped for a reason to get you to come back. I don't think she planned to die in order to do it though. She came up with some very wild ideas though…"

"Oh." I don't know what to say. How Lily knew Jack so well that he's stayed around is a mystery but then with what I'm slowly unravelling nothing will surprise me anymore. "Thank you for telling me, that's a comfort."

"Hmmm." He says gruffly and slams the door behind him.

The water has gone tepid with all the drama. My enthusiasm for lying in the bubbles has waned but rather than give in I fill the bath up further with hot water and lie there for a little longer trying not to think about Jack's glinting green eyes.

***

Jack was in my dream last night.

It was disturbing. Very disturbing.

I was naked.

Obviously.

He was naked.

All of him…naked.

My knees keep going weak and I've repeatedly slopped my coffee over both myself, the dressing table and the floor. It's the eyes. He's hypnotised me. No one should have eyes of that colour.

No one.

He's the devil.

I'm possessed.

I empty out the rest of Lily's cupboard into the bin bags. Nothing worth keeping, mostly half used lipsticks and empty perfume bottles, their colours and scents faded to bland. Turning my attention to the dressing table I move the photos onto the bed and empty it of packets of unsmoked cigarettes, lighters, a half-drunk bottle of gin and a pair of handcuffs.

"Lilian!" I swear I hear a filthy laugh. I decide to keep those.

Opening the dressing room door, I feel the cold hand on my back. "Are you there, Lily?" I ask. On the small table sits a stereo with a tape deck into which I put *Like A Virgin*. I remember the day I bought this tape, it was the same day I'd opened a new bank account in town and I got a voucher for 50p off if I spent £4 or more in *Our Price*. I thought I was so cool buying a tape I knew my parents would disapprove of. When I got home, Lily and I put it on the stereo in the lounge and blasted it out as loud as possible until the Vicar came over to complain.

I turn up the volume as high as it will go and open the window laughing to myself. "Are you singing too?" I ask the empty room before singing along with Madonna. I turn back to the over-stuffed rails. Lily loved clothes. Her dresses are all couture, beautiful works of craftsmanship that tell of bygone eras. I hold a few up against me and wish I was a foot smaller and a couple of dress sizes thinner. With all the willpower in the world, none of these would ever fit me. I deliberate keeping them but these dresses need to be seen. With that in mind I make a quick phone call to the local fashion museum and donate them. I leave them hanging up beside the endless furs. The rest I sort into bags and load them into the car with the videos. The room suddenly feels bare and silent, the music having long since finished without me even noticing. I leave the dressing room and pick up my box, carrying it slowly down the stairs and into the kitchen.

I pour a large whisky and sit down at the table, the box of diaries and Lily's box for me side by side. I can't imagine what she did all this for. Jack said she wanted a reason to bring me back but I can't see it, I can't see what she wants me to know. Outside there is a stillness over the garden, no breeze to bob the heads of the remaining flowers, just the trickling of the sunlight through the trees. I take a larger gulp than planned and cough violently, sending a stream of amber liquid onto the floor.

"Perhaps choose a less grown up drink." Jack says coming in and not bothering to disguise his mirth. "Whiskey? At this time?"

"Dutch courage." I splutter, putting a hand over my nose and mouth. "I need it."

"Slippery slope that..." He says taking the glass from me, his fingers briefly touch mine and I feel a jolt so strong that it momentarily makes me sway. His eyes glitter and I recoil taken aback by the sudden fury in the deep green.

"What's the matter?" My voice comes out in a squeaky whisper and I cough to clear my throat.

"I have to go."

"But you've just arrived."

"I have to go."

"Jack? Will you stay for a bit?" As soon as I say the words I want to take them back. Shock, then surprise flashes over his face and I hunch a little lower in my seat.

"Why?"

"Um…well…" I huff out a big breath. "The thing is, the house is a little lonely and suddenly I just don't want to be on my own. I got a letter from Lily…I don't know what to make of it and…"

"Alright." He says, downing my whiskey. "As long as there is more where this came from?"

"Plenty."

"Selling my soul for a scotch." He mutters under his breath.

"Sorry?" I know what he said but it doesn't make a lot of sense.

"Nothing." He rakes his hands through his hair until it sticks up in all directions. I stare at it distracted, my dream hitting me with the force of a baseball bat. I flush wildly and leap up to get him a glass into which I slosh too much whiskey. "Are you trying to get me drunk?" He asks with a grin.

"Do you want to get drunk?"

"Recently most days it seems."

"Why?" I spoon some melting ice into his glass and fill up my glass with the amber liquid.

"Life." He doesn't say anymore, just sits staring out of the window, his brow furred. I stare at him from under my hair. He is so much more handsome than I remember him to be, but perhaps I was too wrapped up in Nate to notice. His profile is strong, masculine, a straight nose, full mouth, stubble covering his jaw, the same copper colour as his hair. The tell-tale lines of age criss-cross beside his eyes and around his mouth but unlike my own lines, his are attractive, distinguished almost, and I have the strangest desire to run my fingers over them. "Jessamy, why are you staring at me?"

"I'm not."

"You are."

"How do you know, you're not looking at me to know what I'm staring at."

"I can see you reflected in the window."

"Shit."

"Pardon?"

"Nothing." I drink a large gulp of the whiskey and keep my mouth shut tight against the splutter. My eyes begin to water and I feel my internal temperature rising. "Whiskey is vile." I cough. "It must be a drink that men are conditioned to like in their genetic makeup. It's worse than medicine."

"This is a good whiskey." Jack picks up the bottle. "Vintage, smooth and meady."

"Smooth? The inside of my throat has been burnt off."

"Probably because you are a sappy martini drinker!"

"I am not!" I retort outraged. "Once or twice maybe…"

"I remember very well having to walk you home on many occasions after you'd been drinking martini..."

1991
Debbie came round with a bottle of wine and once we drank that we met Tori and Jo on the cliff path and went to the Oak. Nate was in there with Hannah. Apparently he's going out with her. I never did like her, the vain bitch. Anyway, he made a great show of speaking to me until she got in a mega snot and he stopped. But when I looked at him, he looked at me and it was like neither of us could look away. In the end we all went to Exeter. I got so drunk I could hardly walk but I still got off with Jack and Nate got really nasty.

"Jess?"

I start to laugh. "The delightful memories pop back to haunt me every now again!" I empty my whisky down the sink. "I can't drink that shit! I wonder if Lily has any martini."

"Still a sappy martini drinker I see?"

"No! This will be my first martini since nineteen ninety-two! You game?" I giggle as I leave the kitchen for the cellar. It doesn't feel so creepy down here now that Jack is in the house but I still don't linger, grabbing bottles of spirits and mixers into my arms and staggering back up the stairs.

Jack is standing by the back door when I return. "I should go."

"Oh." I feel foolish standing with my arms protectively wrapped around the bottles. I don't know what I was expecting really, having got carried away with the dreams I've been having. Of course he doesn't want to be here, why would he? I rest the bottles down on the

144

work top and slowly unwrap my arms. The martini bottle wobbles precariously but there is no longer any humour in the drink. Now it all just looks a little pathetic. "Ok."

Jack lets out a big sigh. "The garden is nearly done. A couple more days and it should be on its way back to how it was before. Once the plants grow, of course. I'm not sure anything can be done about the tree though, it's in a really sorry state."

"There is still one leaf. I have hope that it will be ok. Thanks for doing it all Jack, you know, for sorting everything and for all you did before Lily died." I get a clean glass out of the cupboard. "One martini before you go? For old times?"

He takes an age to answer and then says. "Just one."

***

1991

We all went out last night. I drank two glasses of cider and was really drunk. Nate got off with Debbie. I got off with Jack.

"Jack?"

"Hmm?"

"I'm feeling a little drunk."

"Me too." He sighs contently.

"Jack?"

"Hmm?"

"I can't drink any more martini."

"Good because there is none left."

"Jack?"

"Hmm?"

"Do you ever think about those summers we all had?"

"I try not to."

"Why?"

"I have to go Jessamy."

"Jack?"

"Hmm?"

"I'm drunk."

"Me too."

"Jack?"

"Hmm?"

"Do you ever wonder why we snogged all the time?"

"I try not to."

"Why?"

He sighs loudly. "Just because."

We're in the morning room. I can't remember when we came in and I've no idea of the time. The room is lightly scented by the roses I've refilled Lily's urn with and a jazz CD is on repeat, playing softly on the small stereo Lily kept in the cupboard beside the sofa. It's gentle music, not the raucous upbeat jazz she was fond of, no, it tells the story of times gone by. I wonder what Jack's thinking of. He's lying on the rug, his head on a cushion, eyes closed, but he's not asleep. I try not to stare at him through blurry eyes but he's drawing my gaze.

"Jack?"

"Hmm?"

"What do you think Lily meant by the box?"

"She meant for you to figure it out."

"Have you figured it out?" I ask him.

"I don't know what's in the box."

"Do you want to see?"

"Not if it's means moving."

"Jack?"

"Hmm?"

"Where's Andrea?"

"I don't know. She left. I got home to a note saying she was leaving me for some bloke she met online. I signed the divorce papers yesterday."

"Oh. Like me then."

"Huh?"

"My husband left me for someone else. I think it was my fault."

"It was my fault too."

"What did you do wrong?" I ask, plumping up my cushion and nestling my head back onto it.

"I didn't give her enough attention. What did you do wrong?"

"I couldn't give him a child." It doesn't seem the right time to mention Nate. "Jack?"

"Hmm."

"Are you sad?"

146

"Not anymore."

"Oh?"

He doesn't say anything, just crosses his arms under his head and stares at a point on the ceiling. His shirt rises up and shows smooth, tanned skin with a smattering of hair across his stomach. There is a sudden, desperate longing to run my fingertips over his skin, feel it warm under my hands. He was never this handsome when we were teenagers, but had he been, would I have even noticed?

"Jack?"

"Hmm?"

"Do you want another drink?"

"Don't you think we may have had enough?"

"Maybe.... Jack?"

"Yes Jessamy?"

"Is it comfortable down there?" I roll over onto my side and look at him, lying out on the floor. Under the rug are flagstones and I rather think it's likely to be cold.

"Come down here and find out." It sounds like a challenge and his smile grows the longer I stay silent. "Are you chicken?"

"Why should I be chicken?" I retort, clumsily getting up from the sofa and wobbling on my drunken legs. "I think I'm more drunk than I thought I was." Giggling I pick up a cushion and step over his legs, sinking down beside him and lying out on the rug. "It's more comfy than I thought. What are you thinking about down here?"

"I'm not really thinking, you keep talking."

"Oh." Jack's eyes are closed but he wraps an arm under my neck and I nestle against him. It feels safe, lying here against his hard, strong body.

"Jack?"

"Hmm."

"Fancy a snog?"

＊

CHAPTER NINE

The feeling of someone breaking open my skull with a chisel and hammer wakes me up. The sunlight singes my eyeballs as I slowly unpeel my eyelids from them so I throw my arm over my face to keep the day out. I'm going to die. My head is throbbing so painfully it's as though a pneumatic drill is punching holes across my brain.

I'm on the sofa in the morning room, under the blanket that normally covers the small chair in the corner. It's itchy, made from course red and silver wool, very decorative but not at all pleasant to sleep under. I shake it off and wish immediately that I hadn't moved. The room spins and my head pounds nauseatingly.

"I am never drinking martini again." I moan through dry, cracked lips. My tongue sticks to the roof of my mouth and I've got a ghastly taste of rotting spirits. Slowly, very slowly, I rise from the sofa and walk joltingly from the morning room towards the kitchen. Each step makes my brain rattle inside my head until I want to cry.

"Oh no." I groan in a scratchy, sore voice catching sight of myself in the hallway mirror. My hair is a matted mess and my face seems to have slipped from my bones and is sliding towards my feet. "Who'd be forty-two?" I mutter harshly at myself. "I never used to look this bad after martini in the nineties when I…Oh fuckaduck." It comes out like a frog wailing, a strange croak of mortification. *Fancy a snog?* Oh…Fuck. Did I? Did he? Did we?

All the blood in my body pools in my feet leaving me icy cold and shaking. Shit, shit, shit, I've no recollection of anything after that. I was snuggled into him on the floor then *fancy a snog* and then…what? Then what? My stomach twists into a knot and I feel the urge to vomit. Vomit and then run away from here. Far away. Run to anywhere that has a human population of zero for me to forever avoid the risk of being a total idiot.

"Shit…" I say under my breath as I walk into the kitchen and come face to face with Jack. He's making coffee. The pot bubbles and hisses as the water heats up and drips through the filter. Jack looks tired, the lines on his face more pronounced and his green eyes have a red tinge.

"H…h…Hi." I stammer sounding like a jabbering idiot. Even hungover he looks handsome…*Oh for God's sake Jessamy.*

"Morning." He pours milk into two mugs and says nothing more, just stands with his back to me watching the coffee pot. The contents of the box Lily left for me are on the table, spread out far more neatly that I'd left them.

"Morning." I reply in a near-whisper, trying to detangle my hair with my fingers before he can turn around. "Have you been awake long?" I've no idea where he slept. The last thing I remember is that we were on the floor but I woke on the sofa. I hope it was me that got there and that Jack didn't get a hernia moving me.

"A while."

"Oh." I pick up the photo album and flick through it. "You looked at this? Does it make any sense to you?" I ask pausing on a picture someone took of Jack and me. I look up to find him staring at me, a strange look on his face. Is there any way of asking him about last night which doesn't make me look like a total fool?

"I think it's pretty clear." He replies switching off the coffee machine and pouring the percolated coffee into the mugs and mixing it with the milk.

"Do you? Really?"

"Yep."

"Oh."

He seems to relent a little but a big sigh is audible before he says. "You just have to look."

"I did look."

"Look harder."

Jack hands me a cup of coffee that I take gratefully. "Thank you." I show him the photo. "Look how young we were...time passes so quickly doesn't it?" I rub my hand wearily over my head. "My head hurts." I say shutting my eyes against the brightness.

"Hungover?" He asks. I gesture to the chair but he shakes his head.

"Very." I sit down. "I've had more hangovers in the past month or so than I've had in the past twenty years. This house is driving me to alcoholism!" I attempt a smile but my lips are too dry and pull against my teeth.

Jack glances out of the window and I turn to follow his line of vision. At the gate between the garden and the farm yard stands a dark-haired man who beckons him with exaggerated arm movements.

"I have to go." He says abruptly and puts his untouched mug of coffee down with a bang onto the table. I barely have the chance to say goodbye before he's out of the door and running over the grass to the gate. I have the sudden image of him striding over the hills, gun over his shoulder, dog at his heels with the same brooding air as…

"Lady Chatterley's Lover." I blurt out, slopping coffee onto the table as I slam the mug down. "Lady bloody Chatterley…" I pick the book up from the table. "It can't be the right answer, can it?" I ask the empty room, hoping for the now-familiar cold hand. I turn the book over in my hand and read the back. Lady of the House and the gardener… Jack? No, I'm misinterpreting things, it's my hangover, Lily wouldn't…would she?

"Morning Jessamy!" Mark walks in with a beaming smile on my face and my heart sinks. "Oh, we're not looking so rosy this morning."

"I don't feel very well."

He glances over at the counter where the empty bottles sit reigning as judge, jury and executioner. Goddamn it why didn't I put them in the bin?

"I spy with my little eye, something beginning with…the banned list." Mark says chirpily.

"I'd hoped you'd forgotten you were coming this morning," I drop my head on the table, "I feel really achy from yesterday so could you be nice and angelic today rather than hell's demon."

"No chance!" He grins and despite liking the man, I'd be quite happy to murder him and bury him under the patio. "Go and get changed, unless you want to be seen in public looking like the sort of person who drinks cheap cider out of paper bags…"

"Can I not just phone in sick."

Mark/Satan raises an eyebrow. "What do you think?"

"You are truly evil."

"You'll thank me when you look fabulous." He says brightly. "I am a gift from the heavens."

"You are the son of Satan."

"I'm waiting…the longer I wait the more painful it will be."

"Alright, alright, I'm going but can we please stay in the garden."

"What do you think?"

I hate him.

***

They are laughing at me. Mark has gone for maximum humiliation and I'm on the beach doing squats while the teenagers look at me with amusement.

"This is the last time I ever work out with you." I seethe between painful pants. "You are a sadist."

"When your bottom is a ripe peach you'll thank me."

"When you've killed me, I will haunt you forever…"

"Very dramatic Jessamy."

"Fuck off." I mutter under my breath. A vision in pink lycra runs past me looking amused before the recognition dawns on her. "Oh crap."

"Morning Jessamy." Tori trots over, her ponytail swinging side to side with a hypnotic rhythm. "How are you? Having fun?"

"Fun is not how I would describe it." I tell her lowering myself into another squat as my knees crack out their protest.

"Squats are the worst," she says sympathetically, "but they do the best things to your bottom. Not that it feels like it at the time." Tori does a few elegant, swan like squats, her perfect bottom resplendent in the lycra leggings she wears. I watch Mark stare appreciatively at her slender form as she goes up and down. Even I'm a little transfixed. "I've been meaning to call round," she continues doing a little jog on the spot while she speaks, which I'm sure is for Mark's benefit. "I'm going out a week on Saturday with Debbie and Jo and I wondered if you wanted to come too? I've not told them you're here, it completely slipped my mind because I've been so busy, but I think it would be the most amazing surprise. Say you'll come?"

"This Saturday?" I ask, stopping my squats. Mark doesn't notice.

"No, next, we're going to the Oak. Not that you'd recognise it, it's been refurbished from the manky mess it used to be, it's more of a wine bar now and on Saturday nights they have a cocktail chap in who does the whole bottle-in-the-air routine. He's hot, gets lots of tips!" She grins. "Will you come?"

"I'd love to."

"Excellent. Let me have your number so I can ring you with the details."

Breathlessly I give her my number that she puts into her sparkly-covered phone.

"Fabulous." She says merrily. "I'll give you a ring next week. Bye Jessamy, bye…uh…"

"Mark." He says.

"Bye Mark." We both watch as she runs across the beach, a steady, graceful run, looking the exact opposite of the bubbly, chubby girl I remember.

"Can I go home now?" I ask hopefully.

"No, drop down and give me twenty press-ups."

"I really hate you."

***

"So, did you snog him or not?" Zoe asks during the most self - pitying phone call I've ever made.

"No idea."

"Are you going to ask him?" She inhales deeply.

"Zoe, are you smoking?" I ask outraged.

"No…yes…I'm stressed. Anyway, don't change the subject, you always do that, switch the conversation when you don't want to answer…are you going to ask him?"

"How on earth do I do that? 'Oh hi Jack, sorry about the horrendous hangover and sorry I made you drink half a huge bottle of godawful martini but tell me, did anything happen?'"

"When you put it like that!" She laughs. "Any joy on the box?"

"I've no idea what the box means, Jack said I need to look harder but aside from the Lady Chatterley idea that's me done. No other ideas. I'm sure she didn't mean Jack."

"How can you be sure? Didn't you snog him every weekend when you were younger?"

"Yeah but…"

"Oh My God." Zoe shouts with excitement down the phone and I have to hold the phone away from my ear. "You're his ghost. I bet he's had a thing for you since the dawn of time. In fact, I'm convinced that's what it is!"

"Don't be ridiculous…"

"Didn't I tell you about my great Grandmother? She was a fortune teller…ooh perhaps I've inherited the gift."

"Zoe…"

"Don't *Zoe* me, I know I'm right."

I blow out a huge noisy breath of exasperation. "Zoe. I'm sure it's not Jack…"

"But it's not Nate."

"Obviously. So not only do I have a box to figure out, I've also got Lily's secret to figure out and today is not the day for any of those things. I've got such a hideous hangover and my workout this morning was brutal."

"I don't know why you put yourself through it. You're a goddess Jess, like a Botticelli painting.

"Are you drunk?"

"At eleven am? That's just wishful thinking!" She groans dramatically and says, "I need to go, I've got a client coming in. Bugger. Just when your life was getting interesting! Ring me as soon as you know anything!"

"I will. Come down soon?"

"Yep! Bye babe."

"Bye Zoe."

***

I'm reading Lady Chatterley's Lover when the doorbell rings. My body groans and complains as I uncurl from the sofa and gingerly walk across the hallway to the front door. Mark has finished me off. Not only is my head still banging despite the endless glasses of water I've had today but my poor body is completely broken after my work out. I'd like to think it will eventually do some good but those days seem so far away into the future I can't see them. The house is still. Like it knows somehow that the last of Lily's things are being removed, that she won't be here anymore. I've not been into her bedroom since the clear out and I feel such anxiety about the final items being taken away. The dresses and furs, they made Lily who she was, glorious, beautiful, glamourous, and for them to no longer be in the house chips away at the final pieces of my heartbroken soul. *They are just things, Jessamy.*

153

The cold hand seems to gently stroke my cheek and I put my warm hand upon the cold. I can feel her so closely. Everyday. I just wish I knew what she was saying. "Will you still be here when I know it all?" I whisper before opening the door.

"Miss Summers?" Two women stand at front door, their name badges on the end of glitzy lanyards. They are impeccable in dresses and little jackets, keeping their smiles in place as they give me the brief look, up and down, up and down. I shift awkwardly, feeling very frumpy in my joggers and oversized tee-shirt.

"Hi." I say reaching out my hand to shake both of theirs. "I'm Jess, please come in."

"Beautiful house." One of them says as she looks around the room.

"Thank you. Can I get you both a drink?" I ask.

"No thank you, time is against us unfortunately."

"Then let me show you upstairs. The clothes are hanging up."

I show them up to Lily's room. I see the house through their eyes, slightly battered but still majestic, sitting high above the bay. It could be very grand again and that's what I want now. To make it grand. To make it live. To end the past and move forward. Fleetingly I wonder what Jack is doing but the squirm of embarrassment low down in my belly pushes the thoughts away.

"Lisa, would you look at these?" The woman with the darker hair gasps as she looks at the couture hanging up in Lily's dressing room. "These are exquisite and...God, they're priceless...are you sure?" She is almost wild with excitement. "I mean, I know they're on loan but..."

"I'm sure..."

"Kayla, look at this one. Givenchy, nineteen fifty or nineteen sixty, I've seen the drawing in the London Museum of Fashion but he made what, two or three, Audrey Hepburn had one and..."

"It's likely this is the only other one." I comment enjoying their delight. "Lily had friends in high places, most of these gowns came from those friendships."

"Are you sure? I mean, sure about lending them to us? We're only a small museum...We're insured and everything but these gowns could be sold at auction, you'd make a fortune."

"I don't want to sell them, I want them to be enjoyed. My Aunt was a fierce supporter of the local institutions and it feels right to donate them to you."

"We have to host an event, Lisa. Something big. You're welcome to be involved in whatever we decide to do."

"I'd just like an invite to opening night." I smile at them. They are trying to kerb their enthusiasm but it's not working, they're jigging up and down like springs. I don't feel as blasé as I'm hoping they think I am. I feel something ripping inside and a painful lump in my throat. I played in this room, I dressed up in the furs and the clothes, pretending to be a character from Dynasty or whichever American drama I was into at the time. They may now be worth a lot of money but to me they are priceless and I'm now wondering if I've made a mistake letting them go. "Let me help you down with them, it's going to take a fair number of trips."

Up and down the stair case is not something my thighs really need after my run-in with Satan but I need to do something otherwise I'm likely to cry. I help with a few trips but my poor body gives up and I leave the women to it. They are puffing and red-faced on the final trip down the stairs, buried under the furs. I watch them load them into the van, holding onto the door frame as wave after wave of sadness comes over me.

"That's it, Lily, it's all gone. Where is the secret?" I ask the empty air.

"Thank you Jess." Kayla comes in with a file. "We'll itemise everything and send you the inventory, just so you know what we have. This is so exciting…I studied fashion and saw some great pieces during my course, but your Aunt's collection is something else. I promise we'll take very good care of it."

"Thank you." I cough to clear my throat. Kayla looks like she understands but says nothing, just squeezing my hand. I'm grateful for the silence.

"I'll be in touch."

"Ok."

I watch them turn the van very slowly on the gravel and drive up to the gates before closing the door and locking it behind me. What now? I need to clear out the final few bits and pieces from Lily's room but that's a job for another day. Right now, I need a sleep.

***

The garden is peaceful. A gentle breeze lifts the scents from the flowers, their heads bobbing delicately and every so often the sounds of the sea drifts over the calmness and reminds me that I'm here. I'm sitting under Lily's oak tree, leaning against the charred trunk, the knots of wood digging into my back, not uncomfortably, more reassuring and grounding, keeping me in the now, the reminders of why I came and the reason I still stay. I feel close to Lily out here. The branches are still empty but the one little leaf has held on tight and it flutters softly in the breeze.

The conversation I had with Rachel earlier has lifted my spirits. My fears that Phil would reject her in favour of his new life have so far proven unfounded and I am forever grateful that he made the journey to London to tell her that she is still as important as ever. She may not be the small child who runs to the door every day waiting for him to come home but the need she has for the father he has always been, remains as essential to her as ever. He's a good man.

I wonder about my replacement and I hope she is making Phil happy. I wanted to ask Rachel about her but I couldn't put my daughter in a position where she felt torn in two and aside from natural curiosity, I don't really need to know. It's a strange feeling, having such definite changes to face and while the ending of my marriage fills me with sadness, I have so much hope for the future. I can feel a change on the breeze, the sounds of the garden seem to reassure me that the next part of my life is on the cusp of being clear. The trees whisper and I strain to hear what they are saying. I close my eyes and lie back onto the crunchy grass. It smells so fresh and is a wonderful colour of green but the sun, having dried out the land, has left it feel crisp under my back.

My laptop beeps with emails and I send a silent curse towards it. I've managed to convince my agent that there is a story here, waiting to be told, and she seems to have been placated by the rather holey outline I've sent her. It should be enough to keep her from having a breakdown, and give me long enough to find out what Lily's secret is. I feel sure it's the story I should tell, but to do so, I've got to find the answers. Everything has been set up but I just can't see what the ending will be. *Look harder.* I roll over onto my stomach, and pick the photo album out of the box.

Then there is this puzzle, the one Lily left for me. What am I supposed to see? What could Jack see with one glance that I am so blatantly missing? I get a flutter when I think of him and it surprises me such that I look around me to see if anyone is nearby to see the flush that spreads across my face as the image of his strong masculine body fills my mind.

Which makes me deplorable and shallow.

And a little bit horny.

Thinking of Jack is making me horny.

Fuck.

Fuck.

Fuck.

I shake my head so fast my brain bounces off my skull.

I cannot think of Jack like this.

I cannot.

I will not.

Oh, but I am!

Jessamy!

"Argh." I yell as loudly as I can, gripping my head between my hands. "Argh. Argh. ARRRRGGGGGGH."

No, no, no, this is a disaster.

"Jessamy? Jessamy are you alright?" The gate swings shut with a loud bang and I look up horrified as Jack runs across the grass towards me. He looks pale and worried. Shit.

"Yes, yes I'm fine." I start to laugh. "I was just…" and then I stop. Jack is wearing a pair of knee length denim shorts and a pair of trainers. Strong brown thighs stretch the denim, shaping the material around the muscles and my tongue darts out to moisten lips that have suddenly gone very, very dry. I don't dare look at his shirtless chest. *Go on Jessamy* the trees whisper, *just one look.*

No!

Go on!

No!

I raise my eyes up. Very slowly. Embarrassingly slowly. My eyes won't move any quicker, even though I'm willing them to skip over his chest and up to his face.

Now!

Come on eyes, now.

Please.

They are not listening to instructions, instead my gaze lingers on each centimetre of his naked skin - naked, brown, smooth skin. I think I may be drooling. Gone are the small sloping shoulders and skinny torso of sixteen-year old Jack, instead his shoulders are encased in muscle, the same toned muscle that covers his entire body, tapering down to a flat stomach and the fine trail of hair leading down from his belly button…

My mouth has gone so dry my tongue is stuck.

He's speaking to me but all I can hear is the thudding of my heart as it picks up a new rhythm. Good God, the man is a…well…God.

"Jess…?"

"What?"

"Have you heard anything I've just said?" He says grumpily. I shake my head. "You are so annoying."

"Yeah…" I cough to clear my throat and lick my dry lips with an equally dry tongue. "Did you want something?"

"I heard you yell. I thought something was the matter."

"Oh."

"Is something the matter?" He asks slowly, as though speaking to a child who lacks understanding.

"No. Not really."

"So why yell?"

"Because I was frustrated with the box." It's a total lie, it even sounds like a lie but it's the best I can do.

"The box? Jesus, Jessamy, I thought something terrible had happened." Jack snaps at me and turns on his heel. His back is decorated with a black tattoo, a sun inside of which is a sword with a snake curled around it in an S. Wrapping around the muscles on his back are sunbeams, the jet black appearing to shimmer as he moves. It's captivating. On anyone else it would look ghastly but the black against the tanned skin…skin so smooth…

Stop it Jessamy.

"You drive me in-fucking-sane." He turns abruptly, berating me with an unexpected anger that stops a nervous giggle in its tracks, leaving it like a brick in my throat. "But then…you always did."

His green eyes find mine, flashing like emeralds under the copper eyelashes.

Oh my God I really, really, really fancy Jack.

"Do you want a drink?" It's the most stupid question to ask particularly to a man who has clenched his fists so tightly the veins pop out of his arms. He stands in front of me looking like he'd happily pummel me to death.

"Do I...? What? No, I bloody don't. That would just add to my problems." He stomps off, wrenching the gate open and slamming it behind him so fiercely it shakes on its hinges long after he's out of sight, leaving me perturbed and more confused than ever.

***

I finish Lady Chatterley's Lover. I can quite see how they went from hating each other to passionate sex to love, except in my head Mellors has copper hair and a jet-black tattoo on his tanned skin.

"Lily I am going to find you in the afterlife." I mutter crossly picking a random DVD from the box. "I am going to find you and I am going to...actually I don't know what I am going to do but it won't be very nice." A cold breeze ruffles my hair. "Don't do that, I'm cross. As if life wasn't complicated enough." I pour a large glass of water and leave the kitchen for the morning room. The sun is setting, sending rays of orange and pink across the garden. It looks magical. In the dimming light, the garden shows no signs of the damage it's recovering from, instead it looks ethereal, the fading sun catching the blossoms and making them glow. I cannot remember a time the garden ever looked like this, but maybe I just didn't look hard enough. *Look harder.* I glance down at the DVD. *Ten Things I Hate About You.* I throw it across the room and it makes a satisfying crack against the stone work. I turn my back on the room and go to the box on the kitchen table and sit down with the photo album.

"Alright Jack, I'll look harder."

I look past Nate, the blond centre of every picture, to the other faces that smile out. Moments frozen in time, changing hair styles, changing fashions but always the same group of people. I'm always as close to Nate as I can be, his arm occasionally around me but mostly around

Debbie it seems. How did I not notice, or was I so blind to him that I never saw? Jo and Andrea are draped over whichever one of the boys they fancied at that time, fickle and flighty, Tori always with Orrion, never apart. I giggle as I look at our faces, all the girls thinking they were something special whilst caked in badly applied makeup and wearing desperately bad fashion depicting the time. Me – thin, mousy, shy, one step behind the fashion, no make-up on my face, glasses and braces emphasising the gawkiness and awkward passage through adolescence. I feel sad for the girl in the pictures, always so afraid of getting things wrong I tried to never make a mistake.

I rub my eyes and go back to the beginning.

This time my focus is on Jack.

Always beside me.

Always looking at me.

Always with a smile for me.

Each picture conveys that which I have never seen. His feelings. The feelings of a teenager with an unrequited affection. Like me for Nate.

Oh, my God.

Is this what you wanted me to see Lily? I feel the cold hand and drop the photo album rubbing my palm as though burned. I can't look anymore.

I leap up from the table. Does he still feel the same?

More importantly, what do I do now?"

***

1990
What am I dreaming for? Dreams don't come true.

"What do you want? Do you need a light bulb changing or something?" Jack stands imposingly in the doorway of the farm house. I'm more disappointed than I care to admit that his body is now covered in a light green hooded sweatshirt. I don't know what I was thinking, coming over here, bare feet covered in grass dampened by the cool dusk. I must be mad.

"I can change my own lightbulb thanks!"

"So, you're here because…"

160

"I don't know really. I was at home and…now I'm here."

"Why?"

I feel foolish. He's glaring at me, a look I should be used to by now but it feels even worse to be receiving it with all the realisations that have hit me today. I've got it wrong. I misread the box. There must be something else.

From inside I hear a woman say, "Jack, sweetie, dinner is ready."

He glances over his shoulder and takes a step forward pulling the door behind him.

"Why did you come?" He asks again, this time a slight urgency creeps into his tone.

"It doesn't matter. I made a mistake coming over. Sorry to have interrupted your evening." I turn to go, leaden with mortification. It could have been worse, I tell myself, it could have been so much worse.

"Jess?"

"What?"

"Have you figured out the box yet?" His voice, soft and quiet, stops me from taking another step.

"I thought so but I got it wrong. Bye Jack."

It's a long walk back to the house and with each step I feel more and more ridiculous. What was I thinking? I have lost complete control of my senses, there is Jack, quite the most handsome man I've ever seen, and there is me, chubby and frumpy. Of course he'd have a woman there, someone like him, looking the way he does, with all his strong, masculine aura and brooding good looks, would not be single for long. I'm confusing the past with the now and clearly trying to finish the puzzle with a piece that could never fit.

I saw in the box what I wanted to see, not what was there. What did I expect I'd find? The beginnings of a love affair? I'm weeks out of a marriage that I thought would last forever, living in a house that I don't know what to do with, desperately missing the one person who always had my back. It is not a good time for irrational thought.

I slam the door behind me with such force the window panes rattle and pace the kitchen.

I have to get out of this godforsaken house, it's sending me crazy.

I dust off my feet, grass falling to the floor in little piles, and pull on my shoes. I grab the car keys from off the counter and wrench open the kitchen door, not bothering to close it behind me, breaking into a half run around the side of the house to the car. Wheels spinning on the gravel, I drive faster than I should to the gate and out onto the main road. I've no idea where to go so I nudge the car forward, sluggish with the boxes in the boot, and put my foot down, leaving a cloud of black smoke behind me. My only destination is to be as far away from the house as possible.

I reach Exeter as the shops are closing, weary looking assistants tidying window displays or hoovering the floors. I park in a back street and rummage in my overstuffed glove box for some spare change. My purse is at home on the table but I manage to find twenty pounds in dusty change under the various wrappers and tissues. I put it in my pocket and exit the car, crossing the road quickly and into the main street.

It's changed so much.

I wander along the street. I don't recognise much of it, shiny new shops replacing the ones I remember spending my allowance in. I follow signs to St Stephens Church and take the cobbled streets beside it and out into the square, passing the cathedral and down towards the river. I want to be lost for a while, forget everything but this area of Exeter, an area I know well, doesn't give me the solace I need so I turn back and find myself outside of the small cinema.

I pay the entry fee for a film I've never heard of and walk into the cool theatre.

I'm the only person in there.

Sitting down, I close my eyes, waiting for the film to start.

***

"Miss?" I feel a shaking and a voice talking to me. "Miss?"

"Huh?" Groggily I open my eyes and wriggle up in the seat.

"Miss, are you alright?"

"Yeah." I look around me and realising with a sinking heart that I'm in the cinema, the light is fully on and the attendant is looking embarrassed.

"Miss, we're closing."

"Oh God, what time is it?" I wipe my mouth and glance down at my watch. It's nearly midnight. I've been in here for hours. "Midnight. Shit."

"We have to close."

"I'm so sorry. Oh, my goodness…" I fumble for my keys under the seat. "I'm so embarrassed, I'm so sorry…"

"Don't worry. I'm just glad I came in to check in here before we all left." She grins at me. "It's usually students we find snoring in here…"

"Oh no, was I snoring?"

"A little." She takes my coat and I follow her out into the foyer. "Are you going to be alright?"

"Yes, I'm fine. Thank you and sorry…"

"Don't be, honestly, it's fine, and to be honest, the film is rubbish." She holds the door open for me and hands me my coat. "There's a film festival on here next week, just bring your ticket for a discount."

"I'm not sure I can ever show my face again but thanks I'll keep it just in case."

"Good night."

"Night."

She locks the door behind me and I wrap my coat around me, tying it firmly in the middle. The outside lights go out and I hurry away from the cinema to the main high street and back to my car. Shouts, hollers and cat calls filter from the street, girls pretending not to notice the boys that call out to them but the age-old game is played out in the feigned disinterest, the subtly exaggerated walk, the occasional flick of the hair, the same games that have been played from generation to generation, games I remember too well.

I start the engine and take a slow drive back to the house.

CHAPTER TEN

1990

This afternoon Nate came round. He stayed until everyone got here for the party and then went home to change. Everyone was scattered around the house and in the garden apart from Nate and I. We sat on the sofa and ended up having a pillow fight before kissing. He made the move. He told me I looked really nice. Then he went weird and just left. I found him in his car about to drive off. I tried to stop him because he'd had a couple of pints. After Jack told me that Nate hated me and always would. I was gutted. All night he was putting his arm around me or touching my leg and when we were kissing he had his hand up my top. I was on air and now I've crashed. It was the furthest I'd let anyone go and now my heart is broken.

The kitchen door is shut and the lights ablaze when I arrive home. Standing in the middle of the room with a glass of whiskey in his hand is Jack, worry etched on his face. He appears to be staring into space, holding the glass half way to his face, not moving. I have the horrible feeling that my overdramatic escape from Otterleigh has caused more concern that it should have, leaving me wishing I'd at least closed the door.

"Here goes nothing." I mutter walking up to the door and pushing it open. "Hi Jack." I say as brightly as I can manage, the feeling fading as soon as he turns his face to me. "Has something happened?" The atmosphere cloaks me with the feeling I am going to get a telling off.

"I was worried." Jack's voice rings in the silent room. "I thought...You seemed upset earlier and the door was wide open..."

"I went out." I pour some whiskey into the empty water glass I'd left on the table.

"That's obvious." He snaps at me, clenching the glass tighter in his hand until his knuckles turn white.

"Have you been here long?" I take a bigger slug of my drink that I planned to and cough painfully.

He watches me. "Yes. I rang your phone but you didn't answer."

"I left it here."

"I know."

"Oh."

"Why did you storm off?"

"I didn't."

"Yes, you did Jess."

"No, Jack, I didn't." I did, of course, I did, I was embarrassed but I'm certainly not going to admit that now.

Jack is looking at me strangely, like he has something to say but the words don't want to come. Eventually he says, "Lily asked me to look after you, next time you go out please at least shut the door because the I won't think you've been kidnapped."

"Don't you think I'm old enough to look after myself." It comes out of my mouth harshly and immediately I want to take it back. I hear Jack take a sharp intake of breath and a very controlled exhale before he speaks. The hand holding my glass quivers a little so I put the glass down.

"You tell me, Jessamy. It seems that you've not changed a lot over the past twenty years. Shall I list everything to date?" He's standing right behind me and I can feel his breath on my hair. I hadn't heard him move. The closeness of his body and the masculine scent of him makes me tremble so visibly that I close my eyes against the humiliation before it can be ridiculed. *Don't say anything, please, don't say anything.* "You are so infuriating, but you always were, infuriating and blind…" The warmth of his body behind mine is replaced by a coldness that gives me goose bumps and before I can turn around the kitchen door is slammed. I feel a cold hand on my arm, pulling me towards the door and the next minute I am through it and hurrying across the grass. *What are you doing?* I ask myself over and over as an unseen force pushes me forward.

It's almost too dark to see. The clouds are covering the moon and I just about make out the tense form of Jack ahead of me. Why am I following him?

"Jack?" I call out and the figure stops.

"What?"

"I'm infuriating? Me?"

"Yes, you."

"If I'm that bad then why bother to come and check on me?" I ask angrily.

165

"Why? Because…Never mind, just go home Jessamy, I'm too tired for this shit." He says with a sigh.

"I am home, this is my garden." It's a stand-off. He's clenching and unclenching his fists and I feel such a pull to him that I have to take a step backwards, for space, or distance…or something. This is ridiculous. It's Jack, my go-to, someone I really thought would be a person I kept fondly in my memory, a good friend, sort of. As good a friend as a weekly snog could be, at least. Now I have these strange feelings for him and I'd like to blame them on the rejection by my husband or the grief I feel for Lily but it would be a lie.

"I have to go." I say quickly and turn away, running over the ground until I tread awkwardly on the indentations left by the fire engine and fall to the ground. "Ow." I cry out gripping my ankle feeling sick as the pain tracks up my leg. "Ow…fuck…ow."

"Jess?" Jack is by my side, lighting the blackness with the torch on his phone.

"It's ok. I just fell over." My voice shakes and the nausea from the pain brings an acidic taste to my mouth.

"Can you walk?" He grips me under my armpit and pulls me up until I'm within an inch of him. His chest is rising up and down quickly but I'm not sure I'm breathing. My ankle hurts and I wince, gripping his arms to steady myself. "Jess?"

I look up at him as the clouds move and the moonlight casts a pale glow over the ground. For a long time we don't move. I look at him, he looks at me and the pain in my ankle is forgotten as the spell cast by the full moon keeps us still. My heart picks up its pace, faster and faster until I feel dizzy, the whooshing of my blood past my eardrums is too loud to hear anything else. "Jack…"

He kisses me.

It's a bruising, demanding kiss, his lips crushing mine, the stubble of his jaw rough against my skin. I lean against him, wrapping my arms under his and holding his shoulders tightly. It's a fiery kiss, angry almost, but the intensity is breath taking, a physical need that takes over my senses and my rationale. If I questioned before the attraction to Jack, this kiss takes the question away. It's real. I do. How he makes me feel in this moment is making me wish I could suspend it in time. His body is hard against mine and I feel an awakening, the flicker of flames uncurling in my belly, that has me pulling him as close to me as

166

I can. This is not the kiss of the teenage Jack that I remember, this is the kiss of a man and I welcome it.

His hands wrap in my hair, twisting and knotting until I can't move. It's exciting. His mouth trails softly down to my neck and I hear a moan, mine, I think, as his lips move over my skin. There's a sigh, a breathy sigh, and my hands find his skin, under the jumper and up over his back. His skin, so smooth, so warm, is electric under my fingertips. Words are whispered, his, mine, whispers so quiet that the words are barely understandable but it doesn't matter. Nothing matters. Only this.

I trace my fingers down his spine and feel the ripples of his skin under my hands.

I want this man.

My body is burning hotter and hotter with each kiss, with each touch of his fingers until it becomes too painful. I murmur, begging and pleading, questioning, his body giving me all the answers I need.

I'm aware of the ground and the cold, damp grass wetting my clothes, but only briefly, as the midnight air begins drifting over my bare body, Jack's velvet skin warming mine. His god-like body is lying over me, my hands tracing the grooves of his muscles down to the V of his abs. His body fits perfectly with mine, his hands stroking and caressing, gentle, firm, mind-blowing touches. We're moving together, our bodies joined, lips not leaving the others, it's a thousand moments in one. There are cries, mine, his, ours, as we move faster and faster, hands on skins, hips meeting hips, the delicious fire burning out of control, inextinguishable, hotter and hotter. Above me the stars twinkle brighter than I've ever seen them, glowing orbs in the black heavens, silence reigning over the night until our heaving breaths fill the air.

Jack lies on me, head buried in my neck, my hands tracing up and down the soft skin on his back. Is this what magic feels like?

"Jack?" A female voice from beyond calls out and a beam from a torch bobs along the concrete of the farm yard just beyond the gate.

"Shit." He says leaping up. I can't bear to watch as he pulls his jeans up and shrugs the jumper over his head, so I shut my eyes tightly. "Shit."

When I open my eyes, Jack has gone.

***

1990
Lily told me that I have to turn off It Must Have Been Love before she loses her mind.

I can't get Jack out of my head. His image is holding on tighter than the little leaf to the burnt tree and every time I blink I can see his face. I've dreamt about him, thought about him and turned to drink to forget about him. A number of times I've reached the gate but I'm too scared to go through, scared of his reaction but more scared that he and voice-from-the-dark are having a love-in, and I'm not sure my fragile pride could cope with that. Over and over I've asked myself if I imagined it, if it was just a dream, a very vivid, very real dream, but the faint bruising from his hip bones on my thighs makes it more real than I wish it to be.

It's been three long days of self-torture. Even Mark/Satan commented yesterday about my lack of bad language and my improved attention to his work-out. I didn't want to give him the satisfaction of saying that I've begun to look forward to the work-outs but I put more into the last one than any of the others because torturing myself was at least stopping me thinking about Jack.

I'm pathetic.

I wonder what he's doing.

You're pathetic.

He's probably doing whatshername.

I want him to do me.

Go and tell him.

Shut up.

I leap with hope when the doorbell rings but it's only two delivery drivers bringing my personal items from the house in Bath. It would have been nice to have had some warning but I make the drivers a cup of tea as they unload box after box into the hallway.

No going back then.

I thought the finality of it all would make me feel sad but I just feel relief. No more lies. No more pretence, just the freedom to move forward and find whatever the fates decree is the life for me. I feel sure, now more than ever, that my future rests here. I just wish I could stop thinking about Jack, wish I could stop thinking about his hands on my body, wish he hadn't left like that.

Be brave darling girl, be brave.

Yes, I'll be brave. I slide my feet into my flip flops and walk along the corridor and out through the kitchen door.

***

I meet Jack at the gate. He looks really tired and his usually sparkling emerald eyes are duller than normal. My heart sinks. This can't be good. I search his face but he doesn't meet my gaze so I find myself taking a couple of steps backwards, needing to put some distance between us.

"I won't be coming anymore." He says softly. "The garden is up together as much as it can be after all the storms, but you may need someone to keep the lawn under control, and the weeds." He squints as though looking at something too far away to see. My heart sinks painfully into my stomach. What did I expect? True love? I know nothing of the life that this adult Jack has.

"Is this because of me?" I ask. "Because of the other night?"

"I don't want to talk about it."

"I'm not asking you to…"

He doesn't say anything.

"Jack, I don't know what I'm supposed to say. It's been nice to have a link to the good old times, there have been too many bad times recently. I…I'm so grateful for everything you did for Lily, it makes me feel better knowing she had someone looking after her, thank you…"

"I don't want thanks…"

"Well what then…" I snap. "Shall I just say thanks for the midnight shag? Go and say sorry to your lady friend for the illicit dalliance under the stars? Shall I write about it in my next book? A quick mistake…is that what it was Jack? A mistake? Because it didn't feel like it at the time."

I storm across the lawn before I can say anything else. I don't need to know what it was for him. My head is a fucked-up place to be and

169

nothing is making sense. I didn't think for one moment that coming here would see the end of my marriage, that I would see someone who meant very little once, in a whole new light, that the house would be mine and the memories so visible. I get into the kitchen and sit down at the table, slamming Lily's box across it forcefully, which knocks the photo album to the floor where it lies open. I look at the photo. I remember when it was taken. We'd spent the whole day at the beach and were looking sun kissed. Debbie has her arms around Nate, I'm leaning against Jack laughing at whatever he whispered into my ear. I look happy.

1990

It's Debbie's birthday today so Nate picked a few of us up and we went to her house. Debbie started taking lots of photos and Nate put his arm around me because he wanted a picture of us in our England shirts. Lily bought mine for me today. The camera ran out so Nate drove me home to get a spare from the kitchen drawer. There was something different about him tonight. He was a lot kinder and less of a shit to me than he normally is.

I've been pacing and pacing the kitchen that I've very nearly worn away the flagstones. I feel so angry and so desperate and so unable to let things go. I've looked and looked at the photo album, checked every picture, looked at every cinema ticket and matched it to dates in my diaries. I'm not imaging things, I know I'm not. I've looked as hard as I can, considered every single option and I can't see past Jack. If I'm wrong, then I'll live with the embarrassment but I know I'm not.

I know I'm not wrong.

***

Jack is chopping wood in the yard behind his house. He swings the axe as if it weighs nothing, but I'm transfixed by the rippling tattoo on his bare back. The sunbeams move as the muscles underneath them relax then contract as he brings the axe down onto the wood. I'm about to speak when a blonde woman comes out of the rear door carrying a large glass of iced water. I turn away too quickly and knock a toolbox off a step, where it falls noisily to the floor attracting the attention of

170

Jack and the blonde woman. I send a small smile towards and say, "sorry," whilst gesturing to the fallen box. Jack drops the axe while the woman stands appraising me, her hands on her hips. This was a bad idea, a really, really, bad idea.

It could be the perfect evening, the setting sun casting pinks and lilacs over the sky, illuminating the wisps of clouds that dot the fading blue. It could be the perfect evening for a romantic stroll along the beach, lovers hand in hand, whispering promises and declarations to each other. It would be less hideous if the slim, blonde, perky, young woman wasn't glaring at me and I was only faced with Jack glaring. That I could just about manage, being used to his broody, angry stance every time he sees me, but having the glares in duplicate has stopped me in my tracks and I now want the ground to swallow me whole. It also doesn't help that Jack's perfect form, glistening with the perspiration from hard work, is half naked and so desirable that I would drool if my mouth wasn't completely dry. The body that I was so intimate with, the body that I would touch over and over again in a heartbeat.

She says something to Jack, too quiet for me to hear and he nods. She gives me a final sharp look and disappears back into the house. For a moment there is total silence, even the nature that surrounds us fades to nothing. I walk forward a few steps and stop. Jack picks up the axe and puts it down again, running his gloved hand through his hair.

"Hi." I say walking further towards him, uncertain if I should still be here.

"Hello." Jack sighs deeply his chest rising and falling visibly. It's hard not to stare at his strong torso, the bronzed skin shimmering in the half light.

Nervously I pick at the skin around my nails desperately searching for something to say that would lighten the mood. Jack says nothing but the atmosphere between us gets heavier and heavier. "I wouldn't have come..." I nod towards the house. "I didn't think...you'd...well I didn't think about you having company."

"No?"

"No. I should have realised."

Jack picks the axe up again and continues to chop the wood. I move around him, giving enough space to avoid the flecks of wood that spray out.

"Careful." He says.

"Jack?"

"What."

"Can you stop that for a moment please?" He throws the axe down and pulls the gloves from his hand and chucks them onto the wood pile. He looks at me expectantly and I attempt a smile. "I came over because I wanted to talk to you about…" I feel the flush rise and my mouth dries further. I swallow but it is painful, the lack of moisture making me feel as though I'm swallowing a packet of razor blades. "…the other night."

"What about it?"

"Well, it happened and then you said what you said and…" I sound like the teenager I once was, trying to make sense of the painful time of adolescence and failing miserable. Adults aren't supposed to do this, to unpick events and make them fit into the puzzle of life correctly. Perhaps I should have just left it as one moment in my life. If Jack and Blondie are together the likelihood of him wanting to even remember the other night is minimal. "I thought we were friends…at least, once upon a time we were…"

"We were never friends." He says angrily. "Never."

"Yes, we were…"

"No Jessamy, not really. I was your Plan B, not your friend…"

"My what?"

"You used me for the all the times that Nate shit on you, or pissed you off, or chose your friends over you. I was your ego-boost, 'look Nate someone likes me' and it was always me because you knew I liked you. The other night, it was just the same. Your husband has left you, your daughter hasn't visited in a while…oh look, Jack will do…"

"Jack will do…" I repeat slowly. "Is that what you think? That it was about 'poor me'? That's not how I remember it."

"Oh?" He says moving towards me, his eyes flashing. "And how exactly do you remember it?"

"It was…" I search my brain for the right word but none seem appropriate. He thinks he was Plan B? I could deny it, tell him that it wasn't true but the words in my diaries have told me that he was. Yet I realise now that he was so much more than that. Jack was always there for me, every time Nate chose my friends over me, he was always there to pick me up, hold my hand, walk me home, give me the drunken kiss I needed to show Nate that someone wanted me. Always. Only I never noticed, blinded by the blond beauty that was Nate, the God I revered who always gave me mixed signals and eventually chose Debbie over me.

"You're right." I say rubbing my eyes. "You were. Not intentionally but you were. It was always Nate, from the moment I met him and to say anything different would be a lie. He bowled me over but I was fourteen Jack, things aren't black and white at that age, it's all grey, because we are working out life, trying to be grown-ups when really, we're still kids. Show me an adult who never made a mistake as a teenager, show me someone who didn't suffer with unrequited love and heart break and didn't hurt others unintentionally. Show me a teenager who didn't need someone to show an interest to make them feel validated. You weren't perfect, you made mistakes, look at Jo and Andrea, they were always vying for your attention. Sometimes you played one against the other..."

He picks up the axe and slams it into the wood. I step back.

"The other night wasn't 'poor me'. It wasn't about Phil or Rachel, it was about me and you. I wanted..."

"What?" he asks lining up the axe for another attack on the timber.

"You."

The words are barely audible but he freezes and I dare not look at his face, barely breathing, hoping that he'll say something, anything, just one word to take this weighty silence away.

He says nothing.

I close my eyes against the word that still hangs between us. Why could I not just have said something cool? Or lied? Even a complete untruth would have been better. I turn enough to see Jack screw up his face and ball his fists into his eyes.

"Jack?" The blonde woman comes out into the yard. "I need you inside for a moment."

I long to yell, 'go away, go the fuck away', at her but instead I take a step back. "I'll see you Jack."

"No," he says sharply, "come inside, I won't be a moment."

173

I follow him into the house. Blondie stands aside for me to pass her.
Jack stops to shrug on a sweatshirt that is hanging from the coat hooks
just inside the door. The small hallway has been painted cream and I
trip over boots and trainers that litter the floor as I follow him through a
door down another corridor and into the kitchen. The cupboards are
cream with wooden counters and its tidier than I would have imagined,
a pile of paperwork the only clutter on the otherwise clean worktops.
Blondie and Jack leave me in here and I sit down at the counter,
looking out over the yard.

Dusk has fallen, the dying embers of the sun sitting on the horizon
taking the day to the other side of the world. I watch the clock. The
second hand seems to zoom around quicker than it should yet the
minutes seem to take hours to change. When Jack doesn't reappear, I
get up to leave, closing the kitchen door behind me and facing three
further doors that lead from the small hallway. I don't know which one
I came through so I open the first one, finding an office, untidy with
papers all over the desk. As I turn to leave the room I notice the collage
of photos on the wall. I feature in some of them and they depict the
memories that are captured in the album that Lily gave me but unlike
the photos I have, in these I am in the centre, Jack by my side, Nate
always on the edge or not featured at all. Next to the teenage pictures
are recent ones, Jack's wedding, Orrion and Tori's wedding, photos of
their children, at least, that's who I assume them to be and on the end a
framed drawing of Jack's back tattoo. I look closely at it and gasp. It's
not a sword in the centre of the sun, it's a J and the snake, an S. My
initials. Surely not. I reach out to the drawing, tracing the outline of
the letters. I'm misreading what I'm seeing. I must be. There is no
way.

"Jess..."

"Jack." I jump, pulling my fingers from the drawing and linking
them with the fingers of my other hand. I feel a flush spread across my
face and Jack looks embarrassed. "I...I...I...I thought it was a sword."
I begin to babble. "It looks more like a J...and...and...and an S, but
it's a sword, isn't it? A sword and a snake...?" His face is set tight but
his green eyes blaze.

"Why are you in here?" He asks.

"I was leaving, I came through the wrong door." He looks beyond
me at the tattoo picture. "Blondie...is she...are you..."

174

"She works for me, she does the admin..."

"Oh, so you're not..."

"No."

"Are you..."

"No."

I look at the tattoo hanging on the wall. "Are these..." I take a big breath. "Jack, are you who Lily wanted me to see? Do you...do you...have feelings for me? Are these my initials?"

He says nothing but the tanned skin reddens a little.

I fiddle with my hair. "Please tell me Jack, please tell me I've not got it wrong. Please tell me that the other night wasn't a mistake, that you wanted it to happen as much as I did? You're not Plan B or whatever you label it, I have feelings for you. I wasn't expecting any of this. I didn't realise that I would come back here, after all this time, that my marriage would end and I would find you. I put Otterleigh into the past, after Rachel was born and Nate died..."

"Nate...what?" Jack stops me shocked. "Nate..."

I interrupt him. "I don't want to talk about Nate, Jack. Not anymore."

"But Jessamy, Nate..."

"Jack!"

"What?"

"I'm not here to talk about Nate. If I've made a mistake coming here and telling you all of this then just say so, I'm a big girl, I can take it. Tell me, are you who Lily wanted me to see, when she left all the stuff in the box? Do you have feelings for me? I need to know Jack."

"I've always had feelings for you. How you felt about Nate was how I felt about you. Jo and Andrea were my Plan B's..." He laughs harshly. "I married Andrea to forget about you, it didn't work, she went off with someone else, I hurt her a lot, it wasn't my intention but it happened. I have to live with that."

I cross the small office to Jack reaching up and tracing my fingers along his jaw, the beard bristly under my skin. He takes a sharp breath in as I draw the outline of his mouth, the full lips opening slightly at my touch. "Kiss me Jack."

"What?"

"I need you to kiss me."

"Need or want?"

"Want. I want you to kiss me. No Plan B's, no teenage teasing, just you and me. Kiss me Jack."

He moves one step closer until his solid chest is flat against mine. Carefully Jack brushes hair from my face, the light touch of his fingers on my cheek sending tingles through my nerves that make me shiver. He smiles as he tucks the stray strands behind my ear and grips my hair into his hand. "Kiss you ey?" He says, "like this…" Gently he kisses my cheek, burning my skin with his lips. "Or here?" breathing against my neck he lightly drops a kiss.

"Oh." I breathe leaning against him.

"Or here." Jack tugs my hair pulling my head back until I'm looking up at him. His green eyes burn and I'm sure mine are blazing back at him as he lowers his face to mine and crushes my lips with his. The kiss is intense, bruising and demanding but I return it with the same eagerness.

Somehow, we end up in his bed. I don't know who led who up the stairs, or who undressed who, but his body is moving above mine, slowly, deliberately, my hands caressing the tanned skin, so smooth and warm under my sensitised fingertips. The room is filled with the intimate sounds of pleasure, moans, gasps and whispers, the heightened sense of our bodies, skin on skin, joined together sends wave after wave through the deepest parts of me, his name never far from my lips, his skin never far from my touch. My body ripples and glows under his hands, awakening in a way I never thought possible. Jack is bringing me back to life.

1990
He kissed me.
I just died.
It was such a soft kiss. I'm the happiest girl alive tonight.

CHAPTER ELEVEN

I don't want to open my eyes. I'm in such a warm, blissful place that I'm scared the bubble I've been floating in this past week will burst. The hammering on the door gets louder and I roll over, burying my head under the pillow.

"Jessamy, your trainer is here." Jack says coming into the room and ripping the warm cover from me. "Come on, lazy bones, up you get!"

"Bugger off." I huff, pulling the cover from him and rolling up in it. "I'm asleep."

"You weren't a few moments ago!" He says tickling my foot. "In fact, you were very, very awake, if I recall."

My reply is muffled from below the pillow. "That was worth being awake for. Torture with Satan is not!"

"Shall I tell him to go then?"

"No." I groan taking the pillow from my head. "No, I'll get up, I'm not going to be thin if I stay here, more's the pity."

"There are better ways to exercise," Jack says dropping a kiss on my ankle. "Think how many calories last night and this morning burnt!"

"If I think about it I'll never get up, and you won't stay dressed!" I wriggle up to sitting.

"That's fine by me." He grins moving around the bed. "I think you look gorgeous as you are! Don't change too much Jessamy." He wraps his hand in my hair and tips my head back, moving his face lower until his mouth is millimetres from mine. My breath catches in my throat as his eyes bore into mine.

"You are so handsome." I whisper. "So handsome, how did I end up with you?"

His mouth finds mine and I melt against him. I had no idea it could feel like this, such an intense connection to someone that buzzes like electricity around my whole being. It's a craving, a drug to which I have become addicted very quickly.

Jack seems to feel it too. There is a fire in his eyes when he looks at me.

It's consuming both of us.

I run my hand along the waistband of Jack's faded and worn jeans. The skin underneath is so smooth, like warm velvet covering the hard muscles of his stomach, but I feel a fire within me as his skin ripples under my touch. "Jack?"

"Jessamy, are you here?" Mark's voice calls up the stairs and Jack leaps back.

"Goddamn it!" Jack mutters crossly adjusting his jeans to hide the erection that bulges under his zip. "Can't you just cancel the bloke Jessamy?"

"When I'm thin!"

"I don't want you to be thin. I want you exactly as you are!" Jack pulls on his sweater. He sighs and says, "The farm calls, I suppose, it won't run itself. I'll see you later."

"Ok." I say, stretching. "Can you tell Mark I'll be a few minutes?"

"Yep." He crosses the room to the door and turns back. "What are you going to do today, apart from work out?"

"I'm going to sort out the art work and get some paint samples. I can't live with some of the paintings, they freak me out, and I suppose I'd better do some writing before my agent sends a hit man! Exciting day hey?"

Jack grins cheekily. "It will be later..."

"Promises, promises!"

***

1989

I changed my posters again today. I've now got Corey Haim, Corey Feldman and Bros. All my Michael Jackson ones are in the box under the bed.

I sit in Lily's room. I've been clearing all the walls in the house of the art Lily accumulated and stacking it all in the hallway which is now looking like an art gallery of modern hideousness. For all her exquisite taste, Lily's choice of art is so dark and disturbing that some of it has made me shudder. She was so bright, so ethereal that the paintings she chose for her home contrast so strongly that I wonder again whether Jimmy's death and her big secret, guided those choices. I know first-hand how the loss of someone can impact on life but the more time I spend with Jack, the more I am beginning to question why I held onto Nate so tightly.

178

It wasn't real.

I don't know why I didn't realise before now.

I think Nate protected me from giving my heart to the wrong person. Holding onto him and the 'what if' meant I was safe from accepting that I chose the wrong husband, that I allowed myself to get swept along by Phil's willingness to take Rachel and I on and to love us. This is the first time I've thought about Nate since Jack and I began our love affair and it feels like he's encroaching. I don't want Nate here. I want Jack.

It feels good.

Lily's photos are on the bed. I pick up the one of Phil and I on our wedding day. It was a lovely day, sunny and happy, and I really did think it would last forever, that it was enough to have deep feelings for him even if those feelings never became love. Not the right kind of love, at least, but I don't have the same guilt anymore. It's gone. I was a good wife, I've realised that in recent weeks and it has been cathartic to analyse my marriage and take away blame. It was a finger of blame that I pointed at myself. It was my own guilt. Guilt because of Rachel and her link to my past. I tried to apologise for something that needed no apology. To pretend my past didn't happen in order to make my marriage work was the worst mistake I made, I should have been honest.

I deserved that.

Phil deserved that.

Now there's Jack.

Gorgeous, wonderful, sexy Jack who doesn't mind my past because he was part of it. I wonder if he'll get on with Rachel, whether he will have any issues with her looking so much like Nate. It's strange that he had the same resentments towards Nate that Phil had, but I wonder if it was worse for him because he knew Nate and he took responsibility for picking me up each time Nate played me off against the other girls.

Jack was always there.

How glad I am now, that he was.

How glad I am that he is here now.

I get off the bed. *This is it Lily, are you sure? Are you sure you want me to do this? Once the paintings have gone, you've gone, there is nothing else to clear.* I can sense her in here with me so strongly that I look around just to check, still hopeful, still praying that she'll be at her dressing table applying bright red lipstick. The room is empty but the cold hand on my arm seems to guide me through to the dressing room.

One large painting remains. I've always liked it, the profile of young woman in a red dress with raven hair sitting under a tree, head thrown back in laughter, a cigarette in a long holder held out as though she is using it to gesture to the artist.

It's Lily.

I recognise the black spiky scrawl of the artist and my heart twists with a strange pain.

Jimmy.

I lift it down from the hook, bracing myself against the weight, my post work-out legs groaning as I use them to ground myself. "Ow, bloody ow, ow, Mark you bastard." I hiss through gritted teeth. I nearly drop the painting when I lower it enough to see the cupboard hidden behind it. I rest the painting to the floor, heavily enough for it to make a thud against the floorboards and let go. The painting falls backwards against the wall but I barely notice.

My heart pounds so violently I wonder if it will break out of my chest.

"Is this it Lily? Is this where I'll find your secret?" The cold hand rests on my cheek and I lay my hand over the top. "Are you sure you want me to know."

The coldness grips my hand and I reach up to the cupboard door. It has no handle and lies flat against the wall, as though it were purpose made. I leave the dressing room, walk through the bedroom and out to the hallway to find another access but there isn't anything but stone wall. I try the spare bedroom next to Lily's but there isn't another door so I walk back to the dressing room and look again.

The keyhole is a unique shape and the hinges don't look as though they'd unscrew very easily and I don't relish the idea of hacking my way in. I have to open it. I realise that but how?

The key! Find the key!

"The key! The key from the safe!" I almost yell at the empty air and hurry from the bedroom.

I run down the stairs two at a time, stumbling slightly at the bottom and jarring my left ankle. "Ouch." I limp into the kitchen and pause beside the key rack. My fingers tremble as I check all the keys hanging on the hook. There it is. The small, strangely shaped key on a ring with no others. I pull it off and leave the other bundles of keys on the work top. Back in Lily's dressing room my hands shake uncontrollably as I put the key into the lock. Am I doing the right thing?

I have to wiggle the key to get the lock to turn and pull the door with force for it to open. It does so under protest, groaning as the stiff hinges move slowly, a rusty dust flaking from them as I pull. Eventually it gives in, one of the hinges breaking under the force. I wonder how long it's been since this door was opened and if I will find anything inside.

I take a deep breath and wipe my sweaty palms onto my jeans. Here goes nothing.

The cupboard is about two feet wide but longer in depth and seems to reach as far as the stone hall wall. It has been laid with wood, oak perhaps, and the sides are padded with covered foam. I reach in hoping that no spiders scurry over my arm. It's too dark to see clearly but I push my arm as far as I can, into the blackness.

Nothing.

I pat the wood and smooth my hand back and forth but feel nothing at all so with breath held I put my head inside the cupboard and squint but it's too dark. "Bloody hell." I huff and stand back from the cupboard. "Lily are you messing with me?" I swear I hear a throaty laugh and I grin. "You are, you evil, evil tease!"

Under all the sinks in the house are the torches that were kept for emergencies such as power outage. We had a lot of those during summer storms. Lily and I used to sit around in the dark, her with a cigarette between long red fingernails, telling ghost stories by torchlight and drinking steaming mugs of hot chocolate that we made on the Aga. I find one that still works and use it to lighten the cupboard.

"Holy fuck!" I exclaim and bang my head painfully on the door frame as I jolt. Hanging from the walls are glistening jewels, stones the size of eye balls and a tray of rings, the colours of the rainbow glittering from in their golden clasps. It's an Aladdin's Cave that would have jewellers drooling into their eyeglasses but my anxiety levels shoot skyward. *For God's sake Lily, what are you doing to me?*

It can't be just the jewels in here. Whilst expensive they are not a secret worthy of hiding, although I understand why Lily would, the vile exes would explode with delight if they saw what was in here.

I flash the torch around the cupboard and hover over a small box at the very back. Had I not had the torch I would have missed it. I stand on the dressing room stool and lean into the cupboard as far as I dare but it remains out of reach.

"Bloody hell!" I wiggle my fingers but no amount of huffing and puffing can make my arm any longer. I shuffle out of the small space, banging my hip as I clamber inelegantly from the cupboard. I scour the rooms on the landing for something suitable to manipulate the box from the back of the cupboard but only find empty cupboards and communes of spiders.

I could wait for Jack to come back from work but the need to get the box is too much to be able to last until dusk. I pull on my boots and leave the house, crossing the grass in a limping run, cursing Mark for my aching thighs, the whole way.

The gate creaks as I push it open. Jack is at the end of the yard grooming a horse. He has his bare back to me and the tattoo ripples as he runs the brush over the animal.

"Jack?" My voice comes out as a squeak.

"Hi." He chucks the brush into a metal bucket and walks towards me. "What's the matter? You look really flushed!"

"I've just run here…" I gasp for breath. "I hate running."

"So why run? Did you miss me that much?"

I attempt a smile but fear it looks more of a grimace. "I found a box." *Pant, pant.* "In a secret cupboard." *Pant, pant.* "I can't reach it." *Deep breath.*

Jack pulls off his thick gloves and shoves them into the pockets of his jeans. He pats the horse and unties it from the iron ring. "I'll be back in a minute." I watch him lead the horse around the side of the house and stand anxiously biting the inside of my lip

He comes back into the yard putting a navy t-shirt on. "Come on then."

I catch my breath. "Did you have to put your shirt on?"

"Yeah, can't have my staff seeing you dribble!"

"You're gross. And big headed."

182

"You keep telling me how hot I am, is it any wonder my head has grown."

"Well you are hot."

"I know!" He grins at me and wraps his arm around my shoulder. He smells earthy and it seems to tug at my insides until I feel dizzy. "Where is the box?"

"In Lily's dressing room."

We walk through the house and Jack takes the stairs two at a time. I limp up behind him.

"It's in there." I point at the cupboard. "Right at the back."

He reaches in. His t-shirt rises up at the back and I have a strong desire to touch the black ink decorating his back. My initials. It makes me grin,

In seconds the small carved box is in my hands.

"What do you think it is?" Jack asks brushing the dust from his hands.

"I think it contains everything Lily wanted me to know."

"What are you going to do with all that jewellery? You can't leave it here now the door is broken."

"I'm going to move it to the safe."

"Do you want me to help you."

I look longingly at the box in my hands. It has to wait.

Goddamn it.

"Yes please." I say.

***

The box is beside me on the sofa.

Jack comes in to the morning room and hands me a glass of whiskey. "I thought you may need it." He says softly.

"Thank you."

"Are you sure you are ready for this?"

"The whiskey?"

He smiles. "The box."

"Oh." I lift it up and place it on my lap. "I don't know. Once I open it, that's it, there is no going back. What if it's something that will change everything? What if it's something I'll wish I didn't know.

What if it makes me think differently of Lily? She was my whole family in one person, my parents and my grandmother…well, they weren't her." I shake my head. "I'm frightened of what I will find."

Jack shifts slightly from foot to foot and takes a long drink of his whiskey. He knows.

"Do you know what is in here."

He gives the briefest of nods.

"Will it change anything?"

"It depends on you Jess. It depends on what you feel, I suppose."

"Should I open it?"

"I can't tell you that." Jack puts the glass on the table. "I'm going to leave you to open it by yourself." He says. "I think it's the right thing, really."

"You're worrying me now."

"Come to the farm when you're done. If you want to, that is."

"Will it change things between us?" I ask feeling cold.

Jack shakes his head. "No, I don't think so."

"You don't *think* so?" My stomach twists painfully.

He gives me a small smile. "Jess, I don't know what you'll think when you open the box. I'd like to think that you'll make sense of it all. Come by when you're finished, I'll wait up."

"Is there a lot in here?"

"Not really, just a lot to take in, I would think." He gives me a quick kiss. "I'll be waiting."

"Naked I hope!" I grin.

"Yes, I'll be naked."

"Good." I watch him leave the room and look down at the box. Hells bells, I'm not sure I'm ready to know anything that could change what I think. It's Lily. She has been my rock, my idol, my everything for my whole life and I can't let that sway in anyway. I can't let anything take her more away from me than she is now.

I take a long drink of the whiskey. "Here goes nothing. See you on the other side, Lily."

I open the box and take out three folded pieces of paper and a photo. I put the papers down beside me and look at the photo. The picture is of a sleeping baby, a mass of black hair and the longest eyelashes, a rosebud mouth slightly opened, porcelain skin with a faint blush.

A beautiful baby.

A baby who looks just like Lily.

I know this is Lily's baby, there is no question but the heart wrenching anguish I feel looking at the beautiful child doubles me up. She never spoke of a baby. *What happened to your baby Lily?* I hold the photo to my chest tightly, willing the intense pain to subside. It's unbearably sharp, a stabbing sadness that seems to wrap itself around me until I can barely breathe. *Is this who Jimmy meant? 'We'll get her back.' Is this your daughter, Lily?* Despite the numerous scenarios that flit through my mind I keep coming back to the same dreadful thought…what if the baby didn't survive.

I think about Rachel. How deep and unconditional my love for her is. How proud I am that she chose me to be her parent and how much I admire the sensitive yet confident woman that she has become. I can't imagine my life without her, and regardless of the enormous and cruel pressure my parents and my grandmother put upon me to terminate my pregnancy, and achieve the law degree they so desperately wanted for me, I will always be thankful that I followed my heart and had Rachel.

I pick up one of the folded pieces of paper, the photo still pressed against my chest. I open the folds and read the faded document.

BIRTH CERTIFICATE
This certifies that
Rose Patience Summers - female
Was born to
Mother – Lillian Elizabeth Summers
Father – Unknown.
On Friday at 20:04 hours on this 25th day of September 1952

There are a series of signatures and a stamp for Exeter Registrar.
Father unknown.
Together we will get her back. Jimmy was coming back for Lily and Rose but fate took him away. Lily always said we were alike, now I understand why. Perhaps this lost child was what prompted her to pick me up as I fell, broken and frightened, catching me before I shattered into a million, irreparable pieces. *What happened to the baby, Lily, where did Rose go?* I drain my glass of whiskey and open the next folded paper.

Lilian

The child will be collected on the 30ᵗʰ October so you will have sometime before she goes to her new family. Obviously, you understand the significance of what you have done and why Mother and Father have left it to me to organise. I don't have to remind you that you have brought great shame on us, but that is to be expected I suppose, given your start in life. The daughter of a whore can never amount to a great deal, even when taken in by the right kind of family. When you come to London it is never to be mentioned and you will tell anyone who asks that you took extended time in Devon to study.

Mother and Father have ensured that the child will go to a good family but that is all they will do. You will return to London and take your place in society as though you were never absent.

Until then,

Ruby.

The daughter of a whore? Lily was adopted? I feel such anger at my family, a wave of rage that crashes over my head and smothers me until I can't breathe, their treatment of Lily, the way they belittled her at every opportunity. How lucky I was to have Lily to fight my corner and how I wish so much there had been someone to fight for her. I pick up the final piece of paper and leave the box on the sofa to pour myself another drink in the kitchen. So much makes sense now, the reason Grandma was so angry when I fell pregnant, the harsh words she spoke to Lily when Lily stood by me, the quiet seething of my parents and the recent conversation with Mum. *You may find your precious Lily isn't what you thought.*

I nurse my whiskey.

Everything seems to fall into place. The roses in the house that Lily insisted on, the expensive carvings of roses on the woodwork, the reason she bought this house even though it was vastly overpriced and falling down, her intense devotion to Rachel and me, and her refusal to see me crumple under the enormity of a baby when I was still a baby myself.

So much love I have for her, my free-spirited, fabulous Aunt. Whether blood related or not, she was my family. I wish I knew all this sooner. Perhaps I could have helped her find the poor lost soul that gave birth to her and helped her track down Rose. What I would give to have the chance to talk to her about Jimmy. It was a love that lasted a lifetime. I understand, very clearly now, why she chose so many unsuitable men but I wish that I'd showed more understanding as she skipped from vile ex to vile ex, not just assumed that she was madly in love with someone else as she flounced away dramatically from another ill-fated relationship.

I wish I could tell her, just one more time, how much I love her, how her kindness and compassion made my life so bearable, how the summers down here made everything else seem less bleak. I wish I could tell her, one more time, that she saved me.

I love you Lily.

I read the letter again. Where did Lily come from? I doubt I could ever find out, the pasts of adopted children were rewritten eighty years ago, records destroyed and the truth buried, but Lily's baby…would there be accurate records in the fifties? There must be someone in the town who knew her then. I drink my whisky like water, the liquid burning my throat on its way down. The Vicar…he mentioned something, didn't he? Something I disregarded at the time but now seems so important. *I'm sorry Jessamy, I was sworn to secrecy.* I scrape the chair on the floor in my haste. No time like the present to find out.

***

"Hello Jessamy."

"Hi Winnie, sorry to come over uninvited." The Vicar's wife stands at the door with a mug of coffee in her hand and rollers in her hair. She touches her head self-consciously. "Is now a bad time? I could come back?"

"No, no, now is fine, come on in, just excuse my appearance. We're due at the annual Devonshire clergy dinner shortly and my hair just isn't doing what I wanted it to, hence the curlers and the complete panic. Come in, come in, I assume you want to see John?"

"Just for a minute if you don't mind?"

"John?" She calls. "Jessamy is here."

The Vicar comes down the hallway dressed casually in a tracksuit and trainers. "Jessamy, how lovely."

"Hi John, sorry to come over unannounced." I say as he clasps my hand between his.

"You're always welcome Jessamy. How can I help?"

"I've found something belonging to Lily, something I had no idea of, but I suspect you may know."

"May I?"

"Yes, in fact, I'm convinced you will know."

"Oh?"

"What happened to Lily's baby?"

He drops my hand and his face looks troubled. "What happened to…who?"

"John, I know you know." I say gently. "The more I think about it the more I feel sure that Lily knew her too, that she is here in the village, or at least nearby, and she was here at the end. You mentioned when I arrived that someone was here looking after her and you were sworn to secrecy. I'm asking you to break that promise. Please John. Please tell me."

"Come in here." He guides me into his office. It's a small room with a desk in the centre and a chair either side. On the walls are certificates and photos that I glance at briefly. "I do know." He sighs. "I can tell you some, but not all. I can't break promises, nor the confidences begged of me inside of the church. I can't, and I won't. You will have to find most of it on your own Jessamy, if you feel that Lily wanted you to know…"

"I know she did John, she left clues. Clues about me, my past and perhaps my future, but also clues about her past. I am in no doubt that she wanted her story known. Tell me what you can, I'll find out the rest."

The Vicar leans back in his chair, takes off his glasses and rubs his eyes. "I met Lily," he says replacing his glasses and looking at me, "in nineteen fifty. I was seventeen and she was around fourteen or fifteen, a whirlwind of energy that was so different to any of the girls that lived here. She had no boundaries, life was to be lived and fun was to be had. We were all captivated by her, the beauty with the brightest smile. I suppose we all fell a little in love with her and she did with us, until the day she met James.

"He lived down on the front, one of six children, his sister Patience became Lily's closest friend. He earned money odd-jobbing around the village, doing what he could to help his parents out, they were so poor, often relying on hand outs from the villagers. His father had fought in the war and saw some horrific things that brought on black depressions. A lot of the time he was unable to work, but unlike some, he didn't ever succumb to the drink. When Jimmy met Lily, something changed. We all felt it. It went beyond infatuation. Then Lily got pregnant. Her parents were outraged and dragged the other girls, Ruby and Margaret back to London, leaving Lily here with a governess, a vile woman who terrified everyone. James was shipped off to Australia, Lily's parents gave a generous allowance to his parents to ensure he went."

"Bastards."

"Quite!" The Vicar smiles. "Things were very different back then, having a baby outside of wedlock was considered a crime against decency."

"I found his letters. He was coming back for her."

"I have no doubt that if he had lived they would have been very happy together."

"What happened to the baby?"

"She was adopted. Lily went back to London. Patience heard from her from time to time."

"Is Patience still alive?"

"Yes, very much so. She settled in Australia, had a couple of children I believe."

"And the baby?"

"The baby is in her sixties now."

"John, did Lily's daughter nurse her at the end?"

"Jessamy, I cannot tell you that."

"By that answer I think you have told me what I need to know. How can I find out who she is?"

"There are ways Jessamy, registers…it wouldn't take much. But ask yourself, what happens when you know? Need I remind you about Pandora's Box?"

"I opened it today John, it will be hard to close now." I stand up. "Thank you for your time and for being honest with me. It's been an odd day, I feel a little like my head is spinning."

He shows me out to the front door. The dog comes bounding along the corridor and leaps up at me making me staggers backwards. "Down Boyd, down, good boy. I expect you do feel a little out of sorts."

"John, did you know Lily was adopted?"

"Yes dear, there was no way she could be related to her family. She had fire, they were nothing but ice." He shudders. "They called themselves Christians but they were the exact opposite."

I pause for a moment on the doorstep. I have so many questions but they will remain unanswered here tonight.

"Bye John and thank you. Enjoy your evening."

"I will. Jessamy?" I stop mid step. "Think very carefully before you look for more answers."

"I would John, but I think she wants me to know."

He shrugs and I walk down the path. The door closes as I reach the gate. I know Lily's daughter is here somewhere, I just know it.

***

I hesitate over the final piece of paper in the box. It's white and crisp, the obvious signs of age missing. The final piece maybe? I unfold it.

My dearest Jessamy

They say history repeats itself and in our case, perhaps it has, the absence of blood ties notwithstanding. You will now know that there was a boy. I loved him my whole life and I will love him well into the next. It is my hope that I see him again, that he is waiting to guide me through death and back out into the light.

You also now know the secret I was never able to tell. My parents held the threat of Jimmy's parents' future in Australia over me and once my parents died, well I worried endlessly about the effect the truth would have on Rose who had a new family who loved her, nearly as much as I loved her. My darling, beautiful Rose that I watched grow from a safe distance, watched as she had a son, watched that son grew into a fine young man, feeling such pride, the same pride I had watching you grow up.

Nothing is ever as it seems, Jess.

190

Have you uncovered the part of your story that I wanted so desperately for you to know? Has the box made sense, do you know what you should be looking for? I questioned how much I should say in the first letter, knowing that the outcome of my death would change everything for you. I knew Phil wouldn't follow you to Otterleigh and that his obsessions would eventually overcome his love for you. I also knew I had to leave enough bread crumbs to make you stay long enough for the next chapter of your life to be visible.

Can you see it Jessamy?

Look hard, darling girl.

Look at what is right in front of you. It holds the answer to your future.

There is one piece left if you choose to find it.

Just don't look too hard for it that you miss what I'm hoping you'll see.

I love you
Lily xxx

***

CHAPTER TWELVE.

"Hi!" I gasp walking into the kitchen and finding Rachel, Zoe and Phoebe drinking coffee at the kitchen table. "Was I expecting you?"

"We decided to surprise you." Rachel says getting up and giving me a kiss. "Is it a good surprise? You look kind of shocked."

"I am…in a good way."

"Where've you been Mum? We've been here ages."

Zoe and Phoebe get up and give me a kiss. I grin at Zoe and she rolls her eyes. "I've been sorting some stuff." It's not strictly true but if 'sorting some stuff' can be roughly translated into 'I've just got out of a hot man's bed' then it's not actually a lie.

"Ok." Rachel says. I pour myself a coffee and sit down at the table with them.

"it's lovely to see you all…"

"What have you done to the house? Everything has gone." Rachel says looking over at my paintings. "Apart from those random attempts. Why are they still there?"

"Lily liked them."

"That's because she loved you…"

"If you loved me Rach, you'd see the talent…"

"It's because I love you, Mum, that I tell you the truth."

I laugh. "Cow!"

"Oh goody, your hot gardener is still around." Rachel sits up and looks admiringly at Jack. He's crossing the lawn from the gate at the back of the garden. Over his shoulder he carries a hose pipe, and in the other hand he holds a large tub of greenery. If he's surprised to see everyone he doesn't show it. I blush and a sly smile crosses his face. Zoe nudges me and gives me a look that says, 'careful.'

I look at Rachel. I had decided that I would hold off telling her about my new romance. She is still reeling from Phil and I splitting, even at twenty-three and independent, she is finding the ease at which Phil has moved into a new life, hard to cope with, despite his assurances that nothing between them will change. There is less light in her eyes and she has lost weight such that her slim body is now leaning towards thin. My heart sinks a little as she stares blatantly at Jack. He smiles a greeting and crosses the garden to the flower border that runs from the kitchen door to the pond, dropping the hose on the ground and fixing the end to the outside tap. Phoebe watches with

192

disinterest, picking up her phone and flicking through social media apps. Zoe looks between Rachel and I, alarm on her face. She sees it too.

Rachel fancies Jack.

Jack comes into the kitchen and stands staring at Rachel, horror on his face and I realise why. He sees Nate. I feel my heart sink into my shoes. I didn't tell him.

I should have told him.

I thought he knew. I thought Lily would have told him.

He didn't know.

Jack's eyes flick between Rachel and me. I smile tightly but he just stares at me, his normally tanned face pale.

Oh hell.

He clears his throat and says a generic hello. To me he says, "Jess, can I show you something?"

"Sure."

Zoe squeezes my hand as I stand up. With each step, I'm feeling more and more like something is about to go boom.

"Hey you!" I say folding myself against him. He's rigid and it makes me nervous. Really nervous. There is a long silence between us, each nano-second counted out by my rapidly racing heart. "Jack…"

"Nate?"

"I thought you knew."

"Nope," he says abruptly, "I had no idea, but not sure why I'm surprised really."

"Jack, she's twenty-three, it didn't happen last week…"

"I can do the maths." Jack turns up the water.

"Jack." I grab his arm. "Please don't be grumpy…"

"Grumpy?" He says crossly. "it's a little more than grumpy."

"Why?"

"Because it is Jessamy."

"Oh, for God's sake." I snap. "I have just come out of a relationship with someone who couldn't cope with the past…"

Jack switches the water off and throws the hose to the floor. "You slept with Nate?"

"Amongst others, do you want their names too?"

"It's not a joke Jess."

"You slept with Andrea…"

"I married her."

"You still slept with her."

"You had a baby with Nate."

"Ok, you win but it was hardly *with* Nate. It would be pretty difficult given the circumstances…"

"The circumstances whereby you ran away from here and didn't come back?"

"I came back." I take hold of his hand. "Look, Jack, the past is long gone. I held onto it for a really long time but now there is you and…"

"And?" He asks moving closer to me.

"And now everything feels like it fits together." I wrap my arms around his neck. "I should freak out, I don't do intimacy…"

"But?"

"But you're so goddamn hot!"

"Come by later when they're all asleep and show me how hot you think I am!"

"If you're lucky!"

He slaps my arse. "I'll make it worth your while!"

The tremble is visible and he laughs.

***

Rachel is sitting in the kitchen looking out across the garden to where Jack continues to water the flower beds. She has a look on her face that makes me nervous, there's a longing in her expression and it bothers me greatly because I, too, have that very same look. He sees Nate in her, that much is obvious, but my confidence has taken a dip and my worry for Rachel being hurt even more than she has been, increases by the second. As much as I don't want to acknowledge my greatest fear it's there at the forefront of my mind, the very idea that the man who I can't stop thinking about, may find that he can stop thinking about me.

Rachel pushes her chair back and, picking up her glass of sparkling wine, leaves the kitchen and saunters over the grass. She has changed so much, gone is the serious girl who studied science like life depended on it, now settled in her training she has emerged from the studious cocoon, beautiful, fiery and full of life. If anyone can change the world, it's Rachel, but as I watch her chatting with Jack, swinging her hair over her shoulder in a coquettish manner, I resent myself for wishing she hadn't come.

"Stop worrying." Zoe says looking over at Rachel. "She looks like his lifetime rival…"

"Is that supposed to help?" I snap and immediately feel contrite. "Sorry Zoe, but you know, it's Rachel, I mean, look at her."

"Have you seen you recently? Whatever that trainer is doing to you is working."

"He's an evil bastard. He's about twelve…"

"That's what old people say about people who are not twelve…"

"I am old." I pull a face and sigh deeply. "I'm old, I have too many chins, I have creases on my chest when I wake up in the morning and I have grey hair. My arse bounces off the backs of my knees and my tits have reached my pants. I'm old Zoe, and seeing Rachel in her perky prime flirting with Jack is making me feel even older."

"Ah, get over yourself. You could always have Botox, breast lift, arse lift and dye your hair if you are that bothered! Or, you could introduce your gorgeous daughter to your gorgeous trainer thus solving the flirting-with-Jack problem! You said your trainer was single…"

"He is but he is also the devil in disguise!"

"Rachel is only here for a few days!"

"I'm not pimping out my daughter!"

"Whatevs!"

"Did you just say, whatevs?" I ask laughing.

"What can I tell you, Jessamy?" Zoe shrugs. "I'm down with the kids!"

I sit brooding. "I could ring him I suppose, although he'll make me do an extra hard work-out if he sees me drinking anything other than water or green sodding tea." Jack looks over and catches my eye. He gives me a brief shrug and I feel somewhat placated. I know it's silly to be worried but it's been a long time since anything made me feel this good. He makes me feel good about myself and I feel good around him. "Do you think I should tell Rachel?"

"I thought you didn't want to?"

"I know but look at her, look at her body language, I don't want her to get hurt."

"His body language isn't mirroring hers, stop worrying! Look, she's coming back now and he's going the other way. It was harmless flirting by Rachel, she's going back soon and very likely she'll get back together with whatshisname and all will be ok."

"You're right." I say resignedly. "As usual."

"I'm always right."

"Shut up!"

"Shutting!"

***

I sprint across the grass to the gate that separates the farm from The White House. Rachel is in the bath chattering with someone, Zoe and Phoebe have gone for a run. The gate creaks as I open it, letting it close behind me with a bang as I hurry across the yard. I find Jack in front of the stables talking on his phone. He gives me a wave in greeting and walks to open the door to the house. I follow him inside. My heart is hammering in my chest and I feel rotten for thinking what I've spent the last few hours thinking. I want reassurance, without having to ask for it, but I have no idea if Jack is the kind of man who notices things. He finishes his phone call and turns to me.

"I can't believe how much she looks like Nate." Jack's brow furrows and he rubs a hand wearily across his forehead.

"I know."

"I just didn't expect…I had no idea."

"Why would you? I wasn't here for anyone to know. Jack, are you bothered by all this?"

He nods his head slowly. "She was coming onto me. Something like that would normally be an ego boost, but Nate's face, on your daughter, things between us the way they are, yeah, I suppose I am a little bothered. It was just a shock."

"And now?"

"Jess, I've waited twenty-seven years for you…" Jack gives me a small smile and my heart leaps. If I came for reassurance, then I have just been handed it on a silver platter.

"Waited?"

"Not exclusively," he grins moving towards me, "because that would have been dumb!"

196

"And now." I'm pretty sure I'm holding my breath because I feel a little dizzy. Jack twirls strands of my hair through his fingers.

"Now? I'm cool with exclusive!"

"Cool?"

"Yeah."

"Don't you mean hot?" I whisper, closing my eyes as his lips meet mine. He reaches inside of my shirt and cups my breast.

"I think you're the hot one." He says in a voice filled with intent. "I'm not sure I can wait until later."

"So, don't." I say breathlessly, "don't wait."

So, he doesn't.

***

I run back to the house, fighting all the way with the smile that won't leave my face. Zoe and Phoebe are in the morning room with a glass each of wine. Zoe looks up at me, her eyes slightly narrowed. "Phoebs, can you get Jessamy a glass please?"

"What did your last slave die of?" Phoebe grumbles, uncurling her long limbs from the sofa.

"Not dead yet darling." Waiting until Phoebe is out of the room she turns to me and says. "Are you intent on taking dumbass risks?"

"What?"

"Disappearing like that. I had to make up all sorts of shite."

"Sorry."

Zoe seems satisfied with the quick apology and asks. "So, I assume you went over there because the old lady sitting on your shoulder had a silly moment?"

"Yeah." I say squirming with embarrassment.

"And?"

"He mentioned exclusive."

"No?" She breathes excitedly. "Really?"

"Yeah," I reply sitting down and biting on a nail, feigning nonchalance. "Then we had a seriously hot quickie!"

"I need romance and seriously hot quickies," Zoe wails.

"You have lots of both, stop being dramatic." I say as Phoebe comes back in with glass and hands it to me. "Thank you." I pour a generous amount of wine into my glass and sit back in my chair, a secret smile on my lips, watching the sky turn from blue to lilac as the sun begins to set. After all the heart ache of recent months perhaps life will no longer feel the need to throw the proverbial spanner in the works.

"You've got a very satisfied look on your face Jess!" Phoebe says smiling.

"Do I?"

"Yeah. Care to share?"

"I was just thinking that everything feels so calm now."

"Careful what you say!" Rachel says coming into the room. "It could be an illusion, the calm before the storm!"

"Don't you think there may have been enough storms for one lifetime?" I ask her.

"It would be nice to think so." She replies sitting down beside me. "Are you planning on going out like that Mum?"

"No."

"Do you think you may need to get changed then?"

"Yep."

"Mum?"

"Yes."

"Go on then! Saturday night Devon style awaits!" Rachel grins. "I've got my waxed jacket all ready."

"You're hilarious."

"I know!"

***

We take the cliff path. Rachel and Phoebe grimacing and grumbling on skyscraper heels more suited to the wine bars and flat streets of London, fall behind, giving Zoe and I time to talk. I feel ludicrously happy. It would have been enough to have my three most favourite people here but Jack is the icing on the cake of delight. It's frightening to be this happy, particularly given my impending divorce, my flirtatious daughter and the passing of Lily, but I am happy and I want to tell the world.

The sun is resting on the sea, casting orange light onto the waves that ripple gently over the darkening water. Down on the beach small

198

groups sit on the sand, the occasional plume of smoke rising to dissipate in the still air. The humidity is taking hold, the air has become more and more heavy as the afternoon went on and now little pools of perspiration are resting on my collar bones. Beside me, Zoe pants and huffs as we take the steps downwards, the air getting more and more oppressive the lower we go.

"I thought there was supposed to be air at the beach." She moans, wiping her forehead with a tissue from her bag.

"The sea is too calm and the air is too heavy…"

"Well the wine had better be cold otherwise I am getting into the car and going home." Zoe says slowing down. "My God, it's so bloody hot. I'm going to be a pool of melted silicone before we make it to the pub. Can we get a taxi back?"

"It'll be fine if a storm comes."

"I'm not walking back in a storm!" She turns to look up the steps. Rachel and Phoebe have taken off their shoes and are stood looking out over the bay. "In fact, I'm not walking back at all."

We reach the bottom of the steps. Laughter reaches us, drifting on the still air, coming from the groups on the beach. Some are smoking, others paddling, some just sitting, leaning against each other feeling all the joy of youth. The flash backs are quite intense, memories I had no idea my brain had stored come back, flashing images of faces and feelings until I feel as though I've sped back through time. A small group of teenagers begin to stand up, likely heading home for curfew, chasing each other over the sand towards us, their giggles bringing a smile to my face.

"Don't you just miss being young?" Zoe asks watching them. "No cares, no stress, nothing but endless time?"

"Sometimes I wonder what it would be like to go back for one day. To see if it really was like I remember."

"Nate?"

"Yeah, and maybe now, Jack too. Reading back over my diaries has thrown up some strange feelings, particularly with the things I wrote about Jack."

"In what way?"

"Well," I pause. "I wrote some terrible things, things like how kissing him was awful and he was too nice. How can someone be too nice?"

"Nice teenage boys never get laid."

"Neither do nice teenage girls."

"You did eventually."

"Yeah," I look up at Rachel and Phoebe who are coming down the final steps. "Thank God! Can you imagine what my life would have been like if I'd not had Rachel?" I shiver. "It doesn't bear thinking about!"

I've lost Zoe's attention. She's staring at the group coming towards us with her mouth dropped open. I follow her gaze and see the boy, the same boy I saw when I was down here with Phil. I have the strangest feeling, one I cannot describe or understand. Zoe's mouth falls open and the colour drains from her face.

"Jessamy? Why does that boy look like Rachel?"

***

We walk behind them along the front and up into town. Zoe is so quiet that I have to keep checking she's here. I thought it was just me, that the likeness was all in my imagination, stemmed from grief and the trauma of a marriage ending, but having seen him again, I know didn't make any of it up.

There is no explanation.

Nate is dead.

Yet the teenager in front of me walks with the same swagger, his physique so like Nate that it could be him and I'm struggling to make sense of it all.

Of course Nate is dead. Debbie told me with tears streaming down her face. It's a coincidence, just a coincidence.

They turn ahead of us, into an alley beside one of the two pubs that sit on the high street. It leads to the beer garden, and from memory it used to be a small, cluttered space littered with cigarette butts and spent matches and the occasionally drunk person crumpled into a heap, the willing victim of the cheap cider.

"Are we going to follow them?" Zoe asks looking from me to their retreating backs.

200

"No! We can't stalk teenagers, Zoe!"

"Don't you want to just have a closer look?"

I nervously chew my lip, covering my teeth with a slick of lipstick. "It's coincidence Zo, Nate died twenty-three years ago, there is a logical explanation, I'm sure of it."

"You don't sound sure."

"Sure about what Mum?" Rachel and Phoebe come to stand beside us. I'm hesitating, going into the former dive of my youth wasn't part of tonight's plan and my insides are churning up so much I may vomit everywhere. My entire body shakes and I feel the beads of sweat beginning to roll down my face. I can't go in.

"Mum?" Rachel asks taking my arm. "Are you alright? You don't look very well."

"I don't feel very well." I gasp as spots begin to form behind my eyes. "I'm going to pass out."

Rachel and Zoe take an arm each and guide me, sweating and shaking, into the pub. It's changed, the rancid smell of old cigarettes and stale beer has gone, in its place are floral scents and the sticky, stained carpet has been replaced by polished wood panels. It would be a lovely venue for a drink if it didn't feel as though it was closing in all around me.

"Do you want to sit outside Mum, get some air?"

"No." I whisper, sitting heavily on a small stool and laying my head on the table.

They talk amongst themselves and a glass of water is placed on the table in front of me. It's coincidence, it has to be. Just a coincidence. I take a few sips of the water and glance up. Rachel is sitting opposite me looking white and concerned. I give her a weak smile and she reaches over to clasp my hand.

"Are you alright Mum?"

"It must be the heat." I mumble. "Where's Zoe?"

"She's gone outside."

"Oh."

There are a few couples in here, looking over with interest, and I turn my face from theirs. I can sense them whispering but I feel too ill to put on a show of normality. I do wonder if it's more to do with Lily and Phil than it is to do with Nate. The mind can play funny tricks on a grieving person but I'm not sure I breathe until Zoe comes back in and sits down.

"There's a woman, dark hair, our age sitting on the next table to them, he's calling her Mum."

"Who is?" Rachel asks. "Has something made you feel ill Mum?"

"I've seen a ghost Rach, nothing more sinister than that."

"A ghost? What ghost? What are you talking about? Have you been taking drugs?" Rachel's voice increases octave by octave.

"I'm going outside." I say firmly standing up. "I need some air."

"Shall I come with you?" Zoe asks. "The girls can order the drinks."

"Yes, please come with me." I hand my purse to Rachel saying, "get the drinks in, make mine a large one." She says nothing, taking the purse for me and turning to speak to Phoebe. I wait until we're in the corridor before I say, "do you still think he looks like Rachel?"

"There's no doubt."

"I wonder what his name is."

"Jed."

"Jed?" I grip her arm. "You sure you heard him be called Jed?"

"Yes. Why?"

"Because Nate always said he'd have a son called Jed…it's a Star Wars thing, he was obsessed…" I tail off as we walk to the exit. "I can't do this."

"Yes, you can." Firmly Zoe grips my arm and leads me outside. The boys are sitting on a bench, all with their faces captivated by their mobile phones. Beside them on the next bench is a younger girl, perhaps twelve, and her mother.

"Debbie?" I gasp.

She looks up and her face fills with a horror that she tries to mask.

"Jessamy?" Shock rings out in every syllable. "When…when…when…"

"Debs?" A voice calls out from the doorway. "Do you want another drink?"

I don't have to turn around to know who the voice belongs to. Everything begins to swim in front of my eyes and I reach out for Zoe, gripping her arm in a vice-like hold. Debbie looks from me to the voice and back again, over and over, making me feel sick.

"You lied." I whisper hoarsely. "You lied to me." Very slowly I turn on the spot and come face to face with the ghost.

"Jessamy? Jessamy Summers?" Nate asks grinning with surprise. "Oh my God, it's been…how are you? Wow, I always wondered what happened to you, you didn't ever come back. Are you at Lily's? It's so amazing to see you, do you want a drink? Jack's at the bar, you remember Jack?" He laughs the laugh I remember so well. "Of course you remember Jack, you two were always getting off with each other, made me as jealous as hell. Jesus, I was not expecting to see you, come and sit with us. It must be twenty years since you were last here." He slows down and narrows his eyes. "Are you alright you look as though you've seen a ghost."

I lick very dry lips with a tongue rougher than sandpaper. "I have," I croak, "because as far as I was concerned you're dead."

Everything goes black.

***

I wake up in my bed, a crushing headache makes opening my eyes painful. Rachel is sitting on the edge of the bed, Zoe on the floor. They both look pale and worried.

"Mum?" Rachel's eyes look sore and streaks mar her immaculate makeup.

I nod but the simple action slams my brain against my skull and a tear rolls down my cheek.

"Did I dream it?"

"No." Zoe says, "no it wasn't a dream. Nate is alive and is downstairs waiting to see you. I expect he's half way down the whiskey bottle by now, he has no idea what has gone on."

"And Jack?"

"He went home. My fault, I went nuts."

"Oh."

Rachel is crying silent tears. I reach out my hand to hers and squeeze it. Her hand is ice cold.

"Rachel…I…I had no idea. None. I just believed what Debbie told me, that he'd died and his family moved away. I had no idea he was still alive."

"Do you think Lily knew?" She asks, a sob escaping as she speaks.

"I don't know." I close my eyes tightly against the extraordinary surge of emotions I feel. Pain, anger and complete shock. My daughter, deprived of a father by someone I thought was my friend. For what purpose, I cannot comprehend. I wriggle up to sitting and ignoring the acute pain in my head, I wrap my arms around my daughter. "Oh, my baby, my baby." I repeat over and over. She feels so small in my arms, small and vulnerable and the surge of hate I have towards Debbie is overwhelming. I rock backwards and forwards like I did when Rachel was a child with a scrape. I hold her as tight as I can, singing 'row the boat' softly in her ear, her favourite song as a toddler, but now it's the only song that came to my mind.

My back is wet with her tears. She makes no sound as they roll down to be soaked up by my shirt. I don't know what to say to her. Everything she has ever known has been turned upside down, first Phil and now the reappearance of a dead father. I want to make it better for her but I've no idea how so I just hold her close and rock her slowly.

Zoe stands up quietly and leaves the room. It's only when the door closes do I give into my own tears.

***

"Jessamy?" Nate stands up as I enter the kitchen. I have left Rachel sleeping, curled up in ball, black rings under her eyes that weren't there earlier. She looked so young as I watched her sleep, her blonde hair spilling out over the pillow. All her life I've protected her but I could never have imagined having to protect her from something like this. I don't even know how.

"Do you want a cuppa?" Zoe asks. I shake my head and leadenly walk to where Nate is sitting at the kitchen table. The photo album is out and I pick it up.

"Fun times." I comment distantly. "Or at least I thought they were."

"They were great times." I'm conscious of Zoe leaving the room. Nate looks at me and sighs. "I just thought you didn't come back." He says quietly. "I thought with Lily onto her next marriage and being in Europe somewhere, you just decided to move your life on."

"Debbie told me you'd died." I rub my eyes, my mascara coming off in clumps on my fingertips. I must look a fright. "I saw her when I came back to tell you about Rachel."

"Why?" He asks aghast. "Why would she say that?"

"I don't know. I've been trying to work it out, trying to make sense of it all and I can't. She had no idea about Rachel so it can't be that reason, it must have been because of me, because she wanted you and...well she got you the minute I got out of your bed so I guess it was just something that came out of her warped mind..."

"I didn't sleep with Debbie after you. I waited for you to come back! I waited all day and then came up here for Lily to tell me you'd left. No goodbye, nothing." He smiles sadly. "I'd waited for that moment for years Jess..."

"Did you?"

"Yeah. We never seemed to like each other at the same time, and you were always with Jack. I used to dream about smacking him in the face." He laughs. "To think he was my best man!" Suddenly sober he says, "your daughter..."

"Is your daughter. That's what I came back to tell you. I was walking to your house when I saw Debbie. She said you'd died, she was crying, said it was a surfing accident, your parents had moved and she'd no idea where. I didn't come back again...not until now. I couldn't. I spent my whole life loving you, and here you are, alive. Your daughter could have known you, you could have seen her growing up." I close my eyes. "I feel so much anger and sadness and grief and rage...It's twisting inside me so fast that I could be sick."

Nate clasps and unclasps his hands. His blond hair is cropped close to his head and around his eyes are the tell-tale signs of age. He looks drained. "I can't believe any of this." He says quietly. "I've got a daughter I had no idea existed, a wife who I thought I knew, a best friend who didn't even tell me you were back..."

"Jack?"

"Yeah."

"Nate? That day, when we slept together, did you sleep with Debbie after?"

"I just said I didn't. I was waiting for you."

"I came back to yours. She came outside and said that you were in the shower because finally you and she had…you know. Why would she have said that?"

"She and I didn't. Christ alive Jessamy, I'm not that much of an arsehole. Most of the time it was all about you, I was just a teenage twat who played girls off against each other and mostly did stuff to mess with your head! Isn't that the rite of passage for all boys? Mess up with girls and somehow live to the tell the tale? But that night, you know, *the* night, I thought that was it, that you and I…now I know why not." He rubs his head. "Shit…shit…" He stands up slamming the chair away from him. "My whole life has been based on a lie. I've got kids…I have to go."

"Nate? What about Rachel?"

"I'll come back. In the morning. Shit…" He reaches the door and pulls it open. "Shit." The door slams behind him and I sit, numb, in the silent room.

***

"I thought you may need this." Zoe hands me a glass filled with ice and a clear liquid. I take a sip and gag.

"That's strong."

"As I said, I'd thought you'd need it." She says giving me a big hug. "You ok?"

"I don't know." I drain half the glass. "Ah, here's to oblivion."

"Jessamy, you have to hold it together."

"I don't know how to. For twenty-three years I thought he was dead, now he's alive and married to the girl who was my best friend, how little you can know someone. And Jack…I thought it was all going my way, that there would be nothing else to hit me, that perhaps I'd had my bad luck and wallop, he didn't tell me that Nate was alive. We spoke about Nate, he knew Rachel was his daughter and still he said nothing."

"Maybe he didn't know how to?"

"He should have just come out and said it. Just like that, 'Jess, Nate is alive.'"

"Put yourself in his shoes…"

"What?" I snap. "His shoes? Why? I could never let someone believe something so terrible."

"Imagine you have spent all your life loving someone, so much that you marry the wrong person just to forget, now imagine that the person you love came back into your life and, despite everything, actually feels for you what you feel for them. Now ask yourself, how easy would it be to come out and say, 'by the way the one you felt so strongly for isn't dead', running the risk, then, of losing that person."

"That has happened. You've just described my life…"

"I've described Jack's too."

"How do you know?"

"Because I have been to see him."

"Oh."

"He's a mess Jessamy. You need to speak to him. He's imagining all sorts."

"Let him imagine…"

"Don't be cruel, Jess, you're being cruel."

"You know what Zoe, there's one more thing that I need to do and then I'm leaving this hellhole behind. If Rachel wants to get to know Nate then that's fine, I'm not going to stand in her way, but I'm going to sell the house and move. This is a bad place, it has a way of taking a person's dreams, churning them up and leaving them as a pile of ash on the floor."

"Oh, for God's sake Jessamy. Are you hearing yourself. You're sounding pathetic. You've never been pathetic, you've always been strong and resilient, this shite you're spouting, it's not you. Just ask yourself, what if Jack was the right one for you, and you walked away because Nate being alive didn't ever come into conversation, that there wasn't the chance to tell you because you didn't listen? He told me how he tried to tell you but you only ever talked over him saying things like 'I don't want to talk about Nate.' In the end, he stopped trying because he figured that in a small town like this, you'd find out anyway. He thought you just didn't want to know and that was ok by him. He made you happy, and you're going to throw all that a way because of an undead bloke you had a crush on twenty years ago? You're nuts Jessamy, completely insane and losing Jack would be the worst thing you could do. The worst. Think about it. Think about what it would really mean and look around you, look at this house, and the town that you've always called home. Phil's moved on, it's time you did too. Hold onto the past, if you must, but keep it as a happy memory, don't bring it into your future, you need a new road Jess, the past is over. Be glad that Nate is alive but go to Jack, don't let him go."

"You don't understand."

"No, perhaps I don't, if I ever saw the father of my child I'd likely kill him."

"I've loved Nate forever Zoe, now everything feels mixed up."

"Darling Jessamy, best friend love of my life, it isn't real. What you felt for Nate wasn't real, it was a teenage dream. You didn't have the chance to fall out of love with him, you didn't have the chance for him to break your heart but you kept him as the reason not to give your whole heart to Phil, but that was because Phil wasn't the one for you. He was safe and, actually Jess, he was as dull as shit."

I smile.

"You have a real chance here for something that could last forever. How Jack feels about you and how you feel about Jack can't be faked. You have a glow Jessamy, well…" She sits back and looks at me through critical eyes. "…today you actually look like shit but I guess shock would do that to a person."

"But Debbie…"

"Is an evil cow who deserves to burn in hell, but she was nineteen Jess, people say things and do things when they have no idea of the consequences. You said yourself that she had no idea about Rachel, had she known maybe it would have been a different lie."

"He said he wanted me…"

"When he was eighteen he did, but he's made a life, had kids, what you want at eighteen isn't the same as what you want at forty. Jessamy…go and see Jack, talk it through, don't let him go, he's too good for that."

She stands up and comes around to give me a kiss on the cheek. I wrap my arms around her slender form and thank the Gods once again that someone so kind and loyal came into my life. "Thanks Zoe."

"Anytime." She crosses the kitchen and opens the hallway door. "Phoebe and I are going to leave shortly."

"It's late."

"I think you and Rachel need time alone." She grins at me. "We'll be back to drink all your gin before the summer ends Jess!"

"I don't doubt it." The door closes softly behind her and I listen to her footsteps walking up the hallway. It's black outside the windows, the stars and moon covered by the wispy blankets of cloud. It looks eerie and desolate. Tiredly I look up at the clock. It's eleven pm, if Zoe and Phoebe left now they'd be home by one. The idea of them not being here is adding to my anxiety.

What a mess.

I feel a cold hand on my arm, but instead of calming me it makes me feel sudden rage. "Did you know?" I ask the empty room. "Did you know and keep it from me? Did you know?" I screech to the air and the coldness on my arm vanishes. What a mess, what a horrible, hideous mess. I've no idea how to play this out, what do I say to Rachel, to Phil? How does he and Rachel move their relationship on from this? Will she still consider him to be her Dad? I burst into angry tears, every emotion imaginable rolls down my face in waves, drenching my face and pooling on the table.

"Jess?" Zoe pops her head in and I lift my streaked face to her. She gives me a sad smile but makes no move to comfort me, which I am glad of. "We're going now. I'll ring you tomorrow. You understand why we're going, don't you?" I nod, unable to speak as the gasps and shudders of crying wrack my body. "I love you Jess, you'll make the right choice, I know it." I bite on my lip and nod again. She smiles gently and the door closes. As soon as I hear the front door slam the tears begin again and this time I don't think they'll stop.

CHAPTER THIRTEEN

Rachel hasn't moved but she doesn't look restful, her body is tense and rigid as I lay the duvet down on her. Her cheeks are wet with tears but she has remained fast asleep.

"Oh, my darling girl," I whisper gently laying a kiss on her damp cheek, "how much I love you." She gives a sleepy sigh and I tiptoe from the room and cross the hall to the spare room. The bed is unmade but I climb into it anyway and pray for sleep to come. Each second feels like an eternity, the endless emptiness of the middle of the night brings nothing but anxiety as I go over and over the events of this evening.

Can such a lie ever be forgiven? Can it be justified? Is there something I am missing that Zoe sees so clearly? In the dark, I think about Jack and what our fledgling relationship has meant to me. I've had such intense feelings, the kind of feelings I would never have expected I'd have ever felt for Jack and now it seems that it was all a false pretence because of Debbie's lie, a lie so despicable, but one I can almost understand. She loved Nate and she wanted him. Maybe she wanted him more than I ever did because I would never lie to have him. Love does funny things to a person's sense and sanity, but for Jack not to tell me Nate was alive hurts. I change position in bed, searching for comfort and finding none. Goddamn it.

Eventually I climb out of the bed, giving up hope of sleep, taking a blanket from Lily's bed and wrapping it around my shoulders. I feel exhausted and icy cold, the tiredness stripping any warmth from my skin. Quietly, so as not to wake Rachel, I walk down the dark stairs to the kitchen.

The lights hurt my eyes so I light the candles that are in a packet in the cupboard and balance them in the empty bottles that line the counter. Putting the coffee on to percolate I open my laptop. Perhaps writing my feelings down will help make sense of it all, but the words are just a jumbled mess that make less sense in black and white than they do fighting for space in my brain.

The candlelight lends a soothing light to the kitchen. They flicker and the shadows on the wall come alive, appearing to reach out to me, making me feel that I'm not alone, a slight comfort against the black night.

210

Nate is alive.

Nate. Is. Alive. His daughter sleeps upstairs, having spent her whole life believing him to be dead. I wonder what thoughts drift through her dreams, how she feels now towards me, to Debbie and Nate and to Phil. What about Phil? A great man who always did his best, the doting father to an adoring child. Memories of Rachel waiting by the window, her blonde hair in bunches, waiting for the sound of his car turning into the road, waiting to regale him of stories about her day.

What a mess.

I stare at the blank paper. What a story it would be. Lily's story and my story, the repetition of history, the ghosts that we carry with us. Does everyone have a ghost? The one overwhelming love that never dies because life didn't will it that way. I sigh and get up to pour the coffee. A movement outside makes me jump and Nate's blond head appears at the door. My heart skips a beat and begins pounding in an unnatural rhythm. Still? After all this time?

"Hi." I say opening the door. He looks as exhausted as me.

"Can I come in?"

"Yes." I stand aside and he comes into the kitchen.

"Candles?"

"The light was too bright." I say, "my eyes sting."

"Rachel?"

"Sleeping."

"Oh."

Nate sits down at the table and looks out into the night. I collect up the coffee pot, cups, milk and sugar, putting them into the middle of the table. I don't ask if he wants one, instead pouring two cups and adding milk and sugar, pushing one over towards him and clasping the other between my cold hands. The clock ticks, breaking the silence, as the atmosphere grows heavier and heavier.

"My whole life," he says quietly, "feels like a lie."

"I think Rachel may feel the same."

"And you?"

"I don't know what to feel. Mostly, I think, I feel anger, toward Debbie and Jack..."

"Jack?" Nate asks interrupting me. "Why Jack?"

"Because he didn't tell me. He knew I thought you were dead and still he didn't say a word, even when Rachel came down and he knew immediately that she was your daughter, still he said nothing. But Debbie...I don't know if I understand why or not. I want to rip her hair out one minute and the next...Oh I don't know, Nate, I never believed this moment would ever happen, that what I believed to be true was nothing more than a massive lie. I spent all this time regretting that Rachel never had the chance to know you and now I wonder what if I'd come back sooner? Would it all have been so much different. Perhaps my own bloody mindedness did this. Lily asked me over and over to come back but I always said no."

"It was all Debbie." Nate says fiercely. "for the past few hours I've asked her 'why' and she has no answer, only 'I don't know.'" He shakes his head. "I'm so angry, Jessamy. I have a daughter that I didn't know existed, who has spent her life thinking that I was dead, if my head is fucked by it all, I can't even begin to imagine how she must be feeling."

I laugh bitterly. "I have a husband, well ex-husband really, who spent our whole marriage being jealous of you. 'My Ghost' he called you, his obsession ate him up and ultimately it destroyed our relationship. Things would have been a lot different if he'd known you were alive and knew there was no reason to be so jealous."

"Did you give him a reason?"

"For the jealousy?"

"Yes."

"I tried not to but I think, even without you being in my head, our relationship was doomed from the start. We were so different and he resented me for having Rachel because he was so desperate for a baby and it just didn't happen for us. In the end, he left me for someone who is giving him the baby he wants so badly. If I'm honest with myself, I'm surprised we lasted for as long as we did."

"And now, now I'm alive and you're back, what do you feel now?" Nate asks huskily. In the candlelight, he looks godlike, the blond of his hair glowing like spun gold. I reach out and run my fingers along his jaw, the beginnings of stubble scraping against my fingers. So many memories, so much love for this beautiful man, so grateful I am that he is still alive but how conflicted I feel. Nate, Jack, Phil, every one of them affected in some way by the feelings I had for this man. He clasps my fingers to his face and I splay them out, touching the smooth skin above the stubble. Nate wraps his fingers in mine and pulls my hand down to the table. He places his free hand over mine until my hand is encased by his.

"Nate..."

"Don't say anything, Jess." He leans over the table, his face inching closer and closer to mine. This is what I have dreamt of for all these years, this closeness, the look he's now giving me and the skipping rhythm of my heart, out of time with the rest of me. So close to me now that I can see the freckles lining his nose, the faint lines around his eyes and the stubble glinting in the light. He comes closer still that I can feel his breath on my face, minty as though he'd planned for this and had brushed his teeth before he came. His mouth, next to mine is mere millimetres away and I feel my lips fall open, just a little but enough to bring a smile to his lips. "Jess..." He whispers.

Suddenly, I long for Jack.

"No Nate. No."

"Jess..."

"No."

***

The house is empty when I wake from a fitful sleep, strange dreams swirling like oddly coloured mist leaving me with no feeling of clarity this morning. I get up fully dressed and make my way slowly down the hall. Passing Rachel's room, I pause to listen but there is only silence. The house doesn't make a creak as I walk down the wide staircase and into the hall. No one is here. There is no sense of the spirits or of Lily, it's as though the house has gone back into hibernation, refusing to reawaken until everything is as it should be.

I don't know what that is.

I cast tired eyes over the hallway, looking at the tired, worn décor. It seems so strange, unreal, cruel almost, that life can change in a blink, a heartbeat, suddenly changing everything that makes sense into a whirlpool of craziness. I've been wondering and wondering if Lily knew about Nate, feeling rage and anger at the idea she did, but I think I just want someone to blame. Lily would never have kept something so important from me. I want to be angry at the house, the worn out, threadbare house, but in truth, the house has been the one constant, never changing as the world turned year on year. If I'd wanted to leave, to run away and never come back, the fact that my daughter's father is here, that she needs to know him and find the part of her that is him will keep me here. For Rachel, the ups and downs she faces in this strange transition, are immense and it is my duty to keep her safe and I'm certain the path ahead for her will be far from smooth.

The biggest question of all is, what do I do now?

He's alive.

The ghost you keep in your head.

Nate has always been the safety net that protected me from giving myself wholly to anyone. The dead love, the romantic memory kept locked safe in the back of my mind, living through Rachel, the mirror image. I can't make sense now.

We nearly kissed.

Nearly.

Kissed.

Fuck.

I walk down the hallway to the kitchen and out of the door. My feet crunch on the shingle as I walk around the side of the house and up the driveway. It's a grey day, with the sun a faint disk behind the haze. At the end of the drive I wrestle with the iron gate until it gives in and opens, closing with a bang behind me. The passing of time means so little that with the conflictions brought on by Nate, I could be a teenager again. Only everything is so different now. I take the steps down to the front. A brisk wind blows up the cliffs from the white tipped ocean below. There is a storm brewing, the cold air and swirling wind lifting the waves higher. The beach is empty, no giggling teenagers playing the games of youth, chasing over the sand and from my vantage point up here, even the town looks deserted. I pull my crumpled collar up around my neck and walk down the steps. I don't have a plan, a destination, nothing to guide me on this brief journey into Otterleigh. I don't know where I am going.

I really don't know where I am going.

A slim vision in pink round the base of the steps and begins the energetic jog up. My heart sinks. It's Tori.

Debbie's best friend.

It's too late to turn and run back to the house.

She's seen me.

Shit.

Tori's pace slows and she looks almost hesitant as she climbs up the steps. I suspect the look of trepidation on my face mirrors the one on hers and I feel my heart sinking to my shoes as she nears me.

"Hi." Tori says with a warm smile. "I was coming to see you."

"You were?"

"Yes, I thought I'd run up, kill two birds with one stone as it were. Are you heading anywhere in particular?"

"No. I just had to get out of the house for some air."

"Like that?" She looks questioningly at my appearance and I grin.

"Yeah, I didn't stop to look in the mirror."

"I can see that," she says not unkindly. "Come on, I'll buy you a coffee."

We walk down the remaining steps to the front. The coldness is sharper here and I wish I'd brought a coat. We cross to the path and walk up beyond the beach huts towards the town.

"So, you thought Nate was dead?" Tori asks linking her slender arm through mine.

"Yes. I had no reason to think otherwise."

"And you've not spoken to Jack since?"

"No."

Tori sighs and says. "I wasn't going to get involved, I said to Orrion that perhaps it was all best left to you, Jack, Nate and Debs but everyone is such a mess that I don't feel comfortable pretending that it's all ok."

"Everyone?"

"Mainly Jack and Debbie." Tori stops beside the cash machine that sits in the wall outside of the small convenience store and taps in her number, waiting for the machine to spit out her bank notes. "Debbie has been hiding out at ours with the kids…"

"Kids? Two?"

"Yeah, Jed and Leila. Jed is fourteen, Leila is ten…nice kids, a little confused by all this but pretty stoic really, you know how kids are, just want to know if they can go out with their mates, pretty oblivious to all the tears."

"Tears?"

"Debbie's mainly. Nate said some terrible things to her."

"Oh."

"And, of course, now she's all bothered about him and you, you know, all that unfinished business, you knowing she lied to you…not that I can understand the lie, I mean, why would she have ever thought saying that was ok?" We carry up the high street to Mrs Thornton's tea toom. Tori pushes the door open and we walk into the cool, air-conditioned room.

"I'll be right with you?" The plump waitress says in greeting. She froths some milk in a metal jug and pours it into two coffee cups. We take a table near the back of the room and sit down.

I'm so tired.

It's a strange tired, a weariness brought on by the turn of events, the odd half-life I appear to be in. It was all so simple just a few weeks ago, married, comfortable, churning out book after book, now I'm separated, torn between the past and the present with no words written. I've never gone this long without having a manuscript on my laptop, it's unnerving how the absence of a story makes me feel bereft. It was the one constant thing I had through all the ups and downs life threw in my direction. When Rachel was first born and Zoe and I were doing whatever we could to make ends meet, I used my writing to fill the gaps between my terrible jobs and looking after Rachel and Phoebe. It came so naturally and my readers lapped them up, sending me emails weekly begging for the next one and now there is nothing to give, no hero to save the day.

Tori sits down and peruses the tea shop menu. "You know, Nate has been a bit of a shit in all this though, playing you against Debs, like he used to, it's as though we've travelled back in time and we're all sixteen again. He always had a thing for you, Debbie used to hate it, she did everything she could to win him, even to the point of shit stirring, sometimes it worked, other times she failed miserably. We all just assumed when you left that you'd moved on and she went all out to get him. It finally worked. Obviously, Jack always had a thing for you, when Lily came back he thought that one day you'd come back too. No one expected you to come back with a child though, least of all Debbie. I mean…" she pauses as the waitress comes to our table with her pen poised over the order pad. We order coffee and I order a cake, Tori shakes her head, smiling sweetly. Once the waitress is back behind the counter and out of ear shot, she continues. "I mean, when did that happen?"

"It was at Nate's, the party he had because his parents were out. We were talking and one thing led to another." I smile. "It was pretty unexpected! The next morning, I went home to shower and was supposed to be at Nate's by ten, we were going to go out somewhere, when I got there, late because Lily wanted me to help her with something, Debbie was coming out of his front door, her hair wet, saying she had just left him in the shower..."

"Oh." Tori breathes and calls to the waitress, "you'd better add chocolate cake to my order."

I laugh. "I don't want responsibility for your increased calorie intake!"

Tori smiles, "every so often I cheat and every sinful mouthful is like heaven on a spoon! Sometimes I long to be fat Tori who eats whatever I fancy!" She gives me a nod. "You're looking well."

"Thanks! It's all down to my satanic personal trainer!" I reply giving Mark full credit. "I was happy being a biscuit eating sugar addict!"

The waitress comes back over with two steaming hot coffees and two giant slabs of chocolate cake. It gives off a mouth-watering scent of decadent yumminess and between us it takes no time at all to demolish, leaving only a few crumbs.

"Are you going to speak to Debbie?" Tori asks, licking the icing from her lips. "She's terrified that you're going to go around and let rip! She's also terrified that Nate will leave her for you."

"Really?"

"Yeah. She thinks she won him on false pretences, which let's face it, she has, and that he'll realise it was you he wanted all along."

"What a mess."

"It really is, the sorriest of messes. Orrion is staying completely out of it. It's hard for him with Jack and Nate being his best friends, he's going away with work, I think he's quite relieved about that, normally he hates business trips!"

"How is Jack? I've not seen him." I ask and brace myself for her answer.

"He's pretty shit. Nate had a go at him too. Of course, they were all 'new man' about it, not one punch was thrown, sadly, I think Nate was ready to pelt him but Jack being so, well you know, buff and muscly, kind of threw a spanner in the works. I was ready to record the fight, thinking it would be something out of the Bridget Jones film, but Nate doesn't have a muscle to call his own, he's a bit puny really, and when Jack squared his shoulders Nate backed down. Nate doesn't understand how his best mate could keep him being alive from you, given how important it is. I guess Jack has his reasons."

"Which are?"

"He thought you would either find out or that you knew and weren't really bothered. He said he tried to tell you a couple of times and you kept shushing him."

"Zoe said the same thing before she went home."

"He should have perhaps come out with it, but you know Jess, he's always had a thing for you, I think he maybe didn't push it because finally he got what he wanted, which was you. He's been really smiley and happy since you've come back, before he was so miserable, think Mr Darcy and you're kind of there. Honestly, he wasn't much fun to be around, although he spent so much time with Lily when she was ill that I'm not surprised he was so miserable, can't have been nice to see someone succumb to cancer."

"Why did he?"

Tori looks uncomfortable for a moment and then says. "He thought it was the right thing to do."

She doesn't hold my eye. "Tori, is there something I need to know about Jack and Lily?"

"Oh, nothing sinister," she says feigning breeziness, "they were neighbours, that's all, had the same sick sense of humour!"

"The vicar said someone else looked after her, he couldn't say who, but, do you know who it was?"

"She had a few visitors." Tori says licking her finger and spooning up the crumbs from her plate. "I'm going to have to run the painful way home to burn off this cake. Are you going to speak to Debbie?"

"I don't know if I can at the moment. I'm trying to understand it all but I just feel completely shell-shocked that I think the best thing to do is stay away from her. I'm too angry to speak to her without losing it and I don't think that is the best outcome for anyone." I spoon up the froth from my coffee and glance up at the big clock that sits on the wall behind the counter. "I need to go home Tori, I need to check on Rachel. She's more freaked out than anyone."

"I expect she is, the poor girl, imagine thinking your father is dead only to find out that, not only is he alive, but you have siblings. Her head must be spinning off her shoulders. It's been nice to see you Jessamy, you know where I am."

"Thanks Tori." She hands a note over to the waitress to pay for the drinks.

I leave the coffee shop and walk up the high street. The sky has darkened. My thin cardigan gives no protection from the chilly wind so I hurry along the high street to the steps that lead up to the top. The sea is a swirling mass of white tipped waves, angry and brutal, beating the sand as they slam up the beach. I hunch my shoulders and run towards the steps, taking deep breathes of the salty air as I run, marvelling at my ability to not pass out with the exertion. Satan is a man of miracles despite his sick, black heart and I resolve to try a little harder in my next session. The path at the bottom of the cliffs is empty and as I slow to a walk so the wind picks up a little more. It's such a change to the weather of late, the warm sunny days and the bright blue skies that has been replaced by the darkening grey that is looming overhead. I cross my arms over my chest and hurry, head down against the wind.

The events of recent weeks are a jumbled mess, swirling with ferocity in my head until I feel dizzy and faint. My thoughts flicker between Jack and Nate, my past and present, until I want to curl up in a ball and sleep forever. "Oh, man the fuck up!" I tell myself beratingly, "honestly Jessamy, you're being pathetic." The sky turns a strange lilac colour, ominous and imposing as the first bang rips across the sky. The humid, heavy air gives way to a sudden downpour of fat raindrops that drench me in seconds, my cardigan giving no protection from the force of the rain.

The beach is empty apart from a solitary person near the shore. The storm rages overhead sending white flashes across the sky while the sea competes by throwing up flotsam onto the sand, strings of dark green seaweed and broken branches littering the beach. The dark grey waves roar and crash, smashing the sand with all the force of the sea, the white tops rolling across the ocean with a fury.

As I walk closer I know immediately that the person at the shore line is Nate. He is wearing a black jacket, his shoulders hunched against the pounding rain, hands stuffed into the pockets of soaking wet jeans. I know I should turn back but my legs keep me walking until I'm standing by his side.

"Jess!" Nate says startled. "What on earth are you doing out in this weather?"

"I don't know." I reply looking from him to the raging sea. "I was on my way home and…"

Nate pulls his hand from the pocket nearest me and takes my hand. His skin is freezing cold and the hand that used to fit so comfortably in mine, seems alien and strange. Nate moves closer to me and wraps his arm around my shoulder, pulling me in until I'm nestled against him. After Jack's bulk, Nate's slender frame feels too slight, too small, for me to fit comfortably.

"I'm so glad you're back." He murmurs in my ear. I turn my face to his, so familiar but after twenty-four years I can no longer see the person that I loved with my whole being, the Nate from back then has been replaced by an adult, one who has lived a life that I've not been part of and I'm surprised by how that suddenly feels ok.

"I have to go." I say shaking off his arm. "I came here to be alone…"

"You can be alone with me. I'm alone, I had to get out of the house, too many people…I couldn't think…"

"What did you want to think about?"

"You."

"What about me?"

"How much I still have feelings for you…"

"What about Debbie?"

"I don't want to talk about Debbie, she's not here, you are…"

He reaches for my face with his hands and presses his lips against mine. I want to feel the fireworks, feel the love for him flowing through me, I want to feel the delight at his words, words I heard in my dreams, the endless, recurring dreams that haunted my sleep.

Instead I feel nothing,

I pull away. "No Nate, don't,"

"You know you want me Jess, you always did, just like I always wanted you." Nate links his arm around my neck and pulls me back towards him. I push at him, leaning back as his invading mouth takes an unwelcome claim to mine.

"Get off!" I hiss through lips pressed firmly together. "Get off me." I shove him and he stumbles backwards. "You can't do this…"

"Jess!"

"No! No, Nate, don't *Jess* me. I don't want this…" I gesture between him and me. "This isn't right, not anymore. I've changed. What I felt for you, it's gone. Over. Since coming back here everything has changed, it's not about you anymore, you and I will never, ever be. It's too late. It was a teenage dream, not the dream of a middle-aged woman. Go home Nate, go home to Debbie, she's your wife, you made that choice a long time ago." I turn away. "There is somewhere else I need to be."

I sprint off across the sand, the rain blurring my vision and I stumble painfully over the branches that have fallen from the trees above. The thunder bangs so loudly my ears ring and the immediate flashes of lightening make the surroundings a mass of shadows. My heart pounds as I run, ducking each time a flash brightens the sky. Behind me I can hear Nate calling my name, his voice being whipped away from his mouth by the screaming wind. I wish I'd not come to the beach but seeing Nate has made everything so much clearer. I have to get home. I have to get to Jack.

The steps up to the top of the cliff are slippery and I grip the rail tightly, pulling myself up. The storm pushes me from all sides, the rain blurring my vision so much that I can barely see. I make the top of the path and look down to see Nate running in the opposite direction, his arm held up sheltering his face from the wind and rain. I watch him a while longer for a reason I cannot fathom until the thundering sky booms louder still and covering my ears, I run back to the house.

Jack is in the kitchen, with a large glass of whiskey on the table in front of him and the almost empty bottle next to it. Rachel sits opposite him, her hands wrapped around a mug. I fall into the house, the wind slamming the door behind me so violently the glass shatters. Jack leaps up from the chair, knocking over his whiskey and stands before me, tense and unsure. I watch the whiskey drip onto the floor in a steady trickle, Rachel stands watching me and no one moves.

"Hi," I whisper, pushing the soaking strands of hair from my face as a shiver rocks my body back and forth. I'm so cold, my clothes are drenched and clinging to me like an icy skin. "I'm so cold."

"Oh my God, Mum, where have you been?" Rachel snaps out of the trance and envelopes me in an embrace. "I've been so worried…we've been so worried, where have you been?"

"The beach." My chattering teeth make talking almost impossible.

"The beach? In this storm? Are you insane? You could have been killed." Rachel admonishes forcefully.

"It's ok. I'm ok." I'm not ok. I can't speak through the chattering of my teeth and I'm shaking so violently that my brain rattles inside of my head. Jack doesn't say anything, just clenches and unclenches his hands until his knuckles turn white. I don't know what to say to him, the expression on his face flicks between relief and anger and loss. I rub my eyes with icy fingers and barely notice that Rachel has let go of me just long enough to retrieve her dressing gown from her travel bag. "Jack? Why are you wet?"

Jack's hair is plastered to his head like a copper coloured skull cap and his clothes are clinging to his body. "I came to find you." He says in barely a whisper. "Tori rang to make sure you got back ok and you weren't here. I went down to the beach…"

"When?" I screw up my face waiting for the answer that I don't need to hear.

"Just."

"I saw Nate there…"

"I know. I saw."

"Mum?" Rachel says interrupting. "I am going to run you a bath, you'll get sick if you stay in your clothes for much longer. Jack, do you need anything?"

Jack waves her question away dismissively. I don't take my eyes from him. I'm conscious of Rachel leaving the room and the sounds of the rain water dripping from mine and Jack's clothing onto the flagstones. The spilled whiskey has stopped tricking off the table and is pooled in the groove of one of the stones.

"Jack…"

"Don't say anything Jess, please. I'm glad you're safe…"

"But…"

"No!" Jack storms past me to the door, his shoes crunching on the broken glass. "No…I saw you Jessamy, I saw you and Nate…"

"It wasn't what you think it was…"

"It looked like it to me." Jack rakes his hands through his hair until it sticks up in all directions. He laughs coldly. "They say history repeats itself, they're not kidding."

"Jack…"

"Don't say anything Jess. Please."

He disappears out into the night, his way across the grass lit by endless flashes from the heavens. Wondering if anything will be alright again, I wearily make my way upstairs to the bathroom and sink into the hot bubbles.

Then I cry.

***

"Where are you going?" I ask Rachel as I make my way into the kitchen. She is putting on her boots, a big, clumpy pair she's had for years. Dressed in a leather jacket and black skinny jeans, Rachel suits biker chick very well. She used to have weekends away with Phil during her teens to watch the motorbikes and it almost came as a surprise when she opted for medicine over mechanics. Rachel tries to mask the guilty looks that spreads across her beautiful features.

"I thought I'd go and see Nate." She says quietly.

"That would be good, you should spend time with him, get to know him…" I flop down on the sofa. "I could murder a drink." I say with a big sigh, "only I've been drinking like a fish and I'm very worried I'm becoming dependent."

"If you need a drink then I very definitely need one." She says standing up. "I'm going to see what's left of the stash."

"I thought you wanted to go and see Nate?"

"A drink will take the edge off my nerves." She looks at me. "Did something happen? With Nate? Is that why Jack went weird and left."

"Ah Rach, it's a strange time, everyone is reacting to it in different ways. Me, you, Jack…even Nate. It's not a situation that crops up very often, is it?"

"A dad coming back from the dead?"

"Yeah."

"No," she says softly, "no it doesn't."

I lean back against the sofa and close my eyes. What a mess this all is. The room is too quiet and from deep along the hallway I hear the cellar door being opened. We need music. This house needs to be heard again. I rummage through the cupboard and find the 'Greatest Hits of the Eighties' CD that I'd long forgotten I'd owned. I turn up the CD player just loud enough that we can still talk and put the disco tunes on. It's not long into the first song that my feet begin tapping out the rhythm.

"Really Mum? We have to listen to this?" Rachel says shaking her head. "It's dreadful!"

"It's Bros!"

"Dross more like!" Rachel has her arms wrapped around bottles of gin and tonic. "These are the last bottles!"

"I told you, I've got a problem!"

"Hmm." She says pouring out large measures of gin and adding equal measures of tonic. "So," Rachel picks up her drink and leans back in the chair. "You have crap taste in music but pretty good taste in men!"

"You know?"

"It's hard not to know when he stares at you like you've fallen from the heavens. Honestly, Mum, it's gross." Rachel grins. "I wish someone looked at me like that, it's limited pickings when you're a med student and work every hour!" She sighs deeply. "I'm trying to get my head around everything but it's like fog has come down. Nothing makes any sense. I keep thinking about Nate and wondering what it would have been like to have grown up knowing him. Tell me about him, Mum...and Debbie, tell me about all of them." Rachel asks, her eyes closed. "Tell me all of it."

"Well," I say, leaning over to turn the music down a little. "I've re-read my diaries, I think it may be different to the stories I told you when you were younger."

"Tell me the truth then, the real stories."

"Nate blew me away the first time I met him," I begin, "I saw him here, in the garden, working with Bob the gardener, but the first time I met him was at the fair with Debbie and Tori, he was with Reef,

224

dressed so suavely, at least I thought so at the time, in a plaid shirt and jeans..."

"Plaid?"

"Yeah! He had a lot of plaid shirts!" I laugh. "And a suede jacket that I always thought made him look the dog's bollocks..." Rachel shudders. "Ah come on Rach, suede was the rage!"

"You're not selling it to me!" She says grinning.

I smile. "Well, I thought it made him something special. He lent me fifty pence to go on the waltzers, I was nearly sick but I didn't stop laughing for ages afterwards. From that moment on, I couldn't get him out of my head. My diaries are full of...well mainly crap actually, the musings of a lovesick teenager."

"So, after that?"

Rachel has heard these stories a thousand times but it seems more real for her now, she knows the person and she listens intently.

"After that I saw him again at the roller disco at the sports centre in town. We were all up in the gallery watching, it cost us twenty-five pence, everyone was there, Nate, Jack, Reef, Rob, Orrion, Debs, Tori, Jo, Andrea and me. Nate got us all thrown out by tipping his squash over some of the roller skaters so we spent the rest of the night in the park. He and I were inseparable. It was the first time I really fell in love with someone. After that it was all very up and down, sometimes he showed an interest, other times he was all over Debbie. I had no idea how dramatic it all was until I reread my diaries, I thought Lily had binned them but she'd left them here waiting for me. Most of the time I ended up with Jack, I always thought he used me like I used him but apparently not. Nate was my whole focus, if I needed a reason for breathing he was it!"

"And now?"

I rub my eyes. "The feelings that I've held onto for all these years, just aren't there anymore." I sit up and look over at my daughter. "He kissed me on the beach and I felt nothing. Nothing. I wanted to, I wanted it to be the same, but it wasn't, well it wouldn't be, would it? I'm forty-two not fifteen, I've changed Rachel, more than I had realised. I think Lily did me a huge favour by asking me to come here, I couldn't see it at the beginning but now, now it's so clear. I belong here, in this house, in this town."

"And Jack? I think he saw you on the beach with Nate, Mum, he went looking for you…"

"I know he did and I think he saw us too."

"Go to see him Mum."

"Tomorrow."

"Go now Mum…"

"I can't…"

"Why?"

"Because I'm scared it's all over and…"

"And?"

"Oh shit, Rachel, I'm in love with him."

***

CHAPTER FOURTEEN

Jack is lying on the sofa in the lounge listening to Oasis. His eyes are closed but I know he's not asleep. His chest rises and falls without rhythm and beside him, on the small table, is an empty glass.

"Jack?" I walk towards him, a little hesitantly as he freezes when I speak. "Can I come in?"

"It looks like you are in." He says. "What do you want? Nate busy?"

"Nate? What? I'm not here about Nate."

"No?"

"No! Look Jack, I know what you saw..."

"Do you."

"It wasn't what you think it was?" I take a couple of steps closer.

"Wasn't it?"

"No."

"So, you didn't kiss him then?" Jack asks quietly. "I imagined it?"

"No, you didn't imagine it."

"I expect that made you very happy."

"Actually, no. No, it didn't."

"You surprise me. I would have thought all your Christmases would have come at once. You know, it being Nate and all..."

I take a deep breath trying to slow the rising nausea. I wasn't expecting this coldness. Jack's mouth is in a tight line and his eyes, while remaining closed seems to burn beneath the lids. His anger envelopes me in a tight, painful grip, that crushes my chest. I have to save this somehow but the expression on his face makes me fear that this is heading towards the end.

"Why didn't you tell me that Nate was alive?"

"Why?" He shakes his head. "Because..." Jack pauses. "Just go home Jessamy."

"Didn't you think I should know?"

"I tried to tell you." He says quietly. "But you didn't ever listen, you always talked over me, so I assumed you didn't care." Jack laughs bitterly. He sits up and looks at me. His eyes are red-rimmed and he looks as exhausted as me. "I didn't mind that you didn't care." He reaches for the glass and refills it from the bottle beside the sofa. "I should have known." He says sadly. "I should have known."

"Nate kissed me, it wasn't reciprocated, I'm not that girl anymore. The feelings I had for Nate, they weren't real…What I feel for you, that's real…"

"Is it?"

"Do you love me Jack?" I ask, biting down hard on my lip. "Do you?"

Jack leans his head back on the sofa and pinches the bridge of his nose. "Do I love you?" He repeats my question and laughs a mirthless laugh. "It's only ever been you. You ruined my life. Mum said it was an infatuation, but I didn't grow out of it and now, just when I thought you…" he pauses and seems to change tack. "But it's always Nate, isn't it? One click of his fingers…"

"Did you hear anything I said?" I snap. "Any of it? Nate kissed me Jack, not the other way around. I didn't want him too but he did. I wasted so much time, holding onto him, grieving for him but I realised what kind of person he really is. Jack, you're the one for me, I think you probably always have been." I sit down in the spare chair and rest my head in my hands. "Reading back through my diaries was the wake-up call I needed. You were always there, always. You never let me down, not once. I thought you were my best boy-friend, but you were so much more than that. Meeting you again and having feelings for you has woken me up to the future that I want. Lily saw it…"

"Lily wanted it."

"What do you mean?"

"How much of Lily's story do you know?" Jack asks.

"Most of it…she was adopted, met someone here, had a baby who was adopted…I think that baby lives here and she was the one who looked after Lily at the end, the one the Vicar was sworn to secrecy about."

Jack takes a deep breath and looks at me, his green eyes flashing. "You were supposed to find this out on your own, it was meant to keep you here." He runs his hands through his hair. "The baby Lily had never left the bay, she grew up here. She found out that Lily was her mother about twenty years ago. She is the reason Lily didn't come back."

"Why?" I ask aghast.

"It was a confusing time, she said some pretty horrible things. Lily struggled enormously with that but eventually they made their peace."

"Who is she?" I ask.

Jack sighs. "I suppose it doesn't matter now."

"What doesn't matter?"

"Keeping you here."

"You don't want me to stay?"

He gives me a tight smile. "I think you'd stay whether we work out or not."

"You didn't answer my question."

"I know."

"So?"

He avoids answering my question by dropping a bombshell I was not expecting. "Lily's baby is my mother."

***

The house is silent save the battering of the unending rain on the windows. Lily's final letter, given to me by Jack, is unopened on the table. I feel like I'm sinking in quick sand, pulled down by the weight of change that is coming too quickly. Everything I've ever known has been turned upside down and crushed to nothing, just a pile of ash on the floor. Rachel is out, presumably at Nate's and despite my darkening feelings towards him I do hope they find a way to have a relationship. I feel a pull to phone Phil but his life has moved on, the divorce papers signed and his new future beckons. He doesn't need me to interrupt even though I long to speak to him. He has always been the one to give me advice, our marriage was great until the past year and he will forever be special to me but now I feel his absence really strongly. I pick up my phone, hesitating over his number before fate takes over and the doorbell rings.

Wrapping my cardigan around me like a shield and smoothing my hair down as much as it will go, I cross the kitchen and walk out into the hallway.

"Hello." I say surprised. Jenny is standing on the doorstep under a bright pink umbrella.

"Hello Jessamy." She says smiling tightly. "May I come in?"

"Yes of course." I stand aside and she comes into the brightly lit hallway, discarding her umbrella on the outside step. I close the door. "Let's go through to the kitchen, it's warmer in there." We walk through the house in silence and with each step I feel more and more nervous. "Can I make you a drink?"

"No thank you."

I gesture to the table and Jenny takes off her coat before sitting down. "Horrible weather." I comment for want of something to say.

"You probably know why I'm here." Jenny says linking her fingers together and giving me an intense look.

"Yes, I think I do."

"Jack told you about me?" It's not a question to answer but I nod anyway. Jenny continues. "I wondered when you'd find out, I wondered why Lily didn't ever tell you but I suppose she had her reasons. I always knew I was adopted, it's hard not to know when I looked so different to my parents, but they were good people, kind, they looked after me..." She pauses and looks down at her hands, twisting her wedding band around and around. "I grew up thinking that Lily Summers was amazing, she was legendary here. We all got excited when she came to town with a glitzy entourage in tow. She always showed an interest in me, how I was getting on at school, was I happy…My mother hated me talking to her and she used to drag me away with the strangest reasons. I was so angry when I found out the truth. It was the lies that upset me, lies from her and from my adoptive parents, they lied all the time. Lies as to why she was speaking to me, why she gave me huge sums of money at Christmas and birthday, why she gave so much to Jack when he was born. I was so angry because the truth was that she had given me away…even in my forties it still felt like the worst type of rejection."

"I've seen the letters, she didn't want to..."

"I know. It's alright Jessamy, we made our peace."

"You were here at the end?"

"Yes." Jenny's eyes focus on the past. Emotions cross her face, anger, sadness, grief, loss and I realise how alike we are, human beings, a mass of feelings and complexities, all with the same raw needs. "I remember when I first saw Lily Summers, glamorous, a cigarette in one hand, a drink in the other, draped in expensive fabrics. She was so different to everyone else in the town that we all wanted to be like her.

So much so that the chemist shop ran out of red lipstick and eyeliner for the first time in history!" She smiles and I'm struck but her likeness to Lily. "My friends would tell me how much I looked like her but of course, you don't see it. My parents did and I think it resulted in my mother's battle with depression. She felt that she couldn't compete with Lily. Mum was beautiful, kind and loving, but normal." Jenny smiles. "She didn't believe me when I told her I was happy with my life. I suppose you wouldn't, would you? It would be like you finding out your real mother was Madonna."

"I wish she was! My parents are awful."

"Lily told me about them. If she'd been religious a plague of locusts would have been sent to their house."

I giggle. "She always cursed them."

"With good reason, I think." Jenny says, and continues. "I came to see her a couple of days after she moved back and we talked for hours. I was here all day and most of the evening. We got through a lot of gin! She told me about my father who she loved so much, who died coming to get us. It helped to know I was wanted and that she came back here for me. Even as a woman in her sixties, I still needed to know that I was wanted." Jenny smiles gently. "I wanted to take back all my harsh words but she waved my wish away as though it held no matter for her. I found myself coming every day. I suppose I was cramming sixty years into however much time was left. She asked me to look out for you because your parents were hideous and she wanted to make sure someone would be there for you after she'd gone. I struggled with that." Jenny confesses. "I struggled because of how much you hurt Jack when you were young. You know well I'm sure, Jessamy, that a mother becomes a lioness where her children are concerned."

"Yes, I know that feeling."

"So, you understand when I ask you to stay away from Jack, unless you genuinely care for him. I know about Nate, Jessamy, and I will not watch you hurt Jack again."

"I have no intention of hurting Jack."

"So why have you then?"

"It's a misunderstanding."

"A kiss is a misunderstanding?"

I keep my voice even. "It's not how it seems, not at all. There is nothing between Nate and I, nothing at all. As for Jack, I do know what you mean about being a lioness but you don't have to worry, I've no intention of hurting him..."

"But you have."

"Only because he won't listen." I rub my eyes before tears can come. "It's been a crazy few days, Jenny. I feel like nothing I've known has been real, that I've been living a life built on secrets and lies. My head aches from the stress of it all. I'm worrying about Rachel, Jack wants to believe the worst of me, so actually, I feel very battered and really alone. My parents would just see all this as another reason to sneer at me, so I can't talk to them, and my best friend decided it would be helpful to leave me to it, right when I needed her the most." I choke on a sob and just about hold it together. "You don't have to worry about Jack, he doesn't want to see me, Nate has seen to that and the worst thing about all of this is that for the first time I actually felt that I belonged with someone. It felt right and I was happy. Now it's all gone to shit and I don't know if there is any way back."

"What about Nate?"

"I don't care about Nate, Jenny. I don't care if I ever see him again." I cough to clear my throat. "How do I even begin to get my head around all this? Lily is my aunt but she's not, Jack is her grandson, Nate was dead but now he's not, Rachel has two siblings and a step-one on the way. It's no wonder I drink!"

She smiles softly at me. "I came here all gung-ho ready to fight for my boy and instead I find unhappy little you." Jenny squeezes my hand. "Go to him, Jessamy. He's loved you forever. Go to him and make him see. I can't have another thirty years of him moping!" She pats my arm and stands up, putting her coat on. "Honestly, I was ready to do battle!" She pulls a scary face and then grins. "It doesn't matter how old they get Jess, the worry never goes away. Don't let him go, he's a good one under all the stubbornness and you're the right one for him, Lily's hope was that you two would get together!" Jenny laughs. "How's that for emotional blackmail?"

"It's worked!" I grin. "Thank you for coming around and for listening. What a crazy world it is!"

"Isn't it just. I'll show myself out. I'll be seeing you." She crosses the kitchen and gives me a small wave as she disappears into the hallway.

I pick up the letter and slowly open the envelope. "No more surprises Lily." I say to the empty room.

My dearest Jessamy

So now you know it all. My whole story, similar in part to yours. History really does repeat itself and you now know that we all carry ghosts with us. Some blind us to the obvious, others guide our life choices for good or for bad. I hope I am with my ghost now and that we can be together for eternity, I'd like to think so. He was my true love, the one my heart sang for but unlike your ghost, mine stayed with me because no one else ever matched up, no matter how much I tried to make the husbands and lovers the right one, they never were.

Your ghost kept you from giving your heart to the wrong person, but now is the time to give it to Jack. He's the one for you Jess, he's always been the one for you. Nate would have let you down and Phil, while nice enough, even you must admit he was dreadfully dull. I could never see it lasting and I always hoped for more for you.

If you have been given this letter it's because my last wish came true, that you and Jack found each other. How like Jimmy he looks, it was quite startling at times.

This is the last letter for you.

I will always be with you Jessamy, always, but I need to move on, now that you have found Jack I can rest in peace (ha who am I kidding, I'm going to cause as much trouble on the other side as possible!). Make the house your home, it always has been yours because no one else could love the house as much as I do. Only you can make it live again. Throw open the doors, pop the champagne corks, turn up the music and dance.

Dance Jessamy, just dance.

I love you

Lily xx

***

Jack opens the door with just a towel wrapped around his hips. He crosses his arms over his bare chest when he sees me standing under an umbrella in the rain. "What do you want?" He asks crossly.

Looking at his half naked beauty it's hard to remember what I came here for. "Um…" is all I manage and he raises a sarcastic eyebrow.

"Um?"

"Um…I came here…" My mouth is dry and my lips stick to my teeth. *Be cool Jessamy.*

Be cool?

Me?

I'm about to make a total arse of myself.

I've never been cool and Jack looking all naked and desirable is just making me hot.

Really hot.

I run my tongue over my dry lips.

"Well?" Jack asks the shadow of a smile on his mouth.

"I…Um…" I change tact and sharply. "I can't talk to you like this." Gesturing at his small towel I continue. "Can you at least get dressed?"

"I'm about to have a bath. I had a foot in…" I look down at his legs to a ring of bubbles around his calf.

"That's not helping." I mutter.

"What?"

"Nothing."

"Do you actually want something? I don't know, perhaps you're hoping my towel falls off?" He's grinning now.

"What? Towel? What? I've no interest in what's under your towel!"

"Yeah, you do."

I concede. "Yeah, I do. But I'm not here about that! Anyway, you've changed your attitude, I thought I would be facing Mr Darcy's grumpier brother."

"I manned up." He says shrugging. "No big deal."

"Are you just a head fuck-upper?" I ask stroppily. "Because you have more personalities than Dr bloody Jekyll."

Jack shrugs again and his face hardens. "So, why are you here?"

He's playing with me.

Bastard.

234

"Well…" I say swallowing hard.

"Well?"

"You're not going to make this easy for me, are you?"

"Nope, I've had twenty-five years of waiting!"

I twist my hair into a pony tail. "Well…" Jack waits patiently so I continue. "Well, the thing is, Jack, it's sort of what I was trying to tell you earlier."

"Go on."

I take a deep breath and from somewhere I hear *tell him Jessamy, tell him all of it.*

"Can I come in?"

"No."

"Please? It's cold and you're distracting me, being half naked and all."

"Delay tactics." He says standing aside to let me in. "Go into the kitchen and I'll go and put something on."

I feel a surge of disappointment.

He disappears up the staircase and I walk through to the kitchen. I take a few wrong doors until I find it and sit down at the table. It's a very tidy kitchen, organised and neat, not like the cluttered kitchen at The White House. I open a couple of cupboards for a glass and, finding one, drink some water, managing to spill some of it down my front. "Great." I moan.

"What's the matter?" Jack asks coming into the kitchen. "I've got stronger if you need it."

"Water is fine."

He takes a glass from the cupboard and splashes a generous measure of whiskey into the glass. "I'm having one, you sure?"

"I'm giving up alcohol as a bad idea." I tell him.

"Whatever." He sits down. "You were saying?"

"I was?"

"Outside."

"Oh, that." I take a deep breath.

"Are you sure you don't want a drink?"

"You're enjoying this, aren't you?"

"Enormously." Jack glances up at the kitchen clock. "I've got a date, Jessamy, is this going to take long?"

"A date?"

"Yes."

"A *date* date?"

"Yes." He drains his glass. "What did you think I was doing? Sitting here waiting for you?"

"I hoped…"

"What? That I was actually waiting for you to come by and flutter your eyelashes?"

"No!" I retort outraged. "I would never think anyone was waiting for me…"

"So, you were saying?"

"It doesn't matter. Enjoy your date. Have a nice life…whatever. I'll see myself out." I knock the table as I stand up and rush across the kitchen to the door. *Please choose the right door, please choose the right door* I repeat over and over as I get to the hallway. The gods are on my side and I bang through the door and along the corridor to escape the house. It's still raining but I don't bother with my umbrella choosing, instead, to let my tears of heartbreak mingle with the rain.

"Jessamy?" Jack shouts through the blackness.

"What?" I shout back, my tongue thick in my mouth.

"Wait."

I slow down and turn to face him. "What do you want Jack? You'll be late for your date."

"How do you feel about me Jessamy? Tell me." He grips my arms between his strong hands. "Please, tell me what you wanted to say?"

"How do I feel?" I repeat desolately. I close my eyes tightly. "I love you Jack. The first real love I've ever felt, how sad is that in forty-two years? I think it has probably always been you, I just didn't choose to notice. I'm sorry that Nate kissed me, I'm sorrier that I didn't punch his face in. Please don't go on your date…"

Jack cups my face between his hands. "There is no date." He says softly. "I'm not interested in anyone else. I've loved you for nearly thirty years Jess…seeing you with Nate was like a red-hot poker through my heart…"

"I wasn't with Nate."

"Shhh." He grins. "I know! My Mum set me straight!"

"Your Mum?"

"Yes, quite simply the most frightening woman in the world."

236

"Jack?"
"Hmm?"
"Kiss me."

***

EPILOGUE

The sun beams down, casting its rays on the gleaming white paintwork. Every window in the house has been thrown open inviting in the scents of the sea brought up from the ocean by summer breeze. Music blasts from the house and all around me are the sounds of laughter and clinking of glasses. The party is in full swing, tables groaning under the weight of Jenny's delicious food and up in the trees the lights hang, ready to sparkle when the sun goes down. I lower myself carefully under Lily's oak tree, movement hindered by my enormous belly, and lean back against the trunk. I rest my hands protectively over my stomach and look up at the leaves. The tree has kept the scars of the storm but nature brought the life back and the branches proudly hold out their green leaves.

I look over at Jack, talking animatedly with Nate and Debbie. I never get bored of looking at him, the copper-haired love of my life. The past year has been more eventful than I could have ever imagined life being and now we're all here celebrating the success of my novel, my agent slowly getting inebriated on a sun lounger by the pond. I turn my attention to Nate. Still so handsome but the pull to him has long gone. It saddens me to see Debbie cling to him so tightly, fearful of an eye that clearly still wanders. It has taken a while but we overcame the lies and now we can spend time together as friends, not close, we could never be that, again but she's my daughter's step mother and a relationship with her is important to me.

Everyone is here, all the old gang, looking older, softer, greyer around the edges but the bonds of friendship remain. Children run around the garden laughing as they chase each other, teenagers sit together, playing the games of attraction that I remember so well.

"Jessamy?" The Vicar stands in front of me, clutching a gin tightly in his gnarled hands.

"Hi John." I say patting the grass. "Are you sitting?"

"I may not get back up if I do."

"Nor I. Come on, take a chance!" I grin as his joints creak. "You sound like me!"

"You have an excuse. Mine is just old age." The Vicar looks up at the tree. "You've brought it all back to life, Jess, Lily would be very proud."

"I hope so."

He smiles gently. "She would also gloat a little." He nods at my massive belly.

"Yeah she would." I say stroking my bump. "It's all come together somehow, the past and present seem to work so well, don't they?"

"At times. We're nothing without our past but we'd be even less without the promises of the future." He looks up at the sky, vivid blue beyond the branches. "Lily will always be part of this house but, I don't know Jess, I feel her less these days."

"I thought it was just me feeling that." I tell him softly. "Since the baby, I don't feel her here so much. It's like she was waiting until she was sure I was ok before she left."

"It's likely she did."

"I hope she found Jimmy on the other side," I say, "I hope she found her happy ending."

"Have you found yours?" John asks me

"Oh yes," I tell him, "I definitely have."

Jack crosses the lawn and stands before us, holding his hand out to pulls me to my feet. "Are you coming to join in?" I stretch my back out wincing at the pull on my belly. "John, do you need a hand up?" He asks.

The Vicar waves us away. "I think I'll sit here for a little longer." He says, stretching out his legs. "But be sure to wake me if I begin to snore!"

Jack leads me back to our friends, his hand tight around mine and as they shift to make room I hear Lily's laugh and the touch of her hand on my arm.

"I love you Lily." I say in barely a whisper. "Thank you for this wonderful life."

A warm breeze flutters over my skin and Lily's laugh begins to fade, the coldness on my arm is replaced by Rachel's soft hand. I smile at my daughter and lean into Jack who puts his arm around my shoulders holding me close. It's taken almost a quarter of a decade but finally I am back in my safe place, except this time, I call it home.

THE END

Acknowledgements

Thanks to:
Rev. Clair S,
Alicia W, Sue G, Melanie C, Lesley E for sending/lending me letters and photographs from the 30s, 40s and 50s
Clare N for lending me a vintage coat to describe.

To Debbie F, Andrea P, Jo V, Vicki G, Micheala G, Lisa T, Rob F, Orrion K and Colin E for lending me your names!

Special Thanks to my fabulous test readers:
Beth, Cinzia, Debbie P, Jenny G, Jenny W, Kate, Mum, Nicola and Teresa without whom I would be a nervous, typo-riddled wreck!

A Note from the Author

I always knew that Jessamy's story would involve flashbacks to her past and when I started writing this book I decided to lend her my stories. Over a five-day period, I read through all my teenage diaries, cringing, crying, reminiscing…but mostly laughing at the madness of a magical time.

All Jessamy's diary entries are real (copied word by word from my journals), the only made up one is marked with a *. They are my thoughts, emotions, highs and lows…and teenage Nate, well he is a mixture of all my teenage love interests! I was fickle back then! Names have been changed to spare blushes, mainly mine, and if you recognise yourself…Ah well!

It is with lots of love that I dedicate this book to all the friends and frenemies I had from 1988-1997 and to the (often terrified) victims of my unrequited affections…To all of you, thank you for giving me stories to tell.

Love Katie xxx
PS – typos are all mine!!!

Contact Katie

Website   www.katiejanenewman.co.uk
Twitter   @KJNewmanAuthor
facebook.com/katienewmanauthor or (profile) Katie Jane Newman
Email   katienewmanauthor@outlook.com
Instagram   @katiejanenewmanwriter